BLESS ME FATHER

Bless Me Father

Copyright ©2019 by Karl Clancy

ALL RIGHTS RESERVED

Including the right of reproduction
in whole or in part in any form.

Karl Clancy has made page three! Fortunately this is a rare occurrence and he's kept his clothes on for once. This may not be repeated but he is open to offers. He is a father of four, has had more professions than are probably useful and rarely knows when to stop talking. This is the main reason for the multiple professions; he talked his way into them, got bored and decided he needed a change. It is said idle hands are the Devil's workshop, but whoever said that obviously never worked as a painter. Busy hands and an idle mind are far more dangerous! His favourite person in literature is Terry Pratchett, whom he considers to be God, ironically, as Terry's views on the subject might dictate otherwise.

Karl Kraus once said *'Every journalist has a novel in him and if he's smart he'll keep it there.'* (Un)fortunately Karl Clancy is not a journalist and so you find yourself holding his thought baby. Please be gentle!

A last thought before you dive in.. you can write your own story or you can be a reader of someone else's but the only way you'll get the guarantee of the ending you want is to be the perpetrator rather than the victim. When you write you have power over the universe and if you don't like the universe you have you can create one of your own. This is probably how (insert deity of your choice here) came up with the story we're all in. I just hope (s)he's a better writer than I.

To my children, Rian, Conor, Leah and Mya
You are capable of anything you want to do in life.

Follow your stars, believe in yourselves, use your many
talents and remember…nothing succeeds like hard work and
total ignorance of the word impossible.

1.

"Bless me father for I have sinned."

A sigh came back in the quiet darkness. "Jesus Christ Eamon, do we have to go through this rigmarole every time?"

"Bless me father for I have sinned" the supplicant repeated in a loud whisper with more than a hint of urgency.

"Fine.. have it your own way.. *my son*.. how long has it been since your last confession?" The soft voice sounded tired in the quiet confines of the confessional but the words *my son* were laced with what the listener took to be sarcasm.

"It's been a month, as well you know" the reply sounding impatient, irritated.

"You either want the official lines or you don't. You're not in the station now, so can we start civilly?" said the priest.

"Fine!" spat the whispered reply, then a pause.

"Fine Brendan, thanks. Sorry. I just don't know where to turn or how to move forward. I'm stuck and I can't seem to get around it" His voice seemed to deflate.

"Still having the same thoughts? The same feelings, urges?"

"Ah for the love of God, do you have to say 'urges' like that? It makes me seem like I'm one of those, those sick fuckers."

From the other side of the opaque mesh separating them the priest snorted, "I see. The answer is yes then?"

"All my life Brendan. God forgive me but lately I just can't keep up the façade anymore. It's too much to bear. After all these years staying silent I just don't know how much longer I can go on."

"You are being tempted but you haven't given in and that in itself earns you forgiveness." His voice carried absolution in every syllable but would Eamon hear it or not? He always felt he wouldn't. Eamon was likely to be harder on himself than on anybody else.

"I'm a married man. I have two grown sons. How could I ever tell them, tell Marie?" the quiet desperation was choked in gasping sobs that ended his questions. Finally a long shuddering sigh brought his body back to stillness.

"She's gone to her mothers and I don't know if she'll be back" Eamon leaned forward, elbows on knees and held his forehead in his hands, massaging his eyes and temples as his shoulders dropped.

"She knows something is happening just not what it is. I keep telling her nothing is wrong, it's all in her imagination or it's just the work is driving me round the bend with stress but she knows it's something else. She asked me if I was having an affair before she left. A bloody affair! I just told her the truth and said I wish I was!"

The priest sighed "She's a clever woman who's known you all your life. You'll have to confide in her and trust that she will have the compassion you need."

"For fuck sake Brendan, how do I do that? How in the name of all that's holy do I tell my wife I'm... gay. After thirty years of marriage and two children?" All sense of where he was forgotten, his words split the air in anger and protest.

It was Father Brendan's turn to raise his voice leaning into the mesh "Quiet yourself and remember where you are Eamon Kearns. You'll show this place the proper respect or by God I'll kick your arse out of that seat and the church."

As quickly as Father Brendan's temper rose it fell and he slumped back in his seat "Jesus Eamon you test my patience, just to prove I'm no saint, no doubt. Go home, tell Marie, trust your wife and God to see you through or don't and just bury it as deep as you can and live out your life as best you can. Lord knows you won't be the first or the last"

"I'm sorry Brendan, I know you listen and try to help, I shouldn't blow up on you" Eamon said "I just have the feeling this'll be the end of me." He stood up, opened the door with a hollow thud that echoed into the empty church and stepped out into the multi-coloured streams of light falling from the stained glass windows and lengthening in the late evening light.

Father Brendan's door opened and he too stepped out, rising to an impressive height at odds with the soft voice in the dark.

"You're a good man Eamon. You'll find a way and I'm here anytime you need to talk" he patted Eamon's shoulder with a large shovel of a hand.

3

"Before you go sit for a minute, listen to what He might say to you" Brendan nodded upward briefly "Oh, and it's a decade of the rosary for the swearing, the blasphemy, losing our temper and general lack of respect. If you can't have it bet out of you you'll just have to pay the price for it." With a last shoulder jarring tap he turned and headed for the sacristy.

"What about your temper, your blasphemy?" he called after the priest.

"I say a rosary every day" Brendan called out over one shoulder as he disappeared.

As soon as the door closed behind him Eamon made for the church door. "Pub, I'll listen better after I've had a few."

Eamon left the pub later that night, working hard to plot a straight line and failing badly in the attempt as he brushed against more than one lamp post. Alcohol had always been his temporary reprieve, his way to numb the pain and guilt. No matter how much he suffered the next day, it served to distract him from the gnawing in his soul. He stopped at the local chip shop where Max, the short, fat proprietor looked up from his paper and simply asked "Ah Eamon, how you doin'? The usual?" over his glasses in a thick Italian accent, though he'd been in Ireland most of his life.

Eamon nodded, not trusting himself not to slur. He suspected, on his more sober visits, that Max doubled up on the accent for the public. No one who lived in Dublin for thirty odd years deserved to get away with keeping their accent. He certainly hadn't, though to hear Max massacre colloquialisms as he did always made Eamon want to tell him to stop. No one had the right to say *bleedin' rapid* in an Italian accent. It just didn't work, no matter how romantic the accent was thought to be.

4

Max was making small talk, complaining about some local kid fighting, "fucking *testa di caso*, beating up other kids around here and taking their money. You should do something about it. You are police, no?"

"I am police, yes, but if you want me to investigate wait until he kills or tries to kill someone. Then I'll be happy to look into it" Eamon said, bitterly. "Otherwise, just go down to Harcourt Street Station in the morning and report him"

He took the paper wrapped package from Max, handed over a five pound note and left, with only a slight wobble at the door betraying his poor condition, or so he thought at least. Max looked at him leave, shaking his head and thinking *if that's what the police are like no bleedin' wonder the kids have no respect, Stronzo!* He sighed and returned to his newspaper.

Outside, Eamon wandered towards home, the smell of vinegar enticing him to delve into the package before he'd gone ten steps. He stopped, picked out a chip and ate it with the slightly exaggerated care of someone struggling to control the trajectory between start and end points. "Good chips" he commented to himself, walking another ten steps before repeating the dance. He was far too engrossed in the twin tasks of walking a reasonably straight line and eating to notice that someone was following him, walking when he did and stopping in time with him also. Eyes that carried conflicting emotions followed him the whole way home, almost as if making sure he arrived unscathed. The figure heard the crunch of footsteps on gravel and the jingle of keys hitting the steps outside the house as Eamon bent down with a grunt to retrieve them and after a brief struggle with the door went inside.

"Oh Eamon, you're going to go through hell, but it'll redeem you or kill you" the figure said quietly to the night air as he observed Eamon's struggle with the front door. "Good night Detective Inspector Kearns" the figure whispered after him, "I'll be seeing you." And the shadow passed Eamon's driveway and continued up the moonlit street at a comfortable strolling pace. Nothing seemed out of place in the neatly maintained Dublin suburb but the figure that slipped away into the night knew that was all about to change, forever.

2.

"Both the Archbishop and the Minister think it would be best if this unfortunate incident were to simply be categorised as a tragic accident. An elderly, frail priest who stumbled, fell and unfortunately hit his head, receiving fatal injuries." The voice on the phone was that of the Commissioner and Superintendent Ray Carroll was in no position to argue.

"Father Mitchell has no family, the Church was his life and it would be better all round if his passing went quietly and without fuss. There are factors to be considered that you don't need to bother with Ray, especially so close to your retirement. Bury the case in whatever way you need to, but bury it." The Commissioner was matter of fact but the implication was clear, this goes away or you might find the next few months to your retirement to be very difficult indeed.

"Yes sir, I understand completely. I will take over from here. The Inspector on the case might prove to be.. difficult though." Ray thought of his most experienced detective Eamon Kearns and his belligerent, thoroughly pig-headed attitude. Trying to get him to back off might be difficult, alright, the kind of difficult akin to getting a Rottweiler to let go of his favourite bone.

"Impress on Inspector Kearns that he has more than enough going on at present and that you are going to transfer the case elsewhere. If he causes any problems I'll come down on him like a ton of bricks and he's been skating on thin ice for long enough not to take that news seriously." The Commissioner knew Eamon's reputation for being both brilliant and a drunken mess in equal measure. The only reason the latter was tolerated was because when push came to shove his results outweighed his drawbacks, just.

"Certainly sir, I'll see to it that Inspector Kearns has his workload lightened. If the files don't reach their destination it's just a case of an unfortunate technical error." Ray wanted this conversation to be done with and the problem to go away. He certainly didn't need the stress after his heart attack and he knew he had only three months left in the job after which his greatest stress would be what golf club to pick next.

"Good man. Send Evelyn my best" and there it was. The phone call ended and he could breathe again.

An hour later and Eamon Kearns was in his office, snarling "What the hell Ray? I had to hear from Gavin that you've pulled us off the Mitchell case." Eamon was pacing the floor in front of his desk and Ray could feel his blood pressure rising. "I came in to find all the case files have been sent to another station, what the name of Jesus is that about!"

Ray tried to placate him "Eamon, calm down will you. You have enough on your plate without adding to the load and let's face it, you've been a little.. off lately. You can enjoy the fact that you don't have even more of a workload, finalise the cases you've got on and maybe take a few days leave. You look like you've been dragged through a hedge backwards."

"There's nothing wrong with me, I'm fine" Eamon snapped.

"This comes directly from the Commissioner. The case *is* being transferred, you *are* taking some time off after you've finalised your current cases and if you don't get it let me spell it out. Either you say *yes sir* right fucking now or the little stint of time off might well extend to a much longer time frame. I can smell your breath from here. I doubt if you'd even pass a breathalyser." Ray was in no mood for Kearns shitty attitude today and shooting from the hip was the only way of getting through to him.

"Yes sir" Eamon was somewhat cowed by Rays outburst. "But you know it looks like there was foul play. I think it was a deliberate act made to look like it was an accident. The assistant pathologist found some injuries that weren't consistent with a fall down a flight of steps, bruising caused by blunt force trauma that just doesn't tally."

"Thank you Eamon, I'm sure that all those details are in the files we transferred so it will be thoroughly investigated and put to bed in due course" said Ray, dismissively and with an edge that dared Eamon to continue.

Eamon could tell from the Superintendent's tone that further argument would be counterproductive, if not downright dangerous for his immediate future. He held his hands up in surrender "Fine Ray, fine. Who am I to argue with the powers that be? May I go, *sir*?" He laced the final word with as much venom as he dared.

"Have it your own way Eamon." Ray dismissed him with a wave of his hand and Eamon stalked from the office. Once he'd gone Ray took a folder from the desk drawer and examined its contents. There it was alright, in the coroner's report. Then he carefully placed the pages into the shredder under his desk and watched as the case disappeared forever. *"That went better than I*

9

expected it would" he thought watching the pages disappear *"But another three months of that arsehole might do for me yet."*

It was a fortnight later that Ray called Eamon into his office again to inform him that the case had been resolved following a thorough investigation and that the coroner's report had probably been in error and that it was simply a case of tragic accident. Eamon had simply looked at him in disbelief and said "if that's what you say, sir." "It is Inspector, and Father Mitchell will have a dignified end and that's all there is to it."

Eamon had left knowing that something was amiss but also knowing that he was in no position to argue when Ray had given him the news that the Archbishop, Minister and the Commissioner were all aware of his contribution and thanked him for his dedication, even if it had been somewhat overzealous. When firepower like that was set up against you, you didn't fight it or they'd just bury you.

Eamon spent the next week in a foul temper. It rankled that the case had just evaporated. He knew someone somewhere was responsible and it was maddening to have to let it go. He'd let things go in the past certainly, everyone did, but not a case that had all the hallmarks of a fucking murder. He decided that if he had to let it go then so be it, he had enough going on in his own life without trying to take on the world but yet every night that week he drifted into his local pub to drown his frustrations and every morning he regretted it, berating himself over and again, yet knowing that his reasons were as much self-punishing as they were easing his anger.

"Another one there Frank and while you're at it a chaser as well" he was slurring slightly but Frank was used to that "No bother Eamon. Call you a cab for closing?"

"Yeah, that'd be great. You're a star. I'll be sick as a dog in the morning but shur fuck it, it has to be done" Eamon lifted the pint of Guinness in salute.

Over the course of the next hour there were three more with three whiskeys to follow. Frank escorted him to the taxi and watched it disappear into the night with a shake of his head. He had given up trying to talk to Eamon about how much he drank. Whatever was causing his excess, be it the stresses of his job or home situation, he'd told Eamon many times it was going to kill him. The reply was always the same "Do you want my money or not? There's no shortage of pubs around here."

The phone rang. Eamon stirred in is sleep. Somewhere in is mind he told himself Marie would get it. The phone was still ringing when he woke, bleary eyed and momentarily uncomprehending. He sat up and looked around. The living room was lit only by the glare of the TV, throwing odd shapes around the room and adding to his disorientation. "*The fucking phone is still ringing*" he thought as he rubbed his face with both hands. Then it dawned on him. Marie wasn't here. Nobody was. The pub seemed like a good idea at the time but not so much now. The remains of a takeaway beside the couch and the end of a bottle of Jameson beside it evidence enough of how he'd finished his night.

"Hang on to fuck", he roared at the phone as he tottered out into the hallway in vest and boxers, groping for the light switch. He found it milliseconds after he'd stubbed his little toe on the phone stand. He hopped around the hall cursing whoever was ringing at this hour while the phone continued to ring, incensing him further. He snatched up the receiver grimacing "What? Who's this? Someone better be dead ringing me at home at.." he paused looking at his watch before exclaiming "half two! For the love of Jesus Christ on a bike this had better be good."

"It's Gavin boss, where have you been? I've been trying to get you for hours?" The voice was that of his young partner and there was a palpable edge to it, anxiety backing into barely controlled panic, Eamon guessed. Something was not good.

"I've been in a bloody cave hiding out with the Mujahideen. I'm at home obviously. Some bloody detective you are!" he snarled. His head was throbbing harder than his toe and his already limited patience was long since used up.

"I'm sorry but I thought you'd want telling immediately. There's been another death, and this one is definitely a murder." Gavin paused and quietly said "It's another priest boss and Christ but it's awful" Gavin paused, hesitating before he continued, as if unsure of his footing. "Boss, I'm not sure but I think it might have been the killer who rang this in. He asked if I'd make sure you got the message. Seemed to want to make sure you were going to be at the scene."

Again Gavin hesitated. He'd taken it on himself to investigate and gone to the Ranelagh address. He knew Eamon could take that well or badly, depending on the mood, or the hangover. "I came down myself boss, just to check it out, it just seemed more than the usual crank calls. I've kept everyone out but rang the pathologist's office and they've just arrived."

Gavin's tone sobered him up in a breath. "Good work. Address?" he snapped. Reaching for a pad he scribbled an address on the south side, thinking as he did it that was a 'good' area... so the media would be all over it in short order. If there were any connection between the two deaths, *murders*, he corrected himself he wanted to get ahead of any hack looking for a salacious headline. The word serial killer sprang to mind and he fervently wished it hadn't.

"You keep the vultures at bay until I get there. I don't want anyone breathing a fucking word before we get a handle on it ourselves, and since you are in the mood for waking people in the middle of the night you can ring the superintendent and fill him in. He'll want to get ahead of any potential fallout before the morning. Enjoy that conversation. I'll be with you in half an hour."

He put down the phone and stood for a moment in silence. One murder was bad enough but two, in little less than three weeks, and both priests, this was a nightmare.

"Fuck" he said limping back into the living room. He caught his reflection in the inky glass of the window. Where he should have been looking at the strong and fit fresh faced twenty two year old he remembered so well there was instead a slightly saggy, paunchy, balding fifty two year old. The harsh lighting from the TV static was doing little to soften the blow, accentuating the furrowed face and the rings under his eyes. A haunted look if ever there was one. He gave the reflection two fingers and realising he needed a shower, shave and some mouthwash, headed for the bathroom.

Detective Gavin Cantwell hung up from taking to the Superintendent. Of slim build and lean, with the chiselled features of a long distance runner, he had in fact run four marathons in the past two years. Sandy hair cut short, of average height and weight he could be missed in a crowd of two, or so said his boss, Detective inspector, Eamon Kearns, god all-feckin-mighty-himself.

He was twenty eight and had been lucky to get his current role as a detective. Everyone had said as much when he was promoted. Four years doing his degree in business and five years on the force and ear marked for progression or so the Super had confided in his last assessment.

"Learn from detective Kearns" he'd said "Both what to do and what not to" cryptically it seemed at the time but now he wasn't too sure.

When he rang the superintendent he knew the reception he was going to get. Yeah lovely conversation alright, he'd had his ear all but torn off by the old bastard. Thanks very much Eamon, for putting me in the firing line again, covering up another session in the pub, he thought. One day soon, they were going to have words and boss or not he was going to let Kearns have it. "I'm sick of always covering your arse" he muttered to no one in particular.

It was an hour later when Eamon got to the scene, a hardly noticeable cul-de-sac in the heart of Ranelagh, where a row of small maisonettes stood surrounded by well-trimmed hedges and lawns. The end house was cordoned off and lit by the patrol cars flashing lights. A few onlookers had gathered just outside the tape, mostly in dressing gowns and slippers. "The blue rinse brigade" he thought "as nosey to know who and how as any detective so they'd have a good story for the queue at the post office on pension day."

In an area like this where violent crime was almost unheard of, thoughts of a murder would cause consternation, for fear they might be next, however unlikely that might be.

Gavin was waiting outside the front door of the house, cutting a grim figure as he stood watch. Eamon noted that for a slimly built man he always wore an overcoat a size too big for him and his suit never quite seemed to hang properly. *He's he scarecrow and I'm the cowardly lion* thought Eamon as he approached.

14

"Jesus Gav.. it's like a scene from *Night of the Living Dead* here" he said, nodding in the direction of the assembled pensioners. "Get one of the uniform lads to send them packing will you?" Eamon stopped when he saw Gavin's face up close, his features pale and his lips thin and set. "Right, what are we looking at?" Best to get Gavin moving and get this scene wrapped up as quickly as they could, he thought.

"The victim is a retired priest boss. Father Buchannan. Lived here alone for the past two years. No one so far seems to know much more. Kept himself to himself and we haven't found anything to indicate next of kin. It's in the kitchen boss… it's a mess.. worst thing I've ever seen" said Gavin haltingly. "I'd really prefer not to go back in unless you really insist." His expression was one that pleaded to be understood.

"I insist. We have a job to do now suck it up. Have forensics finished? Is the coroner here?" Eamon snapped.

A voice called from inside the house "I'm here Kearns, now lay off the lad and get in here." The State Pathologist himself, Richard Cavanagh, thought Eamon, not a deputy, "fuck, this is bad." He went inside and as he crossed the threshold the first thing he noticed was the smell, someone had burned something, the sticky cloying stench assaulted his nose and mouth, causing him to gasp. Few smells were so bad that you could taste them. Burnt flesh was one and here in a peaceful Dublin suburb, someone had charred a human being almost to ash.

It was a scene from a horror movie alright. The body was seated at the half scorched table tied by the ankles and knees to the chair with wire so the flames wouldn't burn through, but that was irrelevant as the victims charred hands had been nailed to the kitchen table, the nails just visible above the table and blackened

15

flesh. *A thoughtfully planned killing*, Eamon noted, *whoever did this knew exactly what they intended* the outcome to be.

"Holy Mother of God" Eamon exclaimed. "What kind of animal is responsible for this?" he knew that the Professor was as shocked as he was even though between them they'd seen many bodies in many scenarios.

"That's not the worst of it. Before he was burned alive, which he was by the way." Cavanagh was as matter of fact in his delivery as though he'd been talking about the weather "If you look you can see where he was struggling to get free and almost managed to pull the nails through his hands before he finally and mercifully expired." He pointed his pen at the wounds. "Well, before that he was genitally mutilated and had his two ankles broken. His suffering must have been unimaginable. The ferocity and malice needed to carry this through would lead one to suspect a very personal motive. There was also a note left presumably for someone to find"

He reached into his leather satchel and produced an evidence bag. There was a piece of paper in it on which someone had scrawled *The sins of the Fathers.*

"Mother of God" Eamon's head was swimming. He needed air, fast. He walked out into the hall where Gavin was waiting and taking one look at the still pale Gavin simply said "sorry lad." Taking a few deep breaths to calm himself he said to Gavin over his shoulder "get yourself home and take a few hours off in the morning. I don't want to see you before eleven. "

"Thanks boss but...."

"No fucking buts, just take a few hours and try to sleep I know I won't be but you should!"

16

"Yes boss" and Gavin walked past him, his shoulders slumped and his head bowed.

"And for God's sake pull yourself together passing the zombie apocalypse. You're a detective!"

He waited for Cantwell to leave, poor kid he thought, not easy doing this job sometimes. Looking out he scanned the faces of the few remaining onlookers but nothing caught his eye. Then with a heavy sigh he turned and walked back inside to see what else he might find.

"It gets worse." The pathologist was looking over his glasses and taking notes. Cavanagh was a short and balding, a portly man with a permanent deep bronze tan from sailing, which he did in every corner of the globe, as often as he could. He was wearing the obligatory white overalls and boots, giving him the look Eamon always thought of a giant Oompaloompa.

"The initial exam shows us that his genitals were hacked off and I'd say possibly cauterised before he was set aflame, with an accelerant, to speed the process. I'll need someone to get me something to cut those nails so we can remove him and I can get a full work up done for the morning" Cavanagh motioned to one of his assistants. "I assume you'll want it first thing so I'll get to work straight away and give you my findings as early as I can." Cavanagh looked over his glasses at Eamon "Your killer watched the whole thing, Eamon, then put out the fire. This is one cold blooded bastard."

Eamon looked around the kitchen, such a normal scene save for the grisly remains stapled to the otherwise perfectly ordinary pine table, on a perfectly ordinary pine chair. What could a retired priest, one of humble means, possibly have done to merit this?

17

The shadow was forming in the back of his mind but he daren't give it voice, let it be anything but that.

He went from the kitchen through the small hallway and into the bedroom. Nothing amiss. ...Nothing unusual. A single bed, still made, a nightstand, a bible, he noticed, opened to Matthew 19. A rosary and a picture of the Virgin Mary. The small room hid nothing, as he rifled through the single wardrobe he found just a few pairs of trousers, shirts, socks and underwear in a drawer. A small existence, Eamon thought, lonely looking even. Not even a family photo to warm the décor. Then he noticed the something that was missing. Above the bed there was a small hole where a hook or a nail maybe, had been removed and the faint outline where a crucifix had hung, long enough to leave an outline. Eamon doubted that Father Buchannan would have moved it. So who did?

He went back to the kitchen where the body had been removed from its restraints and the forensics team had bagged it up. The only signs were the charred table top and chair and a blackened ceiling and walls.

"Thank God for that, there are some things I don't need to revisit. He didn't have a crucifix with him or near him, did he? About eight inches long?"

"Dabbling in clairvoyance now are we Eamon?" Cavanagh snorted holding up an evidence bag "I found this. It had been inserted in is anus. What in the name of God is going on here? Another priest and there is no mistaking this for anything other than brutal torture and murder. This one is far more gruesome, more extreme and violent. You can't possibly hope to keep this quiet."

Noting the look of surprise on Eamon's face Cavanagh pulled him aside and spoke lowly as he continued "I don't make mistakes with my findings, Eamon, not those kinds and your Father Mitchell was, in my opinion, murdered. I take it we both received the same direction from our superiors that it was to simply go away, quietly. I'm not a political animal Eamon, but I do value my position and the lifestyle it affords me. I play ball when I have to and it that case I had to. But this…"

Eamon knew Cavanagh was right but he needed to keep this quiet until he was sure how to proceed. "There will not be a bloody word from anyone in this room to anyone. Not your wives, girlfriends, mothers or the fucking dog. This is simply a tragic accident where an elderly man fell victim to a house fire until I personally tell you different" he snapped at both the coroner and the watching team.

"We know how to do our job Eamon, now you do yours. I'll contact you as soon as I have anything else to offer." Cavanagh motioned for his team to remove the body and with a curt nod, left Eamon standing in the kitchen, seething and bewildered.

Quiet? There was no way in hell to keep this quiet and he knew it. His eyes were burning with tiredness. He needed sleep but where was sleep going to come from tonight? He'd head home for a few hours and try, at least. As he emerged he saw the crowd had disappeared save for one lone figure he recognised all too well,

"Trevor McGinn. What the fuck are you doing here? Nothing happening in gangland tonight? No pimps to expose or good names to smear?" He really detested McGinn, a tabloid reporter without one redeeming feature as far as Eamon was concerned. He would walk over his own mother for a story.

"Ah well Detective Kearns, if they were good names I wouldn't be able to smear them, now would I?" McGinn's nasal, whiney tone always grated on Eamon's ears and the soft Donegal lilt was ever at odds with the ferret faced little bastard it came from.

"Anyway, I'm here because more to the point, *you're* here, and trouble sticks to you like shit to a blanket. Wherever you are, there's bound to be a story unfolding." A little ferret smile, thought Eamon, all teeth and no humour. "Detective storm cloud, or shit magnet I should call you. You do wonders for my career."

"Fuck off you little fucking ferret. There's nothing here for you except the tragic loss of an elderly man in a house fire. Hardly worth a column inch to you, after all there's nothing to profit by doing a sympathy piece on a retired priest now is there. Stick to the gutter where you're comfortable." Eamon's blood was boiling but he hoped he sounded nonchalant enough to put the ferret off for the time being anyway.

"Suit yourself, Detective Kearns. If, as you say there's no story here, why are you here, dragged out in the middle of the night, to oversee a scene were the State Pathologist is in attendance and there's more Garda activity than at *The Pink Elephant* on a Friday at closing?" McGinn could smell a story and he was damned if he was going to be fobbed off just because Eamon Kearns didn't want to play ball.

Eamon lunged forward suddenly, grabbing McGinn's jacket and pulling him almost through the cordon. "If you print anything, ever, that is connected to me" he growled lowly, "my cases or anything even remotely connected to my life, I will fucking end your hack career. Just try me and see how it goes."

"Jesus, alright, now get your hands off me" McGinn pulled away, clearly startled.

Eamon turned away, silently cursing himself for losing his temper. "Just fuck off back under your rock and leave decent people alone." Eamon spat the words with open contempt.

He might as well have shown a red rag to a bull and he knew it but it was too late now. As he walked towards is car McGinn called after him "Hey Eamon, I may well be down in the gutter with the lowlifes, but don't forget you're fucking down here with me, you prick." Eamon felt the barb as if he'd been struck a blow but he simply raised a middle finger without looking back and continued to the car.

As he drove back toward the city centre he gripped he steering wheel as though he was trying to rip it off, his knuckles white and his shoulders tight and already knotting. Fucking stupid, he knew and knew too that he shouldn't have risen to the bait. McGinn would start sniffing like a bloodhound, and like it or not he tended to get results, by fair means or foul. A priest, Jesus tonight why had he said priest? That slip was likely to cost him dear.

He stopped at a red light on an almost deserted O'Connell Bridge and winding down his window, closed his eyes for a moment to try calming himself. When he opened them he saw two young men just on the corner under the streetlight, orange skinned in its harsh glow, noticing that they couldn't be more than late teens or early twenties.

He sat transfixed as they stood hand in hand, unable to shift his gaze as they began to kiss passionately and found is pulse quicken as he watched them. The all too familiar feeling of longing and revulsion washed over him as he felt himself become aroused and yet he couldn't look away as they continued oblivious to the world around them. The spell was suddenly broken by a car behind him blaring its horn, the driver gesticulating at the light which was green. Flustered he started to pull away from the lights only to stall the engine in his panic to flee. He fumbled for the key, started the engine and sped away through what was now a red light again, the other driver left behind still blaring the horn.

He sped down several streets until he realised he had no idea where he had been going such was his haste to escape. He pulled into the side of the street to get his bearings and sat for a moment while his heart threatened to pound its way out of his chest. He took a long slow inward breath but it caught in his throat and with a strangled moan,

Eamon Kearns, father, husband, detective, broke down in uncontrollable agony, huge sobs racking his body, as the hidden truth finally leapt free from where he'd been holding it captive all his life.

3.

"Boss.. boss...!! You're not going to believe this but I think the fucker is on the phone" Gavin whispered loudly in high pitched incredulity, covering the receiver with one hand while beckoning Eamon over.

"What the fuck.. how.. how can you tell" he stammered though the look on Gavin's face gave no impression that he could be wrong.

"He's just told me what the note said verbatim. Only you, me, forensics and this sick fuck know what was written on it." Gavin was white and trembling as he passed the phone to Eamon. "He's asked for you by name."

Eamon leaned over his desk, head bowed, eyes closed, with the phone pressed to his forehead as he strove to calm himself. To an onlooker he might have been praying. Maybe he was in his own way. "This is detective Kearns. It seems you've convinced my colleague that you are someone I need to talk to. What is it that you think I can do for you? More to the point if you are the person I'm looking for why ring in? Why not come into the station and we can talk man to man?" His voice was calm, belying the frantic gestures he was making to the team to get moving on a trace, while his pulse raced and his heart pounded like a hammer in his chest.

"It's Detective Inspector Kearns isn't it? Don't sell yourself short." The voice was muffled as though there was something over the receiver.

You've worked hard to get where you are...*The sins of the fathers*, detective, isn't that the quote, you know your bible... *shall be visited unto the children even unto the seventh generation.* They call us their children don't they, and they are our fathers and so we pay for their crimes?" The voice sneered. "Well this child is going to help them repent their sins to balance the scales so we don't have another six generations of the same thing. I want you to understand detective Kearns, I will only stop when you stop me but why would you want to do that? This is a public service, ridding the world of this evil so it can't feed on the innocent anymore." The voice paused and for a moment Eamon thought the line had gone dead. Then it spoke again, sounding less fevered, more controlled but also, Eamon thought, tired.

"Do you remember what it felt like to be innocent Eamon? Before the evil choked the innocence away? I don't anymore I can only remember being unclean.. no matter how much I wash I'm always filthy.. do you Eamon, do you ever feel clean?" The sound of the receiver hitting home on the end of the line was a thunderclap and Eamon realised he'd been holding his breath the whole time. Exhaling loudly he glanced at Gavin and snapped, "Anything, tell me you got something for fuck sake!" He hissed.

"Nothing boss.. we barely got time to set up. If he calls back again, maybe..." Gavin's tone was defiant and Eamon knew he'd better rein it in or risk deepening the wedge that was forming between them. "Sorry Gav.. he caught me off guard is all. Let's get this phone set up. If he calls back I want a location on him *asap* so we can nail his arse to the wall."

"It's alright boss, he caught us all by surprise it won't happen again. What did he say? I couldn't catch any of it." Eamon looked at Gavin for any sign he was lying but is expression was pale and blank, much like his own but, he suspected, for very different reasons.

Superintendent Ray Carroll chose that exact moment to descend from his office and with a curt gesture to Eamon turned on his heel and climbed the stairs again without a word.

"This day just keeps getting better and better" Eamon sighed and with a grunt rose from his chair and followed, shoulders slumped.

"Ray, listen.." he began while swinging open the door to the Superintendent's office.

Ray Carroll had had a bad morning. His wife wasn't talking to him because that little prick Cantwell had rung hum in the middle of the night. Evelyn was a formidable woman and she had put a moratorium on phone calls after ten at night since his heart attack two years ago. The ultimatum had been simple, do it or she was leaving, because she wasn't putting up with it anymore.

When Eamon barged in he was sitting with his elbows on his large mahogany desk, fingers interlaced and pressed to his mouth. The look he gave Eamon did not bode well. Eamon shoved his hands into his pockets and fumbled with the contents while he waited for the onslaught.

"Firstly, you knock before you enter my office and then you wait" his words flew from between clenched teeth.

"Secondly, it's *Superintendent* or *sir* or *boss*" Eamon stopped dead, a retort dying in his throat.

"Thirdly, sit your arse in that chair" his temper was palpable and suddenly the large office seemed to Eamon to have shrunk. "I've just had the commissioner on the phone. A bloody murder of another priest! This is to go away as fast as it can be gotten rid of before the gutter press start looking at it and god forbid there was any hint of a link. Also, no phrase suggesting any connection between the two, such as *serial killer* will be used either in pursuit of the case or in this office. Am I clear?"

Eamon's heart sank, what the fuck else was he going to call it? The call had said he wasn't going to stop. "Sir" the word was clipped and harsher than he had intended but fuck it, he wasn't going to back down.

"Firstly there is no apparent public link and we haven't released details of the first *death* to the press. At your request and that of the powers on high if you'll recall we agreed that as he had no family and was a retired clergyman no mention of the circumstances would be made known, just a tragic loss of an elderly man living alone. A *dignified end* I believe you called it?"

He saw the words sting as the Superintendent's jaw clenched further and his shoulders tightened. He ploughed on.

"Secondly the press are already sniffing around the latest scene in the shape of Trevor McGinn and that little shit will dig like a terrier after a rabbit if he is given free rein. If you want to delay the inevitable you might consider a word to the editor of that rag he works for but both deaths are going to come out one way or another"

The look on Ray Carroll's face was thunderous but Eamon was intent on sailing headlong, even if just to remind him that Eamon had played the game up until now '*and*' he thought '*you can consider it a warning shot across the bow that I'm not going to just lie down and take your shit'.*

"Thirdly…"

Carroll cut him off. "Sit down and shut up, that's thirdly" his voice was almost strangled. "Now listen you bollix" he stood and slammed his fists onto the table "we all keep our secrets. You think I like being told what I can and can't pursue? This has come down from on high and I fucking mean on high. This goes away, bury it. Feed the reporter anything you like just get rid of it. If it isn't clear already let me make it so, your job and mine are both on the line here and with three months left until I can retire I'm not going to have this, you or anything else fuck that up"

He stood from leaning over the desk and turned away. Looking out the window he sighed "Eamon, get this done. Stop fucking drinking on the job and whatever else it is you're hiding, a bit on the side or whatever. It stops now."

Eamon's surprise was plastered over his face "There's very little I don't know about in my own station, Eamon. Your behaviour lately has been erratic and secretive. Missing afternoons, late mornings but right now I don't give two pence for the ins and outs of your private life, if you'll forgive the pun. I have my secrets in this job and you obviously have yours but right now we either do this or we can both kiss our reputations, careers and I'd say families goodbye."

"Are you threatening me" Eamon was incredulous "Who the fuck…"

Ray cut him off. "I'm explaining the stark realities of life Eamon, the nuances seem beyond you so I'm making it simple. I'm passing the implied threat along. Either we get ahead of this and it disappears or neither of us has a future. The Minister is a devout Catholic; did you know that, Mater Dei schooling and all that shite? His cousin is also some bigwig in the Vatican and I'm not taking on the twin fangs of that serpent, Church and State. Not for two old men nobody really cares about. The official line to the press and public will be that the first is an accidental death due to a fall and the other is going to be an accidental death due to a fire. Now get out and do the bloody job I need you to do for both our sakes."

Eamon's head was spinning as he rose. As he turned the Superintendent called out "Get something concrete, get this bastard caught. If you can't I'll replace you with someone who can. No reports necessary on this one Eamon, no paperwork and keep Cantwell on a short leash. After you've done with this I'll be having a word with young Gavin to impress upon him just how much his future depends on looking the other way in this."

"Yes.. *sir*" Eamon replied "And when I catch whoever's responsible, do I just politely ask them if they'd mind stopping? What's going on Ray? This is clearly covering up something. What aren't you telling me?"

"Just do your part and leave the rest to those in a place best suited to dealing with it" and that was it, Eamon thought, just do the job like a good boy and shut up. He stormed out, slamming the door behind him.

"I'm out for a few hours" Eamon barked at Cantwell when he returned to his desk as he reached for his car keys. "I've got to see a man about a dog." Opening his desk drawer he emptied the contents of his pockets into it, before locking it and giving a tug on the handle to satisfy himself that it was secured.

Cantwell looked at him quizzically "Ok boss, don't need me to drive you then?"

Eamon grimaced "The very nature of seeing a man about a dog is that you do it alone. This man may or may not feel like talking to me but he definitely won't if I bring somebody else. If you want to be useful go down to the Coroner's office and collect the results of the post mortem, by hand, yourself." He turned to leave and then swung round again "and Gav... no one else is to see those results before I do. You get that file and you keep it to yourself until I get back."

Eamon sat into the car and closed his eyes. Such a fucking mess and now it seemed he was going to have to cover the whole thing up. There was hardly a lead to speak of and the two killings seemed so random but there had to be some connection.

A killer who wanted to punish two elderly priests, *God knows I'd sympathise* he thought but as he had done every day of his second life, Eamon buried the rising bile and realising his knuckles were white and shoulders locked rigid, released the steering wheel and took a long breath. "Not me, not my life, not my problem." It had become his mantra for when the dark thoughts and memories of his childhood tried to get a foothold. He started the car "Right, let's see who might know what" and with that the mantle of Inspector descended over him and he was back in control.

It didn't take long to get over to the Northside. He could have found it blindfolded though it had been what, ten years, since he'd taken that drive.

Heading out of town toward Fairview, take a right, a left and another right, down a grubby old street whose faded Georgian façades had better times, a relic of the tenements, turn off left half way down the row and there it was, McGettigans.. A plain looking faded black single storey building squatting between two shops long since abandoned. The pub you went to when you couldn't get in anywhere else. Full of hard men who'd never worked a hard day, alcoholics, bigots, homophobes and would be provos. The kind of place a garda didn't venture alone unless he had a sudden desire to part with his teeth at the very least.

Eamon remembered it with loathing. Years ago it had been the place you'd go to fall off the map. How many times as a young man had he fallen out the side door so drunk he couldn't find his arse with both hands?

He'd been in the gutter then, forgetting and regretting. He stood outside for a minute before the door opened with a crash and someone was thrown onto the street, landing in a dishevelled heap by the kerb.

"And this time fuckin' stay out ya bleedin junkie bastard!" the man who appeared in the door jabbing a finger at the prone figure outside was big enough to fill the opening and his face was whiskey temper purple red. He looked Eamon up and down.

"Yeah, what are you lookin' ah?" His chest expanded and he took a step toward Eamon.

"Good man, fuckin' hate junkies, buy you a pint?" Eamon's approach took him by surprise and he could see the belligerence at odds with the offer as the big face with its many scars broke into a gap toothed grin. "Go on so" and he stepped back inside, holding the door open for Eamon to follow.

"Eamon!" The friendly greeting came from the gloom at the other end of the bar as he stepped inside. "Is that you?" the voice was all too familiar.

"Butler, you still alive?" Eamon jibed with a friendly tone he certainly didn't feel.

From behind the big man's hand landed like a vice on his shoulder "You owe me a pint and its Mister Butler."

The speaker sat on a stool at the end of the bar, newspaper spread in front of him, a teacup to one side. He looked at Eamon over a pair of Lennonesque wire rimmed glasses. "Easy Cyril, Eamon and I know each other for years, don't we Inspector?" the last word was loaded so everyone present would be in no doubt that he was the enemy and Eamon knew it. A false step here and it would not end well.

The big hand gripped harder on his shoulder "Cyril, that pint, yeah?" he offered hopefully. "I don't take nothin' from pigs" the menace was palpable.

"Leave him, now" Butler growled and the hand released. "Take a seat Eamon, you've taken the trouble to come all the way here. I don't want to be rude." He motioned to Eamon to join him.

Butler was a solid block of a man, maybe six foot and with the broad shoulders and big arms of a regular gym user. He slid off the bar stool and took a seat at a low table near the back of the pub. Eamon sat opposite taking in the other man's face, noticing the faint questioning look and the prison pallor.

"You're in good shape Butler. How long you out of the 'Joy?" Eamon knew he was taking a chance but he had to take it and hope Butler would respond to the banter in kind.

"Now Inspector, you know full well that I was wrongly convicted. I was only serving my country in the struggle to free her from oppression" Butler was grinning "Anyway it was only

31

three years, hardly even noticed the time passing. Should've been five but I got time off for my exemplary behaviour." The smile dropped and butler's eyes hardened "You're hardly here for a pint and a walk down memory lane and I know you're not stupid enough to be here waving a warrant card... So?"

Eamon leaned forward and quietly said "It's not for the fond memories or the love of you that's for sure but I need information and if anyone was going to know it was going to be you. Your connections to.. various.. groups means that if someone was active in the city you'd be the man who'd know."

Butler's grin returned "you're hardly asking me to turn informant Inspector. That'd be very detrimental to my reputation" Eamon could see he was enjoying this. "Any supposed links I may allegedly have had to any group are matters of supposition, not fact." He was positively beaming "Open University, Inspector, it's how you kill three years inside, with an English degree."

"Look Butler, don't piss about. I need to know if there's something happening with any of those groups you may or may not have knowledge of. There have been two incidents and I need to stop it before it escalates" it probably wasn't his best tactic but time was critical and Eamon needed to know now.

"You mean have any of the anti-drug lads been busy, or maybe its guns. Is it guns Inspector?" Butler queried with exaggerated innocence.

"Butler for fuck sakes, if you know something just tell me. I can see you do you smug prick." His impatience carried a little too far and big Cyril stood up to approach. A wave of Butler's hand sat him down again but things were definitely balancing on a knife edge. Eamon silently wished he hadn't thought of knives just at that moment.

"Relax Eamon, remember where you are and who you're asking for help. You are asking for help aren't you? I seem to remember hearing a little birdie telling me that you were over in Ranelagh the other night. A poor old man had died in a house fire. Now what would a homicide detective be doing there in the middle of the night? And a little over two weeks ago weren't you over in Walkinstown at another death. They weren't murders were they Eamon?" Butler was looking intently at his face for any sign of the truth.

"You're awfully well informed on my movements Butler." Eamon was rattled but he wasn't going to let it show "Why would that be now?"

"A couple of reasons Eamon. I know the two old boys who died in those unfortunate circumstances were retired priests. I also know that they had both been overseas for almost forty years and one had only returned home to Ireland in the last six months and the other in the past two years. Add the presence of homicide and the State Pathologist and I begin to ask if there are reasons these two died..oddly. If maybe someone had reasons to go after them. Or maybe it's just tragic coincidence" The grin appeared again.

"I think they were nonces, Eamon" he said leaning closer and lowering his voice. "It would certainly explain a lot and if they were nonces then they got what was coming to them and good riddance. I'd like to think of it as somebody doing God's work if that were the case. He does like to move in mysterious ways" Butler waved his arms expansively. "Now Inspector, I think I've done enough of your job for you." Butler laughed at his own cleverness and Eamon silently cursed him.

"Where are you getting this fairy tale, Butler? It's all a bit tea from China."

Butler's smiling face was insufferable "People like to talk to me, a hell of a lot more than they like to talk to you Inspector."

Eamon couldn't take any more. He stood to leave "You should have been a copper."

Butler snorted "too much corruption and not enough money."

Eamon turned to leave to be met by Cyril locking his path.

"Before you go Inspector, remember that you owe me one. I'll be seeing you" said Butler "Bye now. I won't ask Cyril to see you out. That might end badly."

Outside, Eamon sat into the car and left as the figure of Cyril gestured with a middle finger in his mirror. He rounded the corner, headed past the tired Georgians and back into the real world. He replayed the conversation in his head. Butler knew a lot and was egotistical enough to want Eamon to know that, so he'd told him a lot more than if he'd been asked directly. "Fucking asshole" he muttered, thinking that Butler might be right and if he was then this had gotten even more tangled. How was he supposed to catch someone whose basic motivation was so close to his own hatred of the Church? Did he even want to?

He parked in his spot in the station and as soon as the engine died Gavin was knocking at the window, breaking the spell of his dilemma. "Jesus Gav" he said, slumping in the seat "you're going to give me a heart attack. Could you not wait until I at least get out of the bloody car?"

"Sorry boss. Two things, your wife rang to say she'll be home this afternoon. The other thing is we got details back from the pathologist's office and I did some digging myself." Gavin was talking excitedly, making Eamon very nervous.

"What do you mean, digging?" Eamon's trepidation was rising like a geyser.

"The man we thought was Father Buchannan, wasn't. He was Patrick Buchannan alright but he hadn't used that name since he was in the seminary. He took the name Loyola when he was ordained, Father Loyola and he taught in St. Augustine's School, in Raheny, before he went overseas doing missionary work. There were rumours back then that there had been a scandal involving a minor but it had all been covered up and he was moved on. I asked a friend of my mothers who works for the Catholic press office. She's very talkative after a lunch time gin or two. It might be a lead boss, what do you think? Boss? Boss?"

Eamon barely heard anything after hearing that name. Loyola. The name, a long buried ghost in his memory, almost made him faint there and then. He rushed past Gavin, into the station bathroom and unable to hold it any longer, he threw up into the sink, head spinning, before he collapsed on the floor, still retching violently. Loyola, Augustine's… where it had all started and where he had hidden everything for so long, so long ago he thought nobody could possibly know, but now it was all coming back to haunt him.

He couldn't think, couldn't breathe, the weight on his chest was choking him. The only thought in his head that had any clarity was that he was now the lead detective in the case of the murder of the man who had raped him.

Gavin burst into the bathroom "Boss, are you ok? Christ almighty, what's happened? Are you ill?" There was genuine concern on his face as he pulled paper towels from the dispenser. "Here, take these" he said handing them to Eamon "Boss, what

35

the fuck is going on" Gavin squatted down beside Eamon who was still on his knees as he wiped his mouth and spat.

Eamon looked at him and decided there and then he was going to keep Gavin out of all of this, come hell or high water. "Don't drink vodka on an empty stomach when you have an ulcer" he lied, praying it was convincing. He watched Gavin's eyes as the young man searched his face for any other motive.

Eamon remained impassive, hoping, until finally, Gavin stood up and turned his back on him. "I'm fucking done. Go home, sober the fuck up and get yourself some help. It's not just your career you're fucking with. It's mine too and I'm damned if you drag me down into whatever mire you want to sink into." He punched the door. "Fuck it" he sighed looking upward. "Eamon, I'm not going to say a word, just please, go see someone or take time off and straighten yourself out. I'm asking as a friend and a colleague" with that he pushed open the bathroom door with a slam and left.

Eamon knelt, stunned, on the floor, beside a pool of vomit and couldn't even bring himself to stand for what felt like an eternity. He couldn't think. There was too much pressure inside his head. He eventually stood only because his legs were going to sleep.

"Really look drunk then wouldn't you?" He thought grimacing at the stiffness. He made his way to the sink and ran water over his hands, bent down and swished a mouthful before spitting to get rid of the bile. He splashed water over his face and as he stood caught his reflection in the mirror. There it was. The look. The same look of recrimination he'd faced every day for as long as he could remember. This had to end. He looked again. "OK" he said as is shoulders dropped in defeat "You win."

He went home on the pretext of feeling unwell and needing to change his vomit stained trousers. Before he left the station he thought it would be prudent to ring the Portobello Arms, a B&B close enough to the station. He made up some cock and bull story about a water leak and the wife being away. Eamon knew Marie and he could only hope this was going to go better than he expected.

Arriving in the drive his car crunched on the gravel and he realised his knuckles were white on the steering wheel again and between his shoulder blades was burning with knotted muscle. He dropped his hands to his lap and closing his eyes, allowed his head to rest for a moment on the head rest as he gave one long, weary sigh. He got out of the car feeling as though he weighed a ton, every step to the house was heavy, almost funereal. He fumbled for his keys and turned the lock.

"Eamon?" He winced and the sudden sound "Is that you?" "No, it's Gary Glitter." He stopped at the threshold and took one long breath in and out.

"Oh Eamon the place is like a tip." Marie appeared from the living room carrying several takeaway bags "You'd swear I'd been gone a month" Marie tutted while displaying the evidence, shaking the bags at him vigorously.

He sighed "I didn't expect you back" then as an afterthought "so soon."

"Oh for God's sake, I told you I'd be back today. Mum's been back from hospital since last night" she turned busily and he followed her into the kitchen. "You never listen, always too busy, that job'll be the end of you!"

"Marie, can you leave that and sit down?" his heart was hammering in his chest and his mouth was so dry he'd give anything for a drink, but no he thought, not now.

"Ah look at the state of the sink. Did you never hear of a dishwasher?" Marie sighed "And what's on your trousers. Is that vomit? It smells awful. One of them.. junkies.. no doubt." She always gave the word *junkies* its own space in a sentence as if it might contaminate the rest. "Take those off in the utility. You're not wandering round the house like that!"

"Marie! For the love of God, sit down. This is important!" She stopped mid rebuke and with concern crossing her features sank slowly into the chair next to where he had sat at the kitchen table. "Marie, this is hard and it's going to change everything. I need you to hear me because I can only say this once" he blurted. It was now or never and he knew if he stalled he'd lose courage.

Marie lit up "You're retiring! Is that it? I said you should have quit years ago."

"Marie would you shut up" Marie recoiled as though his shout was like a slap in the face.

"Eamon! There's no need for that. Whatever it is can't be that bad" her voice was trembling and a slow realisation seemed to dawn as her eyes opened wide "Oh God, you're having an affair. I was right" she cried.

"I'm NOT having an affair Marie!" Eamon placed his hands on her lap "there is no other woman. There has never been another woman. That's the problem Marie. I don't fancy another woman, or any woman at all for that matter, because I'm gay Marie, I'm fucking gay!"

If he'd hit her it would have had less impact. She froze, open mouthed and wide eyed. He reached or her hand. As he touched her she exploded.

"Don't touch me. Don't fucking touch me!" Marie leapt up from the table and slapped him across the face. "You animal, you filthy animal! Get out of my house, get out, get out!" She was screaming, white faced and feral, visceral in her ferocity "How dare you make a mockery of my life, our marriage. The boys, what will I tell the boys!" Her hands clenched by her sides as she stood over him. To Eamon it seemed as though he was becoming smaller in his own mind and all he could mumble was "I'm sorry love, so sorry."

"You're sorry! Love? Sorry! Just stand up and get out this minute. I can't look at you!" He moved to stand when her fist connected with his face, knocking him sideways. Off balance, he spilled off the chair onto the floor in a heap. He looked up, shocked. In thirty years Marie had never so much as lost her temper, let alone lashed out. She looked ashen and just as shocked as she looked down at him and then at her still clenched, trembling fist. She wailed. A sound that spoke, more than words ever could, of loss, of recognition, of realisation and of a truth that had been spoken and could now never be undone.

Eamon stood, shakily, jaw aching. "Please Marie. I'm still me, still your husband. I just can't live the lie any more. It's killing me!" He was begging as he looked into her normally calm blue eyes, searching for a glimmer of the compassion he wanted but instead he saw only revulsion. A look he recognised too well. Hadn't it been looking out of the mirror at him all his life? "Let it kill you" She hurled the words like knives "Better you die than this.. this.." she trailed off waving her hand dismissively at him "This is too much. Get out. Leave me, now."

4.

He didn't know how he had arrived at St. Peter's church but when he looked up after stopping the car with a jolt, there he was. The headache behind his eyes and the unrelenting pressure were making him nauseous again and he scrambled to remove his seat belt and escape the confines of the car. Panic gripped him as he gasped for air and his heart was hammering in his chest and ears. Hands outstretched and trembling, he leaned on the bonnet, struggling for breath that would not come and feeling like he was underwater, drowning and panicking.

"Eamon? What in God's name are you doing here?" Brendan's voice full of concern startled him and brought him back to the moment. He turned to see the tall figure in black walking quickly toward him. "Jesus man, are you having a heart attack? You look terrible. What's happened?" It was all too much. Eamon's head reeled, his knees buckled and he fell to the ground, his knees crunching on the gravel path. Brendan half ran to him, picked him up as though he were a rag doll and guided him towards the church and into the sacristy all the while quietly soothing him. "Alright, alright. You'll be alright. You just need to sit for a moment. That's it, it's alright." He drew up a chair and eased Eamon down. It was minutes before Eamon could compose himself and began to breathe calmly. Brendan opened a desk drawer and took out a whiskey bottle and glass, pouring a large double measure.

"I told her." Eamon looked up at Brendan who handed him a glass of whiskey.

"Here drink this, I keep it in case of emergency and this is definitely one of those." He patted Eamon's shoulder as he took the glass. Brendan drew up another chair and sat heavily into it "right" he said half sighing "Tell me what's happening when you're ready. Take your time I've got no place else I need to be and I've locked the door so we won't be disturbed." He sat back and watched as Eamon drained the glass in one mouthful, wincing as the fire sank through his chest.

"Pretty awful shite, though on your salary I'm not surprised" Eamon smiled thinly. "Thanks Brendan. I don't know how I wound up coming here but I now realise I have no one else I can turn to or confide in."

"We all need someone we can turn to when things get beyond us or when we feel like we just need someone who can understand why. Why we are how we are or why we do the things we do." Brendan wasn't looking at him but at the crucifix hanging on the wall above his head.

"I'm not in the form for a God lecture on his endless patience, love and the rest of it. I need to get a lot off my chest and God forgive you but you're the only person I can think of who won't breathe a word" he paused "Will you hear my confession?" Eamon pleaded.

Brendan paused and then, pressing his lips together as if to stifle a comment, nodded. "Fine Eamon, but we do it here, man to man, with God watching over us and I'm having a whiskey before we do because I think I will need one before we're done." He stood, went to the drawer and removed another whiskey tumbler. He sat down again, poured a glass and refilled Eamon's. He reached over and clinked the glasses together.

"To the truth Eamon, may it set us free!" He swallowed the whiskey and snorted. "You're right that's bloody awful. After this you can buy me a decent bottle. Call it penance" He smiled. Eamon drained his glass, grimacing again. "You're on."

Eamon began haltingly at first and then as if the dam had broken he told Brendan everything. The first murder and how he wasn't sure if it had been a murder or a home intrusion gone wrong at first until the Coroner's confirmation had left him no doubt. The second murder, the grisly scene, the crucifix, the phone call, the reporter, Butler, the Superintendent's insistence that it be covered up, every detail until he felt he was spent. Brendan sat passively, simply listening, motionless, as though any movement or comment might have closed the floodgates. Only when he reached the point where he went back to the station did Eamon falter:

"Ly.. Lyola." He stuttered the word in a pained grimace, as it tore its way free from where it had been buried for so long. The demon Eamon had worked so hard to forget had finally come out into the open and it was doing what demons do best, torturing his soul.

"There's something I have to tell you. About Augustine's and about me." Eamon felt the lump in his throat as it threatened to strangle him but he knew if he didn't get it out now he never would. "Loyola" he faltered, that name was so filthy in his mouth, even now it filled him with fear, disgust, guilt and loathing, the worst kind, self-loathing. He bowed his head and the story came out, in gasps as he fought himself for control. The story of a young boy who had been put into the Industrial School because his mother couldn't cope and his father was long since gone. The story of falling victim to Loyola and his twisted, evil perverted desires.

"He caught me one day, it must've been after PE, in the changing room. Don't interrupt or I'll stop and I haven't got it in me to do this twice." Eamon took a breath and staring at the floor, uncovered the memory. "He was with his shadow, Morrissey who closed the door while.. while Loyola pinned me to the wall. I was thirteen but I was small, weak and I couldn't move his arm from across my throat. *"Kearns, I've been watching you. Your eyes have started to wander, haven't they, wander to the bodies of the other boys. It's because you're a year older than most of them. You've begun to notice the way it makes you feel, haven't you?"* I shouted *"No Father!"* but in my heart I knew he was right. I was so confused about how I was feeling and I knew it wasn't right."

Eamon sat, elbows on knees and hands hanging low and with another trembling breath he continued "I knew I was different and that I dare tell no one but they saw it in me. Loyola kept me pinned while he grabbed me.. down below.. he started massaging me saying *"oh yes you're a dirty little boy alright. You like that don't you"* I didn't respond. I was frozen in fear, fear of having been found out and fear of what would happen if I admitted it. He grabbed me and pushed me towards Morrissey who caught me and held my arms behind my back. *"On your knees"* Loyola pointed at the floor. Morrissey pushed me and I had no choice."

Eamon swallowed hard, the lump in his throat was almost choking back the words but still he forced himself to remember and continue. *"'You're a part of the Church as much as that chair there. We are the Church and so we will use you as we see fit'.* Loyola's tone was frightening, so eager and malicious. But what he said next was worse *'But you want to be of use to the*

43

Church don't you boy? Yes?' His voice had changed and he sounded like the most reasonable uncle a boy ever had as though he was discussing a match, friendly even. *'You're going to be our special boy. You'll serve the Church by serving us and we won't see your brasser mother out on the streets or your sisters taken into care or tell your little secret to the school board either. That alone would get you put in prison'.* My mother had no choice, you see, she had no man, no money and no skills so she did what she had to do."

Eamon glanced at Brendan for any sign of condemnation. Finding none he continued "If they wanted they could have had her taken away and my sisters put into a Laundry. I couldn't live with that so when he said "beg for forgiveness there on your knees, both for her and yourself." Loyola grabbed my hair and shook my head while all the time Morrissey held me there, breathing hard and leaning over me. I didn't know what was going to happen until he.. they... and to my eternal shame I just gave in and let them." Finally Eamon stopped talking and the silence in the sacristy was deafening, only broken by the soft sobs coming from him, his face buried in his hands and his shoulders shuddering.

After some minutes he raised his face towards Brendan, red eyed and pale as candle wax "Almost two years, nearly every day.. they.. who'd have believed me? I had no one and they had all the power, over me, over my family and even if I had told anyone, Loyola's cousin was the Archbishop. I, I tried to run away once but they caught me and the pair of them beat me senseless. After that they said if I ever stepped out of line again they'd kill me and my family. After two years I was shipped out to another school. I was too old for their... twisted needs and so they got rid of me, but not before they made sure I knew they could always get me or my family."

44

Brendan interrupted "You don't have to go any further Eamon. You've told me more than you need. Don't punish yourself any further." They sat in silence for the next several minutes until the clock on the wall struck the hour with a metallic clang.

It was Brendan who broke the silence first "Jesus Christ, Eamon. I don't know where to begin. No wonder you're collapsing. The weight of all this is unbearable." Brendan reached out and held Eamon's hands in his. Eamon flinched momentarily at the touch but Brendan held his hands fast in a grip that spoke of comfort and acceptance and with a look of deep sadness in his eyes. "Take a minute. When you're ready we'll talk about the job. If nothing else it'll help you focus."

"You know I can't discuss any of that with anyone outside the investigation" Eamon snorted "unless the seal of the confessional extends to chat in the sacristy over whiskey. Though the real sin here is calling that stuff whiskey in the first place."

"Ah, there he is. I thought I'd lost you for a moment. Anything discussed here I will take to my grave you have my word on it" Brendan's tone was as grave as the statement.

"Fair enough" Eamon said, tilting his glass, "Pour some more of that stuff."

Over the next few minutes Brendan sat still as a statue while Eamon recounted the whole sequence of events from the start. Only when he finished with the visit to Butler did he react, a look of distain crossing his face. "Why in God's name would you ever go near that piss poor excuse for a human being?"

Eamon grimaced "The one thing about my job that you know full well is that I mix with some people I'd rather not but it's an evil I accept to get the information I need, and you know Butler hears every whisper of the city. Whatever else he maybe he's better informed that we are in the guards."

"That's as may be but you know you can't trust him to serve anyone's interests but his own. You told me once that he nearly ended your career before it began so *be bloody careful.*" Brendan's finger stabbed the air in front of Eamon's face in punctuation of the last three words.

"I'll never forget that believe me but I'm desperate and needed to know if any of the regular scumbag vigilante hard men were involved. It was a fishing expedition to cross that off my list because right now I'm looking for a needle in a stack of needles." Eamon sighed. The whiskey was making him feel the weight of the tiredness he carried. He couldn't remember his last proper sleep. "I don't think this has anything to do with your run of the mill criminals and it's not the Provos style. If they wanted to kill a couple of perverts they'd do it, take credit and not give a damn."

"Well from what you've told me it's almost as though this killer is looking for you to catch him and you know... that doesn't surprise me.." Brendan said in a quiet, thoughtful tone, his brow furrowing.

"Go on" Eamon looked up, forgetting the tiredness and leaning forward.

"Well, if he's somebody who's religious... and from the conversation you had with him I can only think it's somebody who knows his bible. Then he knows that wilfully killing as he is doing is a mortal sin. He knows he must pay for those sins and you are the instrument of his punishment, if you can catch him."

Eamon was staring at the floor, lips pursed. "It all comes back to the why of it" he glanced up from his reverie. "After so long, what was the trigger? Was it those two coming back into the country after so many years? Is there a link we don't know about between them? I can't see one."

"You said perverts. What makes you think that the first victim, Fr. Mitchell, was a pervert?" Brendan asked.

Eamon answered "Victim? To be honest I hope they roast in hell" Eamon snorted. "It's the only link I can think of although there's nothing yet to say they would have known each other."

Brendan snapped his fingers, a look of realisation on his face "Well actually I think I can shed some light on that. Loyola and Mitchell were both at St. Augustine's. Father Mitchell would have arrived just after you'd left. I knew the name was familiar. There was never any hint of impropriety as far as I know. In fact I seem to remember Mitchell as being an advocate for the boys."

Eamon's look was one of disgust "I'm betting he was just another one. Better at covering his tracks maybe but eventually the truth will out. Someone has made the connection between them, they're both dead but this means it could have been anyone in Augustine's over a ten year period, or someone they told, a friend, a relative... that's one bloody big haystack to search in a few days, either before there's another killing, or I get removed from the case or McGinn, that little bastard, gets something he can print."

Brendan grinned "break his fingers, oh, and while you're at it his jaw too. Not easy to write or talk then I' imagine."

Eamon smiled thinly "The eternal pacifist extolling violence, if it weren't so horrific I'd be laughing."

47

Brendan looked at him earnestly "Eamon, some people would drive a saint to violence but only because it would be a greater sin not to beat the shite out of them. You've got to get something tangible and quick before McGinn gets anywhere with a story or your life will be in a far greater hell than it is at present."

"I know, I know. This has to go away before anyone else gets given this case. If the whole thing unwound in public it might all come out I don't think I could cope with the shame. Being.. this way.. is bad enough but to be seen as a victim would be the last straw. My biggest problem is I don't know if I want to find the man who killed the man who… did that to.. to.. me." Eamon's voice faltered and he held his face in his hands, rubbing eyes that felt as though they were full of sand.

"You do your job, Eamon Kearns. No matter what.. and maybe you'll get justice for yourself and those who came after you along the way. You do not break your oath." Brendan's voice was strident, even a little menacing Eamon thought, as he looked at his friend. "Jesus Brendan, easy big man. You know I'll get to the bottom of it."

"Good" Brendan said quietly, "Its things like this that can bring down the Church, my church, and that I can't reconcile with. She's all I have and all so many others rely on for comfort and peace. How about your young colleague, Gavin? Is he a man you can trust to both see this through and get it out or is he better out of your way? If you *can* trust him he'll be another person you can lean on and another set of eyes and yet if you can't.. well then he's better off being kept at arm's length, both for his protection and yours."

Eamon looked at Brendan as though seeing him for the first time "you're much more suited to police work than the priesthood

48

Brendan2 he snorted, half smiling "always questioning everyone's motives. As for Gavin he's a good lad but I want to keep him out of this, both because he is a good lad but also because I can't tell which way he'll jump if his career's on the line. He might well tow the party line and bury this if he's threatened like me. He has everything to lose and very little to gain"

"Keeping him out of the way but doing the legwork is probably best then" Brendan said and quickly moved on. "Tell me, are you going home?"

Eamon shook his head slowly "No I'm not. I'm going to book into a B&B in Portobello. As far as they're aware it's a water leak in the house and I'm out while it's fixed. Partly true anyway. I'd say I'm definitely out of the house. Christ, the way she looked at me, like I was some piece of shit on her shoe, after thirty years."

"Do you want me to talk to Marie?" Brendan asked.

Eamon slumped back in his seat rubbing his eyes, temples and his jaw which he realised was aching from being constantly clenched. "What would that accomplish? She'll see things differently? Take me back with open arms saying *"Oh you're gay...well, that's ok. At least now I can ask you for fashion advice and actually listen to your answers."*

"I could try to make her see that you're still the same pig headed gobshite she married" Brendan replied, "but that'd most likely send her over the edge altogether" He clapped Eamon on the shoulder with a friendly thump and Eamon wearily stood. "You can be an awful bollix, Brendan. I'm going to get some sleep for an hour or two and try to make some sense of this. As usual, thanks for everything."

With that the big man caught him in a bear hug that Eamon thought would end him before Brendan released his grasp. "As usual, you're welcome" he said, "A decade of the rosary, though, for the swearing."

5.

"Where were you on the night of September 15th?" The sergeant's voice was grave as though communicating the seriousness of the situation. "Specifically between the hours of 11pm and 2am." Hennessey didn't meet Eamon's blank stare, instead shuffling through some papers in a folder in front of him. So intent was his examination of the contents of the folder it was obvious to Eamon that he didn't want to look him in the eye.

"Why am I here? What is this line of questioning about" Eamon was both confused and angry, fucked if he was going to be quizzed in an interview room by Sergeant Hennessey, the big, thick bog man of the station. Hennessey had grown up on the side of a mountain and the joke in the station was that whatever kind of soil they had up there bred big, lumbering oxen, good for heavy lifting but not much else. Right now Eamon wasn't so sure. Hennessey seemed very direct and his huge shoulders were so tight his neck, such as it was, was almost swallowed up. His hands came to rest, leaving down the papers, clenched together as if in prayerful supplication and the backs of his thumbs pressed against his lips. He looked up slowly and Eamon could see the conflict in his eyes.

"Look Eamon, I don't want to be doing this." Hennessey's tone was pleading, "But you're going to have to answer the questions or else call a solicitor. If you can just help me out we can get this over with the least amount of shit."

"What the fuck would I need a solicitor for?" Eamon burst out loudly. "Hennessey, what's going on? Just level with me."

"We'll be asking the questions" a voice came from behind him as the door opened. The slight figure of detective Mullins quietly closed the door behind him and crossed to sit in the empty chair beside Hennessey. He too, had a folder of papers but he didn't even bother to look at it. "By the way it's sergeant Hennessey and Detective Mullins when you're talking to us here, Garda Kearns." Eamon caught the emphasis on the word garda and wondered what Mullins was cooking. Whatever it was it couldn't be good.

"Fair enough, Detective" Eamon loaded the title equally heavily. "But before I go answering any questions I have the right to know why I'm here at least. So I'll know whether to call a solicitor or not."

"How long have you been with us Eamon" Mullins said ignoring his comment. "A year? You should know that when a superior asks you a question you bloody well answer it." Mullins snarled "I have more to be doing than pissing around with the likes of you" He waved the hand holding the folder in a dismissive flick. "This, this is serious and your career and reputation are on the line so answer the questions or I'll personally see to it that you get buried under a ton of shit."

"Eamon, just tell us where you were on the night of September 15th" Hennessey was still pleading, clearly dismayed at the direction this was taking. "There's been an allegation, a very serious one, concerning your activities and your... associations" It seemed as though it was Hennessey had struggled to make the last word fit in his mouth.

Eamon was reeling. What the hell was happening? Clearly this was serious, serious enough to warrant an off the record interview, no rights read, no direct allegation, no evidence produced... so far and he hadn't a clue what the hell was so special about September 15th.

"Hennessey, I literally have no idea what you're talking about. I have no idea where I was on that night. What's so special about it anyway? It's almost two months ago. I've been plenty places since then" Eamon was rising to the bait and he knew it. He should have kept quiet, called for a solicitor or just walked out the door but Mullins had pushed his buttons and he was too angry and defensive to think clearly.

"It was a Friday night. Not long after you'd closed that burglary case. Remember that? You were awful pleased with yourself. What was it? Six houses? You caught the little fucker coming out a bedroom window. In fairness if that had been me he'd have gotten away but you ran him down. A mile of a chase wasn't it? And on top of that he was still wearing a watch from another robbery. A nice little feather in your cap" Mullins voice had become softer, friendly even.

"Nine robberies thought Eamon. *He wants me to correct him so he knows I remember what he's referring to. A shared story, camaraderie and praise from your superiors... whatever this is" "he thinks I'm guilty as sin."* "I have nothing to say. I simply can't remember" Eamon said the words though a terrible realisation was taking shape in the shadows of his mind. Friday the 15th. He'd gotten completely wasted that night with a few of the lads and when they fell by the wayside he headed for the only early house within walking distance. McGettigans. Fuck! What did they know? Had he done something stupid and let the cat out of the bag?

53

"McGettigans" Mullins said as though reading his mind. "Anything in particular you feel like sharing about your visit there. You did go there that night, didn't you?"

"I've strayed in there the odd time after hours for a late pint. As have both of you so don't try to make out it's a big deal" Eamon was lashing out and he knew it but he had lost his composure. "What of it?"

"What indeed. So you admit you were there?" Mullins was tightening a noose and Eamon had just put his neck in it. "It makes no difference. We have a witness who can confirm that you were and more to the point who you were with."

"I probably was, but if I was then I can also guarantee that I was off duty and probably pissed out of my mind. I was celebrating, that's true and as for whom I was with ..." Eamon threw his hands up "No idea. I doubt if I could tell you how I got home either. It was a bit of a long session. Possibly not my finest hour but hardly a hanging offence. So, who is alleging what? Whose shoes did I piss on?"?"

"Well here's the thing Garda Kearns" Mullins was clearly enjoying this bit, the bastard, thought Eamon "that little fucker you caught has an older brother, James. He recognised you in McGettigans and followed you into the toilets with the idea of getting a little revenge. He now asserts that when he entered you were in a cubicle with the door ajar and that you were not alone. He made that allegation this morning, in this station." Mullins paused looking intently at Eamon, searching for any indication that he'd hit a nerve.

Eamon's mind was spinning. He couldn't grasp what Mullins had said. He stared blankly, a rabbit in the headlights, waiting for the killer blow.

54

Mullins however seemed to take his blank stare for incredulity. "I take it you're denying this allegation? You were not in a toilet cubicle on that night, engaged in an illegal and immoral activity with another male? You were just drunk and fell into a cubicle unaware that it was already occupied and in your state of inebriation you took a minute to get your bearings and leave. That's your official statement is it?" His stare bored into Eamon, who suddenly realised the situation he was in.

This wasn't a witch hunt, a casting out of the gay member. This was a cover up. A clear message to Eamon that all the facts were known but they were also being stitched together in such a manner as to be true but useless. "If you say so, sir" Eamon was inexperienced but he was clever enough to know when he was being thrown a lifeline.

"I fucking do say so, Garda Kearns and that will be reflected in my report to the Super" Mullins tone was now completely neutral. "You know that his brother will only be tried on Monday and has been on remand for the past several weeks in St. Pat's because of a backlog of cases in front of the criminal court. I have to think his brother, James, is trying to cause upset that might get his brother's case thrown out and if you were not present to give your evidence due to a cloud hanging over you a judge might well throw the case out."

Mullins turned his attention to Hennessey who sat transfixed. "That seems to conclude our questioning don't you think sergeant? Totally baseless accusations... Sergeant Hennessey, you look as though you could use a cup of tea. Why don't you go take a minute and we'll finish up here." Hennessey looked genuinely relieved. He got out of his chair and to the door with a speed that belied his bulk, not taking so much as a backward glance as he closed it behind him.

Mullins waited, watching the door, until the sound of Hennessey's heavy footsteps faded. Then he turned his attention to Eamon. "Off the record Eamon, I had to show you what would happen if it ever got out that you were a fucking faggot. You know well that's a serious criminal offence and I don't want to be the one who has to prosecute you for it." Seeing the look on Eamon's face he held up a hand "I'm not saying it's true but stuff like that sticks like shit to a blanket and would ruin your career, guilty or not. I took no pleasure in it, believe me, but if Hennessey is quizzed he'll say I went to town on you and that you proved yourself innocent under questioning. He's a slow thinker but a solid, dependable man when you need one." Mullins lowered his voice "I think you're a good cop. I don't give a fuck what you do off duty and in the privacy of your own home unless it harms the force. Then it becomes personal. I won't have it and I will bury you if you make me."

Eamon started to protest. Mullins held up a hand to silence him "I told you I don't give a fuck. You have a wife? Girlfriend? No? Well get one. Get married, have kids, do your fucking job and leave this shit in a sealed box buried way down in your gut until you forget it was ever there. This goes away because I won't have the likes of a career criminal like James Butler or his little brother casting his dirty shadow over the uniform. You watch that one in the future because mark my words, he's trouble."

Over the course of the years he had encountered James Butler more than a few times. For some reason Butler always seemed to get off on some technicality or other, missing evidence or the case getting thrown out. Eamon never wanted to be in a courtroom with Butler because he knew that a cornered rat will bite anything that gets close and he just might dredge up the past out of simple malice.

56

He'd had been very happy to hear he'd gone down for five years for gun running on his last stint, not that Butler was a Provo, he was just an opportunist and a survivor, "Bastard", he thought.

Eamon sat in the car, engine running, outside St. Peter's, his eyes closed, reliving that interview for the umpteenth time. He had of course found a girl, Marie, gotten engaged with plenty fanfare and much back slapping and just a few months later was married, again amidst a mixture of back slapping and comments about not being able to wait for the ride, or was she pregnant that they were getting hitched so soon. Hennessey was the most vocal in both his joking and his endorsement, never missing an opportunity to let everyone be in no doubt as to the manliness of young Kearns.

Eamon looked back on that period bemused. The ultimate irony was that when Mullins had retired some years later, unmarried, and left the country for America to work for some security company, Eamon had learned that he settled in San Francisco and lived out his life with a man he met there. Well this was the nineties and it was almost acceptable now, over there anyway. It never would be here, he thought bitterly.

Eamon had heeded Mullins advice, never acted on his feelings again, became a pillar of the force, a family man and as far removed from those feelings as possible. As far as anyone knew Eamon Kearns was *normal*. He drank too much, but didn't everyone? He worked too hard, but didn't everyone? He provided for his family, sent his sons to college and had a decent life. A life that had become increasingly hollow and empty and only filled with work and the booze and the constant struggle to hide himself from... himself... and everyone else.

"Hmph" he grunted "I don't see me retiring to the States. No matter what this is home and here's where I fight my battles." He started the car and slowly drove away toward the B&B in Portobello, watched all the while by eyes that were as haunted as his own, until his car disappeared into the busy Dublin evening traffic.

6.

Stopping at the first off licence he saw, Eamon bought a bottle of Bushmills. It might be a Protestant whiskey, but damn it, it was good. He left in on the back seat of the car while he walked to the closest greasy spoon and had a good, solid steak and chips, something Marie would have frowned upon he thought sadly with a lump instantly forming in his throat. He paid and left, drove to Portobello in a blur of images from the past few days but there she was, coming back into his thoughts every few seconds. He knew he'd have to call her but dreaded the prospect.

As soon as he'd parked, retrieved the bottle and made his way into the small room. It was well appointed, if dated. Perfectly wallpapered in Laura Ashley, pink velvet curtains and more flowers in evidence on the cushions, pillows and duvet cover than he would ever be comfortable with, gay or not. He sat on the soft bed, another thing he wasn't used to. Eamon liked a firm mattress and the looking around the room he thought that whole experience was at odds with his personality.

He poured a large glass and drained it in one long gulp, feeling the fire hit his throat and the all too familiar warmth in his chest and stomach. "My only friend" he thought as he finished it and immediately poured another. He knew well why he needed them. To face talking to Marie he was going to have to find courage somewhere.

The phone in the room was as dated as the décor, the plastic receiver a jaded, dirty cream. He picked it up and hesitantly dialled. He knew he wouldn't have to wait long if Marie was in. She couldn't let it ring more than three times before she raced to pick up but each ring hiked his anxiety and made his stomach churn. True to form on the third ring the phone picked up but instead of the usual chirpy tone there was instead a deafening silence. His head was swimming as he forced himself to speak.

"Marie, its Eamon" he rolled his eyes at his stupidity, of course she knew who it was. "You don't have to say anything. I just wanted to tell you I love you, have always and will always. I'd never do anything to hurt you, not intentionally. I know this is hurting you and I can only hope you will see one day that I had to finally get the truth out. It's been a millstone around my neck my whole life and it's cost me more than I can ever say" he stopped, wondering if she was still there. There was only silence on the line, then a sigh. "Marie, I'd never want this to come out. I'd never want you or the boys to have to carry the burden but if I don't do something I'm afraid of what it'll mean."

He could feel the panic rising. He gripped the phone tightly, the receiver pressed hard to his forehead and focused, exhaling in a shuddering gasp. "I know this is unforgiveable but I hope that you can, at least enough to be able to look you in the eye and talk to you, to explain, to try making some sense of this, to find a way forward. I'm staying at the Portobello Arms. Can I come see you, talk to you?"

"Mind yourself, Eamon" and with that the line went dead. His head threatened to explode with the pressure he felt and Eamon sank to his knees against the bed, tears coming in between the shoulder wrenching sobs.

It was twilight when he woke face down on the bed and for a moment he was confused, unsure of his surroundings before realisation hit him. At the same moment the half empty bottle of whiskey explained the rest of the story. His head was pounding and he realised that it was the phone ringing that had brought him round. He scrambled off the bed and almost dropped the receiver in his haste to answer "Marie? Is that you?"

"Inspector... Eamon, I prefer to call you Eamon. Two people who share so much should be on first name terms." The muffled voice shocked Eamon to his senses in a heartbeat. "It's been an emotional day for you, Eamon. I hope you are getting enough sleep and if I were you I'd lay off the whiskey." The voice sounded almost concerned but there was a taunt in the tone as well.

"How the fuck did you find this number? And your concern is noted but isn't worth a jot. I don't take advice or counsel from someone who murders and tortures people." Eamon was trying to get his senses together, silently cursing the accusing bottle on the night stand.

"People? Eamon, these animals aren't people. They're a disease, a cancer that has to be burnt out of My Church." The voice was derisory, almost condescending.

"As for finding you, it's not difficult Eamon. I just keep an eye on you. You look tired, but I digress. I'm going to help you Eamon, help you see the truth and you're going to hold that truth up to the light for all to see." The voice had become angry, "And the truth shall set you free. I really believe that Eamon. I also believe that people who interfere in God's work should be punished severely."

"It's God's work now is it?" Eamon was goading the voice, hoping he'd give away something. "I thought this was all you. Now God's getting the blame!"

"Of course cleaning the Church is God's work and I am but his instrument. God brought those filthy animals back to me to cleanse them of their iniquity and everyone else who is complicit in their crimes. When I have cleansed the Church I can finally be clean" Eamon noted that the voice had become sibilant, hissing the words through clenched teeth.

"Everyone? Surely enough has been done. You've killed two people, broken the fifth commandment, wilfully and you must know that's a mortal sin. You can't be absolved of this" Eamon hoped the threat of eternal damnation might sway the bastard, but he doubted it. There was a twisted logic at work and he knew it would justify the killer's actions.

"We all have to pay for our sins in the long run, Eamon. How do you intend to pay for yours?" The voice suddenly sounded weary.

"I haven't killed anyone, when I meet my maker I won't have that stain on my conscience" in Eamon's mind the thought flashed that he'd have enough to pay for as it was.

"The sin of inaction is as bad as the sin of action, Eamon. You will be judged for what you didn't do as much as for what you did." There was a pause then the voice spoke again "Go to Minister Casey. Ask him what this is really about. He knows," and the phone went dead.

"Jesus Christ" Eamon slumped down on the bed, bewildered. His hangover was kicking in viciously and his head was pounding so badly he was having trouble collecting his thoughts. Unsteadily, he stood and tottered to the ensuite bathroom, guts churning as he did. He reached the toilet just in time to empty the contents of his stomach. Then he took a cold shower, the shock of the water hitting his face and body helping in some small way to sober him up. He turned the water to hot and again the sudden change brought relief. A quick shave, new clothes, some mouth wash and a half hour later he felt much more human. He wiped the steam from the bathroom mirror and surveyed his appearance. He'd looked better but he'd also looked a hell of a lot worse.

"Bit between your teeth now, Eamon" admonished his reflection as he poked a finger at it. "No more booze and get this done." With that he called the station and left a message for Gavin to meet him there in thirty minutes. He looked at his watch. It read 10pm. "It might be the middle of the night by the time we get moving but some people are getting woken up." He left his car in the car park and walked the canal from Portobello to Harcourt Street, just to shake off the remaining cobwebs, noting as he did that his step felt a little lighter. It might be a mess but at least he wasn't living a lie anymore and come what may he'd never again be what he was.

When he got to the station Gavin was already at his desk poring over paperwork. He knew they'd have to have a conversation soon but for now he'd just have to concentrate on the job at hand. Gavin eyed him suspiciously, obviously noting the change in demeanour. "Boss" he said simply.

Feeling the awkwardness Eamon looked him in the eye and quietly said "Look, Gav, I'm sorry. We have a job to do and I've let personal issues get in the way. That stops now and so does the booze. I'm on the dry as of this moment."

"Glad to hear it." The relief was palpable in both Gavin's voice and his stance "What's the story?"

63

Eamon recounted the phone call giving all the details except the last bit about Minister Casey. That he was going to pursue alone. "He said something that I can't leave alone. *They came back to me.* Now that made me think that our killer has more of a connection to the two victims than just a religious one. I found out this afternoon that they may have both taught at St. Augustine's Industrial School in the early fifties. The school closed down in eighty two but there is still a church there and there might be someone who remembers them, or someone else connected to them... something, anything that we can follow. I just have a feeling that there's something there. I want you to go over there and rattle the cage of anyone who may remember that time" Eamon knew the lie was skirting the truth dangerously closely but he had to manage Gavin and still get some information.

"What, now?" asked Gavin incredulously. "It's almost eleven."

"Well go wake them up then. We have no time and a lot of ground to cover." Eamon gave a tilt of his head and stood glowering with an expression that defied Gavin to retort.

"Yes Boss." Gavin spat the words between clenched teeth and grabbing his overcoat, stalked out of the office, the slam of the door almost taking it off its hinges as he did.

Eamon sat at his desk, swinging in the chair for a moment, pondering his next call. This wasn't going to be fun but fuck it, he didn't care. If he was going to make any headway he was going to have to upset some of the big wigs. He grabbed the phone and stabbed his finger at the numbers. Evelyn was not going to be happy but Ray was going to get a late night call whether she liked it or not!

The phone downstairs was ringing. Evelyn had taken the phone out of their bedroom after Ray's scare and there was no convincing her to put it back. The ringer was incessant and loudly amplified in the quiet of the night as though the whole house had tensed at the sudden intrusion. Everyone knew not to ring after ten so when the phone woke him with a start and he saw the time Ray was sure, he thought, just how serious and just who it might be. He glanced over at Evelyn still sound asleep thanks to the antihistamine she took for her allergies. He quickly swung his feet onto the cool floor, searching for his slippers and then headed as soundlessly as he could for the hallway. The bedroom door creaked slightly even though he'd lifted it by the handle in such a way as to take weight off the hinges. The protesting creak sent a shock straight into the pit of his stomach as he glanced backwards. Evelyn turned in the bed but thankfully didn't rouse and instead settled back.

Ray made a dash downstairs to where the phone was still clamouring. He grabbed the receiver as though to throttle whoever was on the other end and with a savage, whispered snarl hissed "This had better be to fucking tell me the world has ended or even better, that you're dead, because if there's anything I think has been spelled out clearly it's that I do not get calls at home at this hour. Not for any fucking reason short of Armageddon. I've almost had a fucking heart attack, Eamon. It is Eamon after all. Who else would be such an enormous pain in my bollocks?"

"They don't pay you the big bucks for nothing, Ray" Eamon said casually. He knew he was playing with fire but if he were honest his new found freedom from his personal demons was giving him cause to reflect and what he was finding was that if he could tell Marie, suffer the consequences and be true to himself, he didn't give too much of a fuck what might happen after that.

65

"Have you lost what little of your mind you have left? Are you drunk or just insane? Either would be better than telling me you rang here in the middle of the night just to get a rise out of me. What the fuck are you playing at?" Ray had a feeling that Eamon was sober and that made him even more worried, Eamon sober and ringing at this hour meant that the shit was about to well and truly hit the fan.

"You know I wouldn't Ray, unless I didn't have a choice. I want you to call Minister Casey, now, and tell him I'll meet him in Kildare Street in an hour. I'm not taking no for an answer either, not if you and he want me to keep playing ball. Either he's there in an hour or I'm making a call to McGinn and you can all go to hell together on the front page tomorrow" Eamon's tone was bullish and Ray knew that after all the years of working with him that he meant every word.

"Have you completely lost all reason, think of what's going to be left of your career, not to mention mine?" he hissed down the phone "We all go down together in that case, remember? And what story could you possibly tell McGinn that wasn't already explained or explainable?" Ray had a suspicion that he didn't want Eamon to answer that question and it was confirmed in the next sentence.

"You may have buried the first murder by losing the paperwork in transit but do you honestly think I didn't keep my own copies? I also kept copies of the second and as much of a record as I could of everything else. Enough to go to the press and make a stink that might not touch the high and mighty but it'll bury you, Ray. Now get Fanning into Kildare Street. I know he's in Dublin tonight, I already checked with his Garda detail." With that Eamon hung up.

Ray stood for a moment, becoming aware that he hadn't taken a breath and exhaled shakily, feeling his heart pound in his chest. Kearns, you utter bastard he thought as he began to dial, punching each number in staccato anger. "Minister, we have a problem" he said wearily when the voice answered. "Kearns is insisting to see you in Kildare Street, now. Yes sir, he knows you are. He asked me to inform you that if you don't meet him he's going to the press, publish and be damned. I don't know just how much he knows but it's clearly more than we thought he'd find. Yes sir. An hour. I'll let him know." He replaced the receiver before picking it up again quickly. He punched numbers into the keypad.

At the other end of the line Eamon answered "Detective Inspector Kearns here."

"An hour Eamon, Kildare Street. Someone will meet you there" he quietly placed the receiver back in its cradle and headed back upstairs. If Eamon Kearns survived the night without getting killed, imprisoned, fired or simply disappearing it would be a miracle, thought Ray as he climbed the steps again, his heart still racing

. He was supposed to be the easy choice, a nigh on burnt out detective just punching the clock, drinking himself to an early grave and obviously distracted. Not some single minded crusader from twenty years before. That Eamon Kearns knew how to get results and results, Ray thought, were the last thing he needed on this case.

He slipped back into bed where Evelyn rolled toward him "You ok pet?" she asked in a soft whisper as she put her hand to his face. "Oh you're all clammy. Are you coming down with something?" her concern growing she raised onto one elbow. Ray

67

just patted her shoulder and smiled "Nothing a good night's sleep won't cure. I had a little indigestion but I went down and got some water and an antacid" he lied. She kissed him on the cheek and smiled as she turned back to sleep. "Good night love, sleep well" she sighed and he felt her body settle back into its comfortable rhythm moments later. Jesus, how he envied her ability to do that.

Ray spent what seemed like an eternity staring at the ceiling, a tight knot in his stomach, as he imagined the conversation between Kearns and Minister Casey. It was such a fucking mess he couldn't fathom just how it was going to turn out, except the heavy ache in his chest that told him two things, he was glad his tenure was coming to a close and it couldn't come quickly enough.

7.

Eamon chose to walk to Kildare Street. The late night hum of the city always calmed him and right now he needed to find that calm. Lost in his reverie his feet had carried him to the front of Government Buildings on Kildare Street almost without thinking. He waved his warrant card at the Gardaí on duty and they waved him in. "You're expected apparently" said the older of the two on duty, casting his eyes toward heaven.

"Thanks, I think" snorted Eamon as he passed, crossing the gravelled courtyard to the steps of the building. His footsteps crunched, announcing his arrival as it were, loudly in the night air. Much too loudly it seemed to him. Only a few windows were lit at this time of night, he mused, as civil servants kept the cogs turning that ran the country.

Which, wondered Eamon, of the windows facing him framed his welcome committee and were they watching his advance up the granite steps with any trepidation at all. Certainly he felt the weight of what was about to unfold as he saw it in his mind's eye. What did they know and more to the point what did they suspect? What did they not want seeing the light of day? What did HE not want to see the light of day and could he juggle it all? He sighed heavily, pausing before the main doors *'into the belly of the beast'* he thought and gave a silent prayer that he wasn't going to be eaten alive.

He entered to be greeted immediately by a short, pale, balding man, though Eamon thought *man* might be stretching it somewhat. Despite the receding hairline the lad seemed so babyfaced he didn't look as though he'd left secondary school. The rolled up sleeves on his shirt and loosely knotted tie only served to accentuate the point. He was what Eamon would have called wet or a bit of a milksop.

"Inspector Kearns?" It seemed less of a question than a statement, thought Eamon. "I'm to take you directly to the Ministers offices on arrival. Follow me please." He turned on his heel and began to stride away, an air of impatience in his wake. Eamon stood still, smiling. After about ten paces his usher noticed the lack of compliance and turned sharply "Inspector, please!" he motioned Eamon to him with a sharp flick of the hand.

"Let's start again, shall we?" said Eamon. "I'm *Detective* Inspector Kearns and yes I'm here to see the Minister. However, I've had to walk a bit and as I'm getting on I feel I need a minute before I continue. My heart's not the best, you know… or you will know in about thirty years." Eamon smiled politely, deciding not to play the game. Obviously this young upstart had been given instructions to bring him directly, both to show the power of his host and to get him off balance and on edge. If he'd been ten years younger it might have worked too, but not tonight.

"May I trouble you for a glass of water" he asked innocently.

The babyface looked stricken, confused as this wasn't how the narrative was supposed to play. "Wait.. w.. wait there" he pointed to a chair and again spun on his heel and disappeared.

"Fuck that" whispered Eamon to himself "I might be in the belly but the beast is getting indigestion." It may have been petty but he didn't fucking care. When babyface returned with a glass of water and proffered it, Eamon noticed his hand shaking and could feel the air of impatience and worry coming from him in waves. He felt a small tinge of sympathy for the lad, *just another lackey, same as us all* he mused as he sipped.

"What's your name lad" he enquired breaking the tense silence.

"James, James O'Connor" babyface replied. "Look we'd better get moving. Minister Casey isn't someone to be kept waiting" his voice was tired and the admonition definite. Eamon looked at his face again and saw that young James here had fallen foul of Casey before.

"No point in ruffling his feathers then is there" Eamon pushed himself out of the seat gingerly, his body feeling tired and heavy.

"Lead on McDuff" he motioned with a sweep of his arm.

James O'Connor just cast his eyes slightly toward heaven and set off up the corridor as quickly as he dared without giving his charge a heart attack, it seemed.

Minister David Casey was not a man prone to waiting and that idiot O'Connor was going to catch it in the neck when he finished here. He was pacing the large office over and back, glass in hand, and watched by two seated figures, Archbishop Francis Flood |and Commissioner Sean Flannigan. "That little shit. Where is he?" he muttered through gritted teeth. "I told him to bring Kearns here directly when he arrived. He's taking his sweet time" he glanced at the clock. "It's gone midnight."

"David, David.. calm down" the Archbishop waved his hand in a soothing motion "Kearns is obviously trying to exercise what little power he has in the situation. He hopes to frustrate us so he

71

can control the meeting. Or at least that's what I'd be doing in his shoes. Control the tempo and affect the outcome." He smiled calmly "he'll get here when he gets here and we will hear what he has to say before we decide the next step and how much we can let him know to get the job done."

"I think you've spent too much time in Italy reading Machiavelli" snorted Casey and draining his glass before pouring another whiskey. "What do you think Sean?" Commissioner Flannigan sat impassively, hands folded, seemingly oblivious to the conversation to that point. "I think Kearns needs to be handled very carefully. I remember Eamon well coming up the ranks. He's sharp if erratic, sometimes brilliant and sometimes a bloody mess and his own worst enemy. If he'd been a more politically aware animal he might well be sitting in my seat. Don't underestimate him just because he's too fond of a glass." He nodded at Casey, "You might do well to go easy yourself."

Minister Casey was about to retort when a knock on the door stopped him in his tracks. James O'Connor's face appeared around the opening door, looking tentative.

"Sorry Minister, Detective Inspector Kearns is here to see you." O'Connor cast a quick glance at the other two figures and quickly thought to himself that he wanted to be on the other side of that door quick smart.

Eamon pushed past him, taking a glance at Casey's glowering face "Minister, thank you for seeing me." Recognising the other two men caught him mid stride and he paused momentarily before continuing, hoping that he'd kept the look of surprise to himself, *a bloody ambush*, he thought bitterly. He made a show of taking off his coat and a little theatrically looked around until he noticed a coat rack. He hung the coat ion the rack fussily.

A stalling moment that Colombo would have been proud of he thought as he turned, fixing a pleasant smile as he did. "I wasn't feeling myself when I arrived and young O'Connor here kindly offered me a glass of water and a chair. Thanks for everything James. I'd say you can head off now. I'm sure you have more important things to attend to." He said, giving the young man a wink.

Eamon made a show of the moment just to calm himself as much as to placate Casey's obvious annoyance at his underling. O'Connor, still standing in the open doorway was wishing to be anywhere else at that moment and looked to the Minister for confirmation. Casey gave a curt wave of his hand. With that he disappeared, pulling the door closed quickly. In the hallway he exhaled heavily and walked away as quickly as he could without breaking into a run. *I really don't fancy being in that room, you poor bastard Detective Inspector.*

"Sit down Detective Inspector" said Casey curtly, waving toward the others as he crossed the room and sat down between the two others. "I'm sure you don't have to be introduced to my guests this evening and I'm sure you won't mind them sitting in on our… little chat." He emphasised the *little chat* in a tone Eamon found very disconcerting, as was the vista of this unholy trinity arrayed against him.

"Commissioner Flannigan, Your Grace" Eamon nodded taking the only unoccupied seat, placed, he thought conveniently facing the others as though he was to be interviewed by the panel. "I must say this is something of a surprise, though it at least confirms that there's more to this than meets the eye. I had come here to see Minister Casey regarding a very serious matter and now it seems I was right to do so. May I ask in simple terms? *What the fuck is going on?*"

73

"You will mind your tongue" snapped Archbishop Flood "and show the proper respect for your superiors."

"My apologies, Your Grace" said Eamon with loaded deference "I rarely mix in such exalted circles and my language does tend to be a little.. salty.. occupational hazard" He threw his hands up grimacing "but to be honest I don't give a rattling fuck about protocol tonight. I came here for answers and I'll be damned as will you all if I leave here without them.. so let's cut the pretence and get down to it."

"Easy Eamon" cautioned Commissioner Flannigan "we're all here for the same reasons. We have a job to do in protecting the institutions of the State and you to protect the people." Flannigan glanced from Archbishop to Minister before continuing "This is an extremely sensitive case and we need to be sure you are working in everyone's best interests for a positive outcome before we can make you privy to information that will no doubt assist you in the performance of your duties."

"A few questions, *sir*" Eamon addressed Flannigan directly "Who am I protecting the people from and what are you protecting?"

Flannigan paused, looked at both his companions, and receiving a slight nod from both continued with a sigh. "Before I give you any more details tonight I want to remind you of something you might want to consider. You, as a civil servant, are subject to the Official Secrets Act, 1963. You know that one don't you Eamon, the one that is going to see you in prison if any of this gets into the public domain and we link you to it and by God Eamon, we bloody well will. You'll do time and your family will be disgraced. I don't think Marie or the boys are up for you committing professional suicide, and who knows what else might come out in the wash. The press can make a story out of the slimmest details, it seems, these days." He looked Eamon straight in the eye, holding contact as though to drive the implied threat home or glean a reaction.

Eamon broke eye contact and smiled at the three in a friendly, even jovial tone. "Right, now we've gotten the threats out of the way and you've pretty much stitched me up if this goes wrong what do I need to know so that I can bring this killer.. potentially a serial killer mind you, to some kind of justice"

Through the smiles Eamon was barely holding his contempt in check, but by the looks on the three faces opposite him, they were in the same boat.

8.

Gavin had crossed town in both record time and with some belligerence toward pedestrian, cyclist and driver alike. He wasn't sure which version of Eamon drove him more mental, the drinking version who didn't really give a shit or the thinking version that seemed to hate everyone and not give a shit. *Either way,* he thought, *I get the shitty end of the stick.*

He arrived at the old Augustine School, now mostly used as a community centre, Alcoholics Anonymous meeting point or for numerous clubs.

"After all this I might need to join AA myself as a precaution" he muttered.

Mass was still said in the Church but the signs of the buildings decline were evident. Broken windows boarded up rather than repaired, weeds poking through the cracks in the old paving slabs of the courtyard and a general sense of being forgotten.

Maybe that's exactly what the Church wanted after everything came out there a few years ago mused Gavin as he crossed the courtyard, moss growing in the joints of the old brickwork on the verge, telling of further disuse. He headed toward the only light still on, illuminating the front door and porch of the priests quarters. They weren't going to thank him for this visit at.. he glanced at his watch.. *nearly midnight.. Jesus Eamon this is just bloody great..* with another grimace and a sigh and he knocked on the door, banging the old brass knocker, itself in need of a good cleaning. It was a minute before another light illuminated a window upstairs and he saw a figure twitch the curtains.

The door opened slightly, revealing a tossed white haired and bleary eyed, elderly man, wearing typical striped pyjamas and a dressing gown that was probably as old as himself. He hadn't undone the chain lock on the door and eyed Gavin suspiciously until he produced his warrant card.

"Detective Gavin Cantwell" he said holding up the warrant card "I really am sorry for calling this late Father" Gavin was pouring the apologetic tone on quite heavily and hoping he wasn't going to be told just where to go. He quickly added "but it's in connection with a very serious case and if I could have a few moments it might help me a lot."

The older man had been about to say something but Gavin's tone seemed to do the trick. He shook his head and opened the door, ushering Gavin inside.

"Come on, come on. I don't know what brings a Detective out at this time of night or why it can't wait until daylight but if it's that important you'd better get on with it" He sounded as old and care worn as the rest of the building Gavin thought as he stepped inside. "Go through into the kitchen, second door on the right in the hallway." The priest ushered him forward, waving a finger feebly toward the gloom of the unlit hallway. "The light switch is there on your right. We don't use it much, save electricity and all that" he called after Gavin as he shuffled along in his wake.

They entered the kitchen and Gavin flicked the light switch. The overhead light was hanging from a long cord over the kitchen table. Without a shade the naked bulb cast a harsh light. The priest shuffled slowly over to the counter, flicking on a desk lamp. "Turn that off, will you, it hurts my eyes. I keep meaning to buy a new shade but it never seems to be the right time." He shrugged apologetically. "Now, tea?"

Gavin had been through the ritual with older people many times and whether you wanted tea or not, you didn't refuse. To do so would be to defy tradition and possibly insult your host. When you wanted to open a conversation, a good cup of tea was better than any badge.

"That would be great, if it's not too much of an inconvenience" he said apologetically.

"No more trouble than getting me out of bed at this hour" the old man smiled "I'm Father Buckley by the way, and you are Detective.. Cantwell, was it?"

"That's right, and I really do apologise for getting you out of bed. It wasn't exactly my choice but we're investigating the unfortunate death of a priest and we're looking for help to tie up some loose ends. My gaffer, I mean my superior is pushing me to get it wrapped up so we can move on to other cases." The lie was almost true, with a little spin to soften the edges.

"Oh that unfortunate fellow in Ranelagh was it?" Father Buckley. He noted Gavin's puzzled expression with amusement. "We're old, retired or mostly retired priests with dwindling congregations, dwindling responsibilities and we gossip more than we should when we meet. It was the talk of the Community for a week or so. The poor chap. Not how I'd envisage shuffling off this mortal coil, I can tell you."

If only you knew thought Gavin, *or perhaps you do and it's better to pretend you don't. Maybe it was an idea to test the waters.*

"Yes, that's him alright, Father Buchannan", he confirmed "terrible business and I agree, awful way for a man to end his days, having given so much to the community and the Church. You didn't know him yourself then?"

"I'm afraid the name doesn't ring any bells, though perhaps thankful too. I have seen my fair share of friends pass over the past few years, time and tide waits for no man, though I'm sure a young chap such as yourself doesn't yet feel his mortality" The older man smiled thinly, as he pottered for cups and tea bags. "Is that why you've come, doing the rounds to see who might know him? We're of an age I suppose. I can't think of any way in which I could help you otherwise."

"My boss seems to think he might have been here when the school was open, a long time ago and wondered if someone might still be here that remembered him or any of his family." Gavin looked at Father Buckley's face for any signs that he might know or be hiding anything, but he seemed genuinely surprised.

"Buchannan, you said, well I can tell you that there's never been a priest of that name working or living here in the forty six years I've been in the parish and in this house." He seemed perplexed, asking "Are you sure your boss didn't mean a different parish?"

"That's quite a boast, to have been in one location for so long and I'm sure you've seen all sorts come and go. Is there any way he might have slipped your mind" Gavin asked softly, no point in offending the old man.

"Young chap, my body may be failing and almost done, but my mind is as clear now as it was on my first day here." He snorted with a slight shrug of his shoulders "More so probably and that is the most ironic thing about growing old, young fellow. Wisdom, experience and learning to burn and a body that won't let me take advantage of it" he chuckled slightly. "God moves in very mysterious ways, I just hope he knows what he's doing."

Gavin smiled "I'm sure you have many years ahead of you yet."

"Oh Lord, I hope not. I've paid my dues and I've a prostate the size of an orange, or so my doctor tells me. It won't kill me anytime soon but it does make certain bathroom functions quite, uncomfortable." Father Buckley placed two cups on the table with the teapot, a small glass jug of milk and matching sugar bowl. "Help yourself, its self-service around here" he smiled. His smile was a very open one Gavin thought, and his whole demeanour matched it, like an open book. This elderly gentleman had nothing to hide. His candour was evident and Gavin was sure there was nothing else to be gained but before he left he wanted to see what the old priest's reaction might be to Loyola's name dropping into the conversations.

"Father Buchannan had been out of the country for many years, travelled all over the world and only returned two years ago. No one seems to remember him" Gavin paused "he didn't always go by Buchannan, it seems he took a religious name as a young man."

"Some did, I never saw the point myself, but horses for courses, I suppose" he sat down to the table as Gavin poured two cups of steaming tea.

"I hope you like it strong because that's the only way I make it" again the old man chuckled. "I take it black and without sugar myself. I must like penance. What was his name did you say, maybe I'll know him after all"

"Loyola, Father Loyola" Gavin said, adding sugar to his own. The old man's cup stopped an inch from his lips. He placed it down on the table again "Oh dear, him" he said quietly. He sat back in his chair and a tortured expression crossed his face as though he was struggling with some unseen force.

Gavin froze momentarily, his spoon hovering about the steaming cup. "Go on" he said quietly seeing the priests shoulders sag and his hands shake "you do know him then?"

"Not *do*, but yes I did. It's a name I'd hoped never to hear again and one I can't say I'm happy hearing now. Though the circumstances of his death do lend me some small, if perverse, comfort" Father Buckley looked at Gavin intently, his eyes bright and alert, at odds, Gavin thought, with his aged, liver spotted skin. He continued "I know wishing ill on someone is sinful, petty even, but if anyone ever deserved to get his comeuppance it was that… bastard" the word spat from his mouth, surprising Gavin more because of its vehemence and its origin.

Seeing his expression Father Buckley reached out a leathery, worn hand and gently tapped his arm "I wasn't born saintly and I am human. If ever a person deserved to be cursed it was that demon. There's very little of me would mourn over the world losing one such as he. I just pray he suffers more now than he ever did in life."

There was such bitterness in his voice Gavin knew he wouldn't have to push very hard to get the back story he was looking for. Loyola or Buchannan or whoever he was certainly seemed to have been the type that made enemies and maybe this fishing expedition would turn something up after all, long shot or not.

"Loyola, that animal was priest in this parish for four years before I came here as a young canon. Even then he liked to throw his weight around, with the boys in the school and with the staff, he paused shaking his head "In those days both the Christian

Brothers who taught in the school and the parish priest lived in this house, sometimes up to ten of us here, besides the lay teachers in the school and they were glad they only had to put up with occasional visits from him, I can tell you." Father Buckley sounded indignant, as if he were a man remembering an unresolved slight or insult.

"He was moved on to missionary work in.. Gambia I think it was... out to minister to the heathens as it were, though what he could have ever taught anyone about the grace of God I can't imagine." He stopped, wringing his hands, a silent wish perhaps, to wash them even as Pilate had. He reached out and shakily picked up his cup of black tea and took a sip before sighing and continuing, looking down into the steaming, black tea.

"From the moment I arrived here I knew two things, firstly who was boss and secondly that something wasn't right here. The atmosphere of repression and quiet fear was unlike anything I'd ever encountered" another sip, before placing the cup back on the table.

"He intimidated everyone, and you must understand that this was when his word was absolute law in the parish and not only that he was a cousin of the Bishop and made sure everyone knew it." Father Buckley's eyes were beginning to well up and he wiped them on the sleeve of his old robe before continuing.

"It wasn't long after I arrived that I had a run in with him for beating a schoolboy" he recalled, closing his eyes as though to see the past in a clearer light, or maybe so as not to see Gavin and any silent judgement his face might betray. "He'd really given the poor lad a hammering and when I challenged him he became nothing short of apoplectic, shouting in such fury that his face went white and his body rigid. After that I was left in no doubt as to who was in command, especially when I was given a talking to by the Bishop for trying to undermine his authority."

"So he'd have had a few enemies here in the school" Gavin interjected, "was there anyone who might have been especially aggrieved. Enough say to hold the grudge to the present day?"

"Almost everyone who worked here or attended the school would have had some form of enmity toward him, though most if not all of the staff have passed away at this stage so I'd doubt it would be one of them" he paused, as though realising something.

"He didn't die accidentally did he?" Father Buckley's expression became intent, earnest "you're here because someone killed him." Seeing Gavin's stony expression he tapped his forearm several times "I'm old, not slow. You can tell me anything you'd like safe in the knowledge that it won't ever cross my lips. I have a lifetimes experience in keeping secrets" he smiled thinly and seeing Gavin's brow furrow "confession my son, I hear more than you'd ever possibly imagine. I'd write a book if I could." Again he smiled "maybe I will, before I give up the ghost."

It was Gavin's turn to smile "I'm sure it'd be a page turner. Though you'd probably get paid more not to write it."

"I'm sure I would" Father Buckley replied his eyes twinkling momentarily before the moment passed and the light faded "Can you tell me what happened?"

"I can't but safe to say you are not slow and should probably have been a detective" Gavin gave a short, sharp tap on the table with one knuckle to punctuate the point.

"If there's anyone you can think of who Loyola might have had a serious grievance with could you let me know? I don't care how

83

long ago or insignificant you might feel it is. Anything at all could be pivotal."

Father Buckley leaned forward, catching Gavin's forearm in a grip that belied his age and leaning his careworn toward the younger man his voice dropped to a whisper.

"He was *moved on*" He spoke in what was barely above a whisper, conspiratorial and intense "In those days, far more than now, a potential scandal or priest acting in a manner unbecoming was dealt with.. differently. A big fuss would possibly embarrass the Church and certainly the Bishop. So when a priest was moved on, it was a euphemism used to cover over his indiscretions" he put his hand to his eyes, rubbing them before continuing.

"He was moved on because of a young priest who saw that he had... interfered with boys... boys in the school" he breathed out a heavy, quivering breath, whether in fear, anger or relief Gavin couldn't say.

""Father Mitchell was his name. He made accusations directly to the Bishop and was knocked down hard for his trouble. He was sent away himself, though God knows where, the whole thing hushed up and every one of us hauled in front of the Bishop with threats of dire consequences if we ever opened our moths about any of it", he paused, took a sip from his tea and pursed his lips as thought lost in thought.

After a few silent moments he looked into his cup and set it to one side. "I'm ashamed that I've never done more than wish I'd done more with my own suspicions, but in those days to go against the Bishop was madness. He controlled both Church and State. I put up with Loyola's insufferable smugness after that. He knew he couldn't be touched and I think it brought out the worst madness that was in him. Rumours occasionally surfaced but if a

84

child spoke up they simply vanished and if a staff member spoke up they knew they'd lose their job and possibly never get another, such was the Bishops power."

"And now? Gavin ventured "Would you consider laying this open now?"

"Quid agas predenter agas et respice finem" replied the old priest, his voice softening "Whatever you do, do with caution and look to the end" he looked at Gavin's confused expression. "Let sleeping dogs lie." Father Buckley shrugged, "The Church, this church especially has seen enough and had enough revelations of brutality and impropriety, though Loyola's name was never connected to later events that tarnished us, it was he who created the culture in the first instance."

"You are referring to the claims of abuse that were made by some past pupils" Gavin made the statement, not a question. It had made news for a few weeks but because there were only two former students making the claims while the vast majority of their compatriots denied any issues whatsoever, the claims had simply petered out or perhaps had been paid to do so.

"Lone voices in the wilderness" Father Buckley said, shaking his head. "We were all glad when it blew over, for many reasons. Mine being that the Church would be blamed but the Church is not at fault, her agents were. I have come to regret that belief over the years, as the Church should have done more as an institution with a duty of care for its flock, but I'm too old and tired to fight against the way things were and indeed, are still."

It was Gavin's turn to reach out his hand, squeezing the old man's in his own. "You sound as though you did your best in difficult, unforgiving circumstances."

"I did far from my best, because I was afraid, afraid of losing my place, being ostracised or cast out. This place and my work have been my entire life." There was a plea for understanding and perhaps forgiveness in his voice, Gavin thought.

"We all compromise, Lord knows I do. My own boss is demanding, brilliant, a drunken mess and impossible to please" he confided "I have to make decisions I'm not happy with and that often conflict with my conscience but I do it because in the end he gets results and justice is done."

Father Buckley smiled thinly "Thank you for trying to absolve an old man of this sin, but I'll have to face my Maker soon enough and see if he's as understanding. Your boss.. he's the one who has you out here in the middle of the night, is he?"

Gavin grunted "Oh he is, Eamon's Cantwell has no mercy for man or beast when he gets going. He'd wake the devil himself if he thought it would help him connect the dots in a case" seeing the expression on the priests face he added hastily "Not that you're the devil!"

Father Buckley's eyebrows shot up and his face registered surprise "Eamon Cantwell" he paused thinking "It's not possible he's the same Eamon Cantwell who was here in nineteen fifty?"

"I doubt it, Father, why do you ask?" but a thought had sprung to life unbidden in Gavin's mind and he was counting back the decades mentally. He had only started working with Eamon two years ago and there had been a big blow out for his fiftieth. *It would tally* he thought. *Eamon would have been twelve or so.*

"Because" the old priest said "It was an Eamon Cantwell that Father Mitchell spoke to the Bishop about. He was the first person in this school to have suffered Loyola's wrath. The poor lad was beaten half to death for trying to run away and yet we did nothing, to our eternal shame." He slumped back "I'll never forget that name" he said quietly, guilt resting heavily on shoulders that sank lower as he spoke. "He came back to the school from hospital and it was as though something had broken in him. The light was gone out in his eyes. If it were him he'd be what… fifty two or so and I could see him as a Guard, righting wrongs and bringing justice. It would seem fitting."

Gavin hardly heard the old man as his head swam trying to put possible pieces together. If the thought festering in his mind, one he dare not even give credence to yet, proved true, was Eamon Cantwell involved in more ways that he had let on? Was he somehow the nemesis to these old men, reaching out through time to exact revenge for.. for something.. Gavin's thoughts veered away from that precipice. "Thank.. thank you for your help" he stammered standing too quickly and knocking the chair backward with a loud clatter. The sound focused him and he looked at the old priest, who seemed to have become smaller in the light of the conversation, and more tired, Gavin thought, feeling a pang of both empathy and guilt for him. "Probably better if you don't discuss this with anyone" he cautioned "at least until our investigation is concluded. I'll be in touch if I need anything more. Thank you again father and sorry for keeping you up so late."

"I've kept all this bottled up for over forty years. I can guarantee you that it would be forty more before I voluntarily discuss it again." Father Buckley stood up gingerly and with a stiff grunt. "I'll see you out."

When they reached the door the old man stopped him as he walked out into the wet night "Detective, are you a believer?" he asked gravely.

87

"I am" Gavin replied, unsure what direction this was taking.

"Then whatever you do, do it in line with your conscience but also in line with the best interests of the Church."

Gavin opened his mouth to reply but Father Buckley cut him short "We all have to carry burdens from time to time. I have kept this burden for the sake of the Church and I will pray that you will do likewise. I can't guarantee that I will remember everything as clearly if called on in future. I am very old" he paused a moment, looking at Gavin grimly, before continuing "I have told you what I know, or knew of that man and that time. I fervently hope you catch whosoever is responsible and bring them to justice. I simply ask that when you do that you consider the wider implications for the future of the faith. It has been rocked badly of late. More nails in the coffin, so to speak, are the last thing it needs. Good night, Detective, and thank you for calling." He shut the door and Gavin heard the locks sliding home.

When he reached the car Gavin allowed himself a moment of breathing in the cool night air to wonder how he would broach the subject with Eamon and indeed if he should at all. Should he go directly to Superintendent Carroll and lay his fears out for him to make a judgement call? He was so lost in his reverie he never heard the figure quietly approaching or see the swing of the hammer in the figures gloved hand. It hit him on the back of the head, his knees buckled and he fell to the ground, immediately unconscious, which was a mercy as the figure didn't stop however smashing the object heavily into his prone, limp body. There was an inky pool spreading out from Gavin's head, slowly growing larger but yet again the hammer landed. Several times, each accompanied by a dull thud or a sickening crack as the weapon broke bones.

Breathing heavily the figure stood over the limp body "*The Lord detests lying lips, but he delights in people who are trustworthy.* Proverbs twelve twenty two" the figure said conversationally, looking down at Gavin's unmoving form.

"You can't stand in the way of this truth and by God I'll make sure it comes out and that everyone who wants to cover it up pays with their lives!" A final kick at the broken body and the figure walked toward the Church, nonchalantly hefting the bloody hammer is it crossed the paving and rang the doorbell. A light appeared again upstairs and after a moment the door opened.

"Detective, I've..."Father Buckley stopped mid-sentence, a perplexed look on his face as he stared at the figure silhouetted in street lights "Oh it's you" the look changed to surprise and then for a brief moment, to terror as the hammer descended..

9.

Eamon sat watching the faces of his three inquisitors. There was a short silent pause where they seemed to debate mentally. It was the Archbishop who broke the silence, albeit with obvious reluctance.

"Some weeks ago I was having breakfast in my study, on a Monday morning as I normally do. I had my post delivered to me, the usual kinds of things I might expect, and one package." He cleared his throat, somewhat more nervously than he was accustomed to Eamon was sure and the thought brought him both comfort and concern. If Archbishop Flood was nervous then at some point in this tale, Eamon knew he would be even more so. At this moment though, he was relishing the thought that Flood was feeling out of his comfort zone, *the fat prick.*

"I thought nothing of it for a moment and set it to one side. My secretary called me and I left to attend to some church matter." He threw up his hands in a gesture of *mea culpa.* "In truth I forgot all about it until that evening I received a phone call. The person on the line asked if I had examined the contents, or to be precise, had I *watched* the contents."

He was clearly uncomfortable, thought Eamon, who by dint of experience in interviews and watching countless confessions over the years, could see all the hallmarks of someone who has a story to tell, who doesn't want to but still feels the need to unload the unburden, while trying not to incriminate themselves. *They're all the fucking same* he thought *guilt looks the same on the face of the high and mighty as it does on the face of the low life.*

"I had no idea what the caller meant, or what I was supposed to have watched and when I told him so he become quite agitated, to the point of being disrespectful." The Archbishop sounded quite incredulous at this affront.

Eamon could barely stifle the smile as he noted Flood's annoyance. *No you wouldn't be used to that*, your Grace he thought, *more like you'd be used to having your ring kissed by simpering lackeys, in more ways than one.* The thought had come unbidden and Eamon had to clear his throat to mask the desire to chuckle at his own humour. At almost the same instant he wondered if people found out about him would they make similar veiled jokes at his expense.

"His exact words were to get off my arse and watch it and when I had he would call again. I had one hour to do so or he would take this rather unfortunate and explosive tape to the newspapers." The Archbishop again cleared his throat before continuing as though the truth threatened to choke him. His collar seemed a little tight as he spoke and he turned his head from side to side to loosen it, his jowls and fat neck wobbling as he did so, looking, Eamon thought, like a turkey gobbling at Christmas. It was to no avail so he was forced to reach up and undo his dog collar and top button, sighing in relief as he did. "He also warned me that I'd be better off watching the contents… privately" The Archbishop said, choosing to emphasise the last word.

"I'm sorry, your Grace" Eamon interjected as diplomatically as he could "Did you recognise the voice?"

"Not at all" the Archbishop replied. "It wasn't until later that night when he did call back, on my private number too if you don't mind, that he told me exactly who he was, bold as brass."

"Loyola" breathed Eamon, contempt filling the air as he spoke.

"The very same" agreed the Archbishop, mistaking Eamon's reaction for one that matched his own. "He asked if I had watched the recording, sneering with every syllable" he curled his lip in disgust. "I have" I replied.

"What was on that tape Eamon" the Archbishop said leaning forward, gripping the arm of his chair tightly with his left hand and jabbing a finger at Eamon " was a very poor recording, though its content was probably best viewed in that context as what I had to watch was not fit for anyone to see. Depravity such as that has nothing to do with humanity, but the work of the Devil himself and those in it were no more than demons made men."

"I'm sorry again, your Grace, but I'm not here to debate the finer points of philosophy or theology. I only want the facts as succinctly as you can give them to me. I must confess though, that in my experience, the Devil and all his demons are no match for so called humanity. To call men demons is to excuse them of their responsibility to behave in a way that is in fact, human." Eamon had had enough of this pompous fool's breast beating.

Archbishop Flood raised his eyebrows as though in surprise and immediately furrowed them again, not taking the bait that Eamon was dangling. "I won't argue theology tonight either, Eamon, but I would caution you to remember that life continues for us all when this matter is resolved."

Minister Casey interrupted, perhaps sensing that a change in direction was needed. "The bastard sent me the same tape, the same message and the same went to Commissioner Flannigan."

Casey's outrage was controlled, thought Eamon. *He's the far more dangerous of these two.*

He looked at the Commissioner for confirmation, receiving a single nod of affirmation in return. *The old man saying less than the other two together* thought Eamon ruefully *I'm being cautioned to tread carefully here.* He gave a single nod in reply to which the Commissioner may have smiled ever so slightly, a faint twitch at the corner of his mouth betraying his acknowledgement.

"I'm sorry your Grace, Minister" said Eamon deferentially, nodding to each in turn, "I'm not here to argue and it isn't my place to do so. I just want to get to the bottom of this and to stop the sick bastard who's murdering people, whatever they may have done."

"It goes further than you understand, Eamon said Casey "We've all seen the tapes, we all know things now that we wish we didn't" his tone had become ominous and the atmosphere in the room almost funereal. He continued, swirling the drink in his hand and looking into it instead of to Eamon "The tape.. the tape" he said quietly " It shows acts against a young boy" he hesitated, finished the contents of his glass with a grimace and again plunged forward "it seems that Loyola, Buchannan or whatever you choose to call him, not only abused children in his care but he also allowed others to do so, often, it seems, actively encouraging them. What they didn't know was that he was also filming their atrocities." The words spilled quickly, disdainfully from his mouth, as though he hated the very taste of them.

The room suddenly seemed unbearably oppressive. Eamon thought he would faint. Panic clutched his chest, his heart pounded impossibly loudly and he was unable to catch his breath. His mouth was dry and the metallic taste of fear. Surely the three of them could hear the hammer in his chest as loudly as he could hear the pounding of his pulse in his ears. He was fighting to keep upright, to focus on the Minister's voice as a forty year old secret threatened to have even wider and graver implications that he ever envisaged it could. His hands clenched and eyes closed he steadied himself, taking several moments to let the feeling subside and to feel like he wasn't drowning in snatches of old memories, rising like a tide to claim him, threatening all the while to drag him under.

"Jesus Christ" he exhaled slowly, realising as he did that he'd been holding his breath the whole time. He forced his body to appear relaxed as he noted the concern on the three faces opposite. "This is a lot to process and it is outrageous that he would do such a thing." The three men exchanged glances once more before Casey continued, somewhat more warmly and softly, Eamon thought. He was right. Minister Casey seemed to have mistaken his stunned and disbelieving reaction as one of simple dismay and perhaps even solidarity.

"Take a moment and a drink if you need one Eamon" he offered, nodding to the decanter on the side table.

"Thanks Minister, but I'm on the dry" Eamon explained simply, "Please go on."

"It's even worse and a lot more delicate than you know to this point." It was the Archbishop who cut in "On that tape were some.. people.. men.. men who would not enjoy the limelight if this were to emerge" he looked at Eamon as though making sure he was getting a point across "Men who are still alive for the most part, or whose offspring are, at any rate. Men who.. " he trailed off, unable to bring himself to finish.

"Men who are some of the most powerful, well thought of, well

94

positioned and respected in Irish and International society" It was the Commissioner who spoke "Men whose influence casts a very long shadow on every facet of our society.. and yet men who have everything to lose if this scandal gets out." The Commissioner's tone was grave, his face set in stone and his body bolt upright as he went on "These men are some of the most highly placed members of the Clergy in Rome now, though they would have been far less senior then. Members of the judiciary, the police force" he gritted his teeth at that personal attack on his uniform before adding "Business, politics, law, clergy.. we can only guess how far this goes." He stopped, giving Eamon enough time to catch up and digest all this.

Minister Casey cut in, "We are looking at the ruination of the fabric of our whole society if this ever gets out. Your job, Eamon, is to find the original versions of those tapes and to destroy them or bring them directly to us, to no one else and to then forget that this ever happened, for the sake of all concerned."

"A few things, gentlemen, firstly you mentioned versions of tapes. I take it there is more than one?" Eamon hoped his voice didn't betray his desperation to be wrong. A tape was one thing but several only added to the possibility or probability that he was on one of them. The very idea sent a cold bead of sweat down his back.

"Also, there was nothing to suggest tapes or a camera or anything to point to the location of any originals at the scene of his death. I'd have noticed something like that, even if I didn't know what it was I'd have wanted to see if there were anything on a tape that might help my investigation." He was explaining for the benefit of the Archbishop and Minister, to confirm to them he actually knew how to do his job. "So either he had them secreted in a different location or whoever killed him could have taken them from the scene if he knew what they were."

Commissioner Flannigan interjected "You might not be aware, but the copies we received were just that, VHS copies. The originals would have been old reels of film. If these still exist they need to be found also. He obviously managed to transfer the originals onto VHS cassettes so there may be several copies and maybe even an old 8mm projector. I'm sure you'd remember if you saw one of those from your school days perhaps. I can't imagine he would have allowed anyone else to do it for fear they'd see the content."

Eamon nodded. "Well I'm positive there was nothing of that nature at the scene, but I will go back and look to see if they had been secreted anywhere less obvious" he continued, "I'd also like to know why Loy.. Loyola.." again the name caught, as if barbed, in his throat. "I'm sorry" he stammered, "It's been a long day and night." He cleared his throat and asked again "What do you think he hoped to accomplish, sending the tapes to all three of you?"

Minister Casey offered the explanation. "He wanted to blackmail the State and the Church. He sent me the tape to make sure I knew what was on it and to insure himself against simply getting arrested and left to rot in jail." The Minister's tone indicated that was exactly what would have happened if it were at all possible. "Yes I'd have had him locked up in a mental institution and thrown away the key. If he weren't insane going in he soon would be and good riddance", the Minister confirmed as though reading his thoughts.

"The other copies were to the Archbishop as our country's most senior cleric and to Commissioner Flannigan as the head of the country's police force. If nothing else Loyola had covered his arse. We all received the same calls and were left in no doubt that the original tapes were very much intact and that if we didn't acquiesce to his demands quietly he'd sell them to the newspapers. I must admit" he snorted derisively "The moment I heard he'd died in a fire I was relieved, but that was short lived when I heard the circumstances. Better the devil you know Eamon" he shrugged "At least I could have bought his silence and this could have all been dealt with quietly. At this moment we don't know where the tapes are or who might have them or what he intends to do with them, if anything. This is why we need you to get to the bottom of this quietly and to do a great service to your country both in secular and religious terms." Minister Casey eyed Eamonn with a mixture of supplication and desperation and Eamon liked it.

"I'll get to the bottom of this but as I asked my Super, what do I do when I find this murderer? Get the tapes if he has them and then let him off scot free?" Eamon was getting irritated. Catching the bad guy was supposed to be the job, bringing him to justice and for everyone to see justice being done. In this case justice was getting done alright, done out of the process of law, and yet though it rankled his professional soul, the part of Eamonn that wanted this to just go away was relieved when the Minister said "Don't worry about whoever it is, just find him. Within hours he'll be in a padded cell for the rest of his days and fed more drugs than a junkie on Sheriff Street."

"I will find him" Eamon stated flatly. There was no room in his tone for doubt or failure "And if he has these tapes I will find them and destroy them then and there. I'm not risking even bringing them to any of you, besides incriminating you and myself it would serve no purpose. You're all going to have to trust that I will do this quietly and in return I think I might like to retire upstairs to Ray Carroll's job."

"You're bargaining with us?" The Bishop's voice was incredulous. "How dare you. Surely you'll do this for the same reason we're doing this, to protect our country and The Church?"

Eamonn spoke quietly but as clearly and with as much matter of fact as he could muster. Though he was close to exploding on the inside he knew it was important to punctuate every syllable, so no one could be in any doubt as to the undertaking. "With respect, your Grace, Minister, Commissioner, you're covering your arses, you're covering your benefactors arses, you're covering up generational abuse on what you say is a grand scale and you're asking me, *asking me* mind, to turn a blind eye while you incarcerate some lunatic with so much as a trial, ride rough shod over law, justice and everything I believe in. I'm exacting my pound of flesh as bloodlessly as I dare. I'm no shylock negotiating with you. I'm bloody well telling you that I'm coming out of this smelling of roses or you can all go to hell!"

His voice had remained neutral until the end. He hoped his words were landing as intended, loud and clear. "Well gentlemen, are we in agreement?" he looked from face to face "I find him and you deal with him. The tapes are properly dealt with and we all walk away into the sunset, like it never happened."

The three looked as though they would happily have thrown him out the window to his death but after a moment's hesitation the Minister smiled "You'd have done well in politics. We have an agreement." He held out his hand to Eamon who looked at it as though it were a grenade about to go off, before taking it and shaking once. He tried to withdraw but Minister Casey held him firm in a grip he hadn't expected to be as powerful "But Eamon, if you fail or if this does get out into the public domain, I will ensure that you fall harder than the Devil himself cast out of heaven and the hell I'll put you in would have His sympathy." He

98

pressed a slip of paper into Eamon's hand. "It's a number for someone you may need if there's anything that needs cleaning up discreetly." He simply shrugged at Eamon's shocked expression.

Eamon pulled his other hand free, slipping the paper into his pocket. "I'll do my job and you make sure you honour your end, all three of you. We'll all just have to live with the outcome."

As he stood up the Archbishop handed him a slip of paper "That's the address of the only other person that Loyola had any time for, his protégé, a man named Morrissey, the right hand of the Devil." Eamon took the paper. "He's not a Christian Brother anymore, hasn't been for many years and doesn't go by Morrissey either" the Archbishop continued "he left the order some few years after Loyola was sent away. He actually married and has lived quietly under our noses for many years, in Delgany. Quite a nice life or so it would seem. No children but teaching in a secondary school" noting Eamon's shocked expression he snorted "a girl's secondary school. No point in wasting his talents as a teacher it seems. He was moved on at the same time as Loyola but since there was no evidence that he had actually done anything improper he simply moved diocese and after a time returned as a lay teacher. Working in an all-girl school was seen as making sure he wasn't going to be tempted to put his hand back into the cookie jar, as it were. His tastes it seems ran strictly to young boys"

"Just like that" Eamon was disgusted and he wanted the old bastard to know it. He was fighting the urge to kick in that fat head as much as he was striving to contain the panic, the revulsion and the intolerable urge to run away from all of this. Every mention of their names sent bolts of lightning through him, through his memory and images, moments of clarity were trying to break free from where he'd kept them imprisoned for so long.

99

"It was before my time and things operated.. differently back then. The sanctity of the Church was important to everyone and to protect it was seen as paramount. Regretfully, I see that devotion is waning" the Archbishop replied, seemingly unaware, thought Eamon, of the indescribable horrors he was forgiving in one sentence. *Or maybe the sanctity of his Church is more important than any amount of human suffering and he just doesn't care.* He knew at that moment that whatever God was responsible for allowing this to pervade the Church was no God he ever wanted anything to do with, not ever again.

The Archbishop was droning on, oblivious. "We must all do whatever is necessary to preserve the Church and in turn the State. One is nothing without the moral guidance of the other. Without faith in the Church, the country would descend into chaos. When you interview him, impress upon former Brother Morrissey the full weight of what will happen if he doesn't aid you in any way possible.

"I know how to do my job and my part in all this" Eamon was edging closer to the precipice "but I wonder if you all truly know your respective parts and if you're prepared to live with the aftermath." The three looked at him blankly, faces set in stone.

"Good night Eamon" said the Commissioner, taking his arm and walking him to the door. Opening it he leaned toward Eamon and quietly said "I trust you'll find your own way out. It's late and I'm sure you'll want to get home to Marie. She must worry about you" he squeezed Eamon's arm tightly, out of view of the others who had turned and made their way toward the side table and the decanter.

"To borrow from a famous quote, *speak softly* Eamon, you're in a house of cards and I'd hate to see the lot fall on you. Get this done, write your meal ticket and put it behind you. We all carry skeletons as we ascend to loftier perches, you don't want any of yours to see the light of day and more than I do, but if you don't play the game you're going to come off worst and I think you know that. If nothing else think of your family and their future as well as your own. We can all get a win from this."

Eamonn was left wondering if Flannigan knew more than he was letting on or was he referring to what had just transpired that night. He nodded curtly and the Commissioner freed his arm, his face stony and unreadable.

"You only used half the expression there, Sean. *Speak softly and carry a big stick. You will go far*. Isn't that it? President Roosevelt I believe." He gave a smile he did not feel or believe and taking his coat from the peg on the rack, threw it over his arm and made his escape.

When Flannigan turned and closed the door the other two were standing by the window, tumblers of whiskey in hand. Minister Casey gestured to the desk where a third sat.

"Sharp indeed, Sean, your boy is sharp indeed and somewhat caustic with it. I approve, I like to see a man with both backbone and self-interest. I can trust those traits" said Casey. "I actually think he's the man for the job, despite my initial reservations. If he's prepared to play ball and we keep this arrangement do you think he'll see it through?"

"Like a dog with a bone" replied Flannigan "Though I must admit he caught me by surprise, asking for the Superintendent's job. He's got more ambition than I would have credited and behaved more.. politically sensitively than I have known him to be in the past. Perhaps he's learning that playing the game gets us what we want, even if it has its costs." He sounded thoughtful.

"Are you concerned? Should we all be?" Archbishop Flood queried, alarm in his voice. "The little shit should learn to know his place and respect his superiors. Did you hear how he tried to bait me?" His eyes widened and voice rose in volume and pitch, clearly indicating his displeasure and indignation.

"I did, and I think he was simply letting us all know that he does, in fact, have us in a tight spot where we are relying on him to be the left arm of Satan and to act in ways that may at the very least, bend some laws. Something Eamon has never been good at in the past. The fact that he's prepared to do so now means that either he's getting old and tired and wants away from the front line, or that there is more to his involvement than he's telling, some personal motive that makes him want to play this our way" said Flannigan, "I feel that I may want to make some discreet enquiries myself to determine which of those avenues he may be taking. That way we will at least have a contingency plan in place if anything goes awry. A fall guy as it were"

The other two nodded ascent and all three watched from the Georgian window, their silhouettes throwing long shadows out onto the courtyard as the figure of Eamon Kearns crossed, descended the steps onto the gravel drive, walked through the main gates with a wave to the guards who were on duty, hailed a taxi and disappeared into the Dublin night. Each was having his private thoughts about Eamon Cantwell but other than in the completion of his current task, not one of the three wished him well in any compass whatsoever.

10.

It was six am when the phone call woke Eamon from a deep, dreamless sleep in his hotel room. He raised himself on one elbow and reached to the stand by the bed, picking up the receiver. "Yes?" he barked, looking at his watch and trying to focus "For fuck sake Gavin what do I have to do to get a single night's sleep. I only got in at two. Come get me will you I left my car at the station last night."

"Sir, its Dempsey. There's been an.. incident" the voice was that of the duty sergeant, Kevin Dempsey, an old campaigner who had been there, seen that and bought the t-shirt. For him to sound as rattled and grave as he did, shook Eamon to attention in an instant.

"Go on, Kevin" he said flatly.

"It's Gavin, sir, he's.. in hospital, in a bad way, critical in an operating theatre as we speak. It seems he was mugged and left for dead last night out in Raheny. I thought you should know immediately but I didn't have a number for you besides your home number and it rang out. I went to Beaumont Hospital myself after work, just to check if he was going to be alright and by sheer luck met your friend Father Quinn. He told me where you were staying while your leak was being fixed." His voice faltered, alarming Eamon even more as his stomach knotted and a cold dread rooted him to the spot. "Christ Eamon" Dempsey's voice was just above a whisper "whoever did this left him in a right state, he's broken up, skull, collar bone, cheek, jaw, shoulder and four ribs. His lung was punctured and he lost so much blood they're afraid he'll be brain damaged. If he wakes at all." His voice trailed off waiting for a response.

"I'll be there as soon as I can, thanks for letting me know. Can you send a car to get me? I left mine at the station last night." Eamon was struggling to remain controlled though his thoughts were racing ahead. He slammed down the phone and jumped up snatching his clothes and dressing as quickly as he could, all the time the knowledge that this was most likely connected to the case was growing into a huge pressure in his head, *my fault, my fault for sending him there alone with a fucking psycho on the loose.*

Eamon waited impatiently for the car. Five minutes had passed since he stepped out into the cold autumn morning. The rheumy, thin sun was low in a grey sky, casting precious little warmth. The minutes seemed to pass as though the cold was slowing them down, like honey in winter. A Ford Sierra squad car rounded the corner at speed and came to an abrupt stop directly in front of him.

"About fucking time" he admonished as he sat into the passenger seat "Beaumont Hospital, and drive like your life, job and mother depended on it and get those fucking sirens going."

The driver had obviously been briefed as he simply nodded and grunted "No problem, Sir, get a seat belt on and hold onto something." He hit the accelerator and the car lurched forward even as Eamon was reaching for the belt. They crossed town faster, Eamon thought, than he'd ever moved before. This young lad driving was certainly capable. He was feeling a little disorientated when they pulled up at the hospital, but was also silently thankful as he'd been too concerned with not screaming as the young garda drove at breakneck speed, throwing the car around city streets with abandon, sirens wailing. More than once he thought they were going to crash or kill someone but through skill or fortune, they screeched to a halt and the young garda nodded "safe and sound, sir." Eamon undid the belt and shakily stepped out of the car. As he did the driver called out "Sir?"

"Yes lad?" Eamon leaned against the door as he peered into the car, glad of the momentary support.

"When you do catch whoever did this, and I know you will, do me a favour and give him a few extra kicks from me" he said vehemently. Eamon simply returned a thin lipped nod and pushing the door closed, watched for a moment as the car took off again as though the hounds of hell were in pursuit.

Eamon took a breath as he watched it disappear. The driver may have been a hothead but Eamon was determined to follow through on his request. He started up the steps, two at a time. He made straight for reception where a young nurse took one look at his face and brought him directly to the waiting area outside the surgery room, where Brendan sat sipping on a cup of tea. He stood as Eamon approached with a haunted look in his eyes.

"Eamon, thank God they got through to you" He put his hand on Eamon's shoulder as though to steady him "the nurse just left theatre. She told me its touch and go but they think he could pull through, mostly because he's so fit and young. It's a terrible business." He sighed, rubbing his forehead. "I was here with a parishioner, a dear old girl who was receiving last rites when your young colleague was brought in. The surgeon asked if I'd say a prayer over him on the way in and that's when I recognised his face, or just about recognised it. The poor lad was beaten to a pulp" He was looking at Eamon but his eyes were focused on the memory of what he'd seen. It was obviously affecting him deeply.

"Easy Brendan, he'll be alright. He's a tough fecker. Let's sit down and just wait for the good news." Eamon was praying for an outcome he wasn't confident would occur but what choice did anyone have in those circumstances, *you wish for a miracle and pray harder than you ever prayed before*, he thought, closing his eyes and silently asking God to intervene, *while at the same time knowing that I've seen so many people do the exact same thing and receive a terrible outcome anyway*. They sat in silence. Fear, worry and guilt gnawed at Eamonn in turn as he watched the clock on the wall slowly mark time.

Eventually, after two more hours, the surgeon came out, removing his mask. He raised his head and shrugged his shoulders, stretching to relieve the tense, knotted muscles in his neck and upper back. He at glanced the expectant, fearful faces of Eamon and Brendan, a look he was so familiar with sometimes he forgot how harrowing this moment could be. "That lad's a fighter" he said approaching the two men. "I've seen less extensive head injuries in a high speed crash, not to mention the rest of him, but he's stable, critical but stable. I've done what I can and the rest is between him and God." He exhaled, looking exhausted "If you'll excuse me I'm going home. I've been here for the past thirty six hours and I doubt if I can even see straight at this point." With a handshake to both men he turned and left.

"His parents are on their way" said Brendan quietly "They should be here soon. At least it'll be some bit of good news rather than what might have happened."

Eamon spoke in a loud whisper, shaking his head in frustration and guilt. "Jesus Brendan, I sent him over there last night, to talk to the priests in Augustine's."

"Sending him there to do his job is hardly something you can blame yourself for, is it Eamon. I think you're beating yourself up over something that might not even be related. |This could simply be a case of being in the wrong place at the wrong time." Brendan tried unsuccessfully to placate Eamon but his agitation only seemed to grow.

"For fuck sake, He might have died out there and I sent him there alone" Eamon was pacing to and fro, fists clenching and unclenching as he did. "It's on me if he doesn't make it and I swear to God I'll put a bullet in the bastard that did this if I catch him" his voice was a strangled hiss and his face had gone from red to pale white in fury.

Brendan caught him by the shoulders, his grip like a giant vice "Calm down would you!" he said sharply, shaking Eamon like a rag doll. He glanced at the nurse who had appeared in the corridor, giving her a quick, nervous smile. She nodded back at the sight of the priest consoling the patient's colleague and disappeared again. "There is literally nothing you can or could have done. Gavin was a detective doing his job. The best way for you to use this.. this anger, this fury is to calm down and get to the bottom of it. Did he even go to Augustine's or did this happen before he got the chance? Is this related to your investigation or simply a random attack, probably a mugging where Gavin tried to fight back and got beaten? Was there more than one? Until you have the details don't be going off half cocked!"

"Hey *Steve McGerritt*, would you let go of me, you're crushing my fecking shoulders" Eamon smiled thinly, the rage passing with the abrupt shock of being man handled. "You really should have been a detective, Brendan" he said, straightening his jacket, "You're a natural" he shrugged "The priesthood's gain was *Hawaii 50's* loss."

Brendan smiled "There's the sarcastic prick I've come to know. There's obviously something happening for you since we last spoke. You're balancing on a knife edge. It's obvious, from your temper alone, even if your face didn't tell its own story. You look like shit. I think I preferred it when you were drinking heavily. At least then I could smell the reason for your foul mouthed outbursts and offer up a prayer now and again."

"Well yes" Eamon replied "I met Minister Casey. He had company in the shape of Commissioner Flannigan and Archbishop Flood" Eamon shook his head and motioned to the seats in the waiting area. He and Brendan sat, Eamon quietly recounting the night before and the meeting and its outcome, Brendan listening intently, motionless as a church statue, as though not to break the spell that allowed Eamon to unburden himself. When Eamon finished Brendan sat still, his hands folded in his lap. The only tell-tale sign of his emotions was the slight flaring of his nostrils and the bunching of his broad shoulders. "What will you do?" the question came as a low growl.

"I'll find the killer and I'll hopefully find those tapes before they get into the public domain because not to find them along not with finding the killer, spells disaster for me personally and professionally." Eamon scanned Brendan's face for any hint of emotion but he was stock still. "Look, I know you want me to do the best for all concerned, but those tapes ever see the light of day it will have unimaginable consequences and so when, not if, *when* I find them I'm going to destroy them. It's for the best."

Brendan's voice was measured but Eamon could hear the absolute disgust. "The best for whom? For you? For the trio who want this to go away so they can continue to preside over the tarnished State and the Church, my Church, as it gets dragged into the gutter?." The incandescent rage emanating from his friend, Eamon thought, might set the chair alight and yet his hands were the only tell-tale sign. His big fists were white knuckled and held in front of him like a shield.

"What happened to calming down" Eamon asked "You know, all the shit you tried to fill me with?"

"Did it work?" Brendan asked caustically.

"Not one fucking iota" Eamon said.

"Well then, fuck off" Brendan said, venom in every syllable.

"Easy big man, what would you have me do?" Eamon was alarmed at Brendan's ferocity. "Show me a solution and I'll take it!" he pleaded, "because I can't see any way to go about this that ends well unless I just make it all go away, like they want, and you know I hate the very concept of being a puppet in a cover up but I can't do what you want without losing everything and even then I'd have no guarantee that it would work, that they wouldn't just cover it up or scapegoat me. I have a responsibility to keep the secrets as well as seek justice. That much I'm in no doubt about, if I try to go public they'll have me rotting in prison, one way or another and that's shame I can't live with."

Brendan sat back in the chair letting his head fall back, face to the heavens and eyes closed. His hands had relaxed and he took a few long, deep breaths to compose himself. He pulled himself forward, stood, towering over Eamon, though there was nothing but resignation in his eyes "Do what you have to Eamon, I will pray for you and I'll pray for guidance for us all. Now, go home."

He extended a hand to Eamon, who took it and Brendan hauled him up from his seat. The handshake lasted a moment longer with Brendan placing a hand on his shoulder. He looked deep into Eamon's eyes, his own softening with compassion for his friend, "You haven't been dealt a great hand, Eamon, and it's a chalice I'd gladly see taken from you but if our Lord could endure to the end I will pray that you find the strength to follow suit."

"Thank you, Brendan, but I don't think prayer will help me this time. I fear I'm damned if I do and damned if I don't." Eamon sighed, "Worn out at ten in the morning. I will go get an hour I think, I can hardly even function. Then this afternoon I have to go find that other bastard, Morrissey, though if he were tortured and set alight like.. the other one.. well I doubt if I'd sleep any less soundly for the loss."

"God speed and good luck Eamon. I'm sure that with God's help a path will become clear, now go rest." He patted Eamon's shoulder again and said "I'm going to wait for the young lad's parents. It will be little comfort but it's something I'd like to do. He shouldn't be left alone until they get here."

Eamon nodded, "You're a good man, Brendan. The Church is lucky to have you"

"Sure don't I know" Brendan smiled in return "but don't extoll my virtues too heavily, pride goeth before a fall."

"Oh don't worry, I still think you're a bollocks" Eamon grinned, tiredness making him feel giddy. At that he turned and left.

Brendan watched as his leaden footsteps retreated until he disappeared from view.

"Oh Eamon" he sighed "It's a heavy load and I fear it'll only get heavier. May you have the strength in the end to do the right thing, make the terrible choices and not falter, this will be the making or breaking of you, and I fear the outcome either way." He looked to the heavens "Give us all the strength to carry the burdens placed upon us and not to succumb to the iniquities of our souls, through Jesus name I pray, Lord" and he made the sign of the cross, lifting the crucifix round his neck to his lips and kissing it.

A nurse approached and Brendan asked "Would you mind if I sat with the young man and perhaps said a prayer or two?"

"Of course not Father, I'm sure he could use all the help he can get, the poor lad. He's been taken to ICU, I'll show you the way" she smiled, somewhat sadly "Though to be honest it's not looking like he'll be round anytime soon. His head injuries have left him in a coma and we don't even know if he'll ever wake up."

"With God all things are possible" Brendan smiled back "He'll pull through if it's His will" he pointed upward. The nurse smiled again and led him toward the ICU.

11.

Eamon hailed a taxi outside the hospital and the driver had tried to engage in small talk, however his fare had fallen asleep almost as soon as he had sat into the back seat.

"Rough night, then" the driver grunted "Just as well you gave me the address" he chuckled to himself heading Southside at a leisurely pace. After forty minutes of crossing Dublin's traffic, the taxi pulled up and the driver turned to Eamon, who had just woken, somewhat startled.

"Alright pal, that's seven pounds. Was it your own or a grandchild?" seeing the confused look on Eamon's face "Well coming outa the hospital lookin' knackered, and fallin' asleep as soon as we moved, I bet myself it was a grandkid, no offence but you looked a little.. long in the tooth for it to have been one of your own."

Eamon finally realised what the driver meant. "Grandkid, yeah, that was it." He really didn't feel like chatting so the best policy was to agree, pay the guy and leave. He took a tenner out of his wallet and handed it to the driver "Keep the change" he opened the door and stepped out, expecting to be in Portobello, but instead he found himself standing outside his own house. Looking back into the taxi he asked "Are you sure this is the address I gave you?"

"Well of course it is" said the driver in a thick Northside accent, "I'd hardly be droppin' you in the middle of the suburbs for the craic. It's not bleedin' *Beadle's About*" he chuckled at his own humour. The taxi's radio crackled and the driver called out "Right pal, gotta go, cheers" and with that he motioned for Eamon to close the door. Eamon pushed the door closed and watched, bemused, as the taxi moved off.

"Now I know I'm exhausted" he muttered, realising he'd given the address out of habit and tiredness, working on autopilot. "Well I'm here now, might as well see if she'll talk to me or let me use the phone at least." His feet made their familiar crunch on the gravel, feeling so comfortable and familiar that for a moment he forgot everything else.

The front door opened. Marie stood there in the doorway, a sentry blocking entrance to the unwelcome. She took one look at Eamon and her face, at first stern and still full of hurt, completely changed expression to that of concern and worry. "Oh Eamon, you look terrible. Come in. I'll put the kettle on" she turned, leaving the door open for him to follow "but take off your shoes, I've just polished the hall floor" she called as she walked to the kitchen. By the time Eamon had removed his shoes and followed her into the kitchen Marie had already put the kettle on and taken down two cups from the cupboard. He felt uncomfortable, like a stranger or first time visitor, the atmosphere certainly didn't feel like his home. "I'm sorry Marie. I didn't mean to come here. I jumped into a taxi at the hospital and must have said the wrong address. I can go" he apologised but the last word was left hanging in a void.

"Sit down, you fool, before you fall down. I'll make tea" Marie said dismissively "I haven't seen you look this bad since David had meningitis as a child. I don't think you slept more than minutes at a time for the duration, so this must be particularly bad." She stopped mid-way between picking up the kettle and pouring water into the teapot. "Wait, you said hospital. What's happened? Who's in hospital and why in God's name didn't you phone me?"

She was giving him the expectant look she used when he was reluctant to confess about one of his many escapades or adventures coming from the pub. Those little adventures had earned him that look far too often in the past, especially if the conversation started with "So.. what time did you wander in last night?" He'd learned not to lie or try to obfuscate as his wife's hearing rivalled a bats, any day of the week.

Seeing how tired he was she turned back to the teapot, finished making the tea, stirred the pot, brought it to the table and set it in front of him, along with his favourite cup and sugar. "I've made the tea, pour it yourself, and mine too while you're at it." She waved theatrically. "Then we'll talk." She sat in the seat next to him and put her hand on his arm. The touch shocked him momentarily, his mind flashing back to the last moment they sat in the self-same spot and the result. "We can talk about.. other things later, after you've had time to rest." Eamon tried to protest but she simply cut him off "No arguments Eamon Kearns. I'll not have you keeling over in my kitchen."

Eamon told her about Gavin and his injuries but chose to omit both his own crushing guilt or the wider circumstances of investigations for the sake of brevity and because he was genuinely petrified that it would swing the conversation around to him and Marie would want to talk about his revelation. That was a conversation he could go a lifetime without having and feel none the worse for it.

114

"The poor chap, I've always liked Gavin. He's such a good young man. I'll have to visit the hospital. When do you think they'll allow visitors? Should I bring anything? Do his family know yet?" Marie's chatter, which normally drove Eamon a little mad, now made him smile a tired smile as he realised life was somehow *less* without her and her idiosyncrasies.

"You look awful. When did you get a night's sleep last?" she asked.

"I can't remember. This case I'm working on is.. difficult" he was skirting the truth but Marie didn't seem to want to press too hard. Eamon was both glad and regretful in equal measure as he didn't have to discuss it but she didn't seem too bothered which prodded a nerve of longing, of wanting her to care.

"I think you need a couple of hours sleep Eamon, away from everything and everyone. You'll feel better for it and.." Eamon opened his mouth to object .".*and*" she reiterated forcefully, holding her hand up to stop him before a sound escaped his lips "If you push yourself to exhaustion you'll have a heart attack, or stroke and then you'll be no good to anyone."

"You could at least claim on the life insurance" he smiled wryly.

"I would too. You owe me that much." Her point made Marie stood. "The spare room is made up. Throw yourself in there and I'll wake you in a couple of hours"

He stood, placed the cups in the sink and headed to the hallway. Marie remained sitting at the table. Just before he left the kitchen she called him.

"Eamon, I will always love you but we have to talk soon about what happens next and going forward. Maybe after this case is finished for you we can discuss things. To be honest I've needed the space to think so it's been better you not being here, but sleep now, you'll thank me for it later."

"Just an hour or two then I have so much to do to track down.. all the leads and now.." he stammered, "without Gavin.. it's even more difficult, but you're right. I can hardly stand let alone think. Thank you, I really don't know what I'd do without you."

"Clearly" she replied, sarcasm clear in her tone "look at the state of you. Never could iron a shirt. Take it off and give it to me. You'll get it back clean and pressed at least."

Dropping his head, Eamon went to the spare room upstairs and took off his shirt, socks and trouser. She called up the stairs "Throw down the lot. I can't bare the thoughts of you parading around Dublin looking like a homeless person."

He didn't even argue, just gathering everything up into a ball, picked a robe out of the wardrobe walked downstairs and handed the bundle to her. "Thanks" he said, feeling unusually shy.

"Go. Sleep" Marie commanded and turned into the kitchen. He heard her pottering in the utility room as he went back upstairs and into the bedroom. He lay on the bed and by the time the washing machine started he was fast asleep.

The phone ringing, *so bloody loud* he thought, woke him. For a brief moment he thought he was back in Portobello, before the familiar smells of his own home, fresh sheets and lavender, reminded him differently. He could hear Marie's muffled voice in conversation.

How has life come to this he thought before Marie called him. "Eamon, it's the station." Feeling better rested than he thought possible after only a couple of hours sleep, he grabbed the robe and quickly descended the stairs, took the receiver from her, answering the call flatly.

"Yes, Kearns here" he felt a gnawing in his stomach, both fear because the last time he answered the phone in the house was the moment that set everything in motion and he also suddenly realised he was ravenous and hadn't eaten since yesterday. Marie had gone back into the smell something cooking, making his mouth water.

"Kevin Dempsey here sir, I have to say, you're harder to track down than *Shergar*, but it's good to see you're back home. The water leak didn't do too much damage then?"

"Funny man, but yes it's good to be back" said Eamon "it could have been a lot worse, but it certainly did enough damage."

"Fair play" said Dempsey "An odd coincidence popped up this morning while you were out. There's a report in of a missing priest on the same street that Gavin was assaulted on. An old chap from St Augustine's, that old church and school in Raheny. Apparently he went to bed last night around ten, as normal, but someone called late and he's missing this morning."

Dempsey sounded curious and the last thing Eamon wanted right now was curiosity around any of those events. Of course the assault would have to be investigated but if it were random then it would either be cleared up quickly, as most of these things were, and if it was somehow connected to the disaster he was embroiled in, he doubted if anything would be found at all, unless he was the one to find it.

"No eye witnesses to Gavin's assault?" Eamon queried.

"Not a one, it was raining heavily around that time so no one was on the street. A perfect opportunity for someone to jump him" Dempsey's voice had an edge to it. "It may well have been random but my money's on someone he had sent down recognising him, following and waiting for a chance to catch him on his own."

"Maybe" Eamon agreed "You're probably right. The bad guys don't fear the law like they used to. Too many of them connected with the IRA nowadays, thinking they're fucking invincible." He hoped he was convincing.

"We thought we'd follow it up anyway, the missing priest that is, so we're canvassing house to house and I'm sending a uniform to Beaumont to get Gavin's notebook and see if he'd left anything in it we can use."

Eamon's heart sank. *The bloody notebook.* Gavin was such a boy scout he might just have notes in it, even though Eamon had told him not to. The first instinct was to take notes. It was always helpful later in a case if suspects or witnesses stories didn't match original accounts. The fact that he was so badly beaten suggested to Eamon that he might well have uncovered something. What that something might be made him feel nauseous. *I should have gone myself, I should have kept him out of it like I said I would* he silently berated himself, holding the receiver to his forehead.

"Don't worry about sending a uniform, I'll get it myself. I'd like to check in with the doctors anyway, see how he's doing" Eamon tried to sound nonchalant.

"Not to worry, one of the lads just left. He'll be over there in a half hour what with traffic at this time of the evening" Dempsey assured him. Eamon however, was far from reassured. He needed to get to that notebook before the uniform got there.

"Right" he said quickly "well I'm out to Delgany this afternoon following up on that awful house fire, so I'll be back in the office about six."

"Six? Sir it's after four thirty now" Dempsey sounded confused. Eamon glanced at his watch. Four thirty four! He'd been asleep all afternoon. "Jesus Christ" he exclaimed "bloody watch has stopped again. Think I need to invest." "You'll get a new one at retirement" Dempsey joked, "At this stage you're as well to wait until traffic calms to head that direction."

"Yeah" Eamon forced a superficial laugh "Thanks Kevin. See you later." He hung up the phone, slamming the receiver down and racing into the kitchen. "Jesus Marie, I only meant to sleep an hour, two at most. I'm seriously fucked!"

Marie handed him his clothes, neatly folded. "Don't you dare Eamon Kearns" she said sternly "I let you sleep because no matter how bloody urgent your job may seem, the world will still turn without you for a few extra hours. It's about time you learned that. You've been a slave to it for far too long." She turned away as he dropped the robe, hurriedly dressed and then squeezed her elbow "I know love, I know" Eamon said in apology "and I'm sorry, sorry for all of it."

"It's only taken you thirty years to see, there may be hope for you yet" she said turning to him and handing him a set of car keys. "I presume you've got to go save the world and you won't get far on foot."

"You are a godsend" he said, hugging her to him quickly. Her scent was a balm for his raw nerves, *always has been*, the thought occurred, *if I'd just been clever enough to see it*. Just as he passed the phone in the hall it rang out. He grabbed it without thinking, "Yes Dempsey?" he asked impatiently.

"Eamon" the voice on the line was most certainly not Dempsey. "You're stirring up the hornets' nest aren't you?" That smug tone made Eamon see red.

"You fucking bastard" he hissed "You might have some twisted grievance with Church, with those animals but that young lad.. that was something else. You tried to murder him, a decent lad, who, by the way, *is* a fan of your Church. All this chaos, this evil is all to get to some fucking tapes to hide the Church's corruption and rotten core isn't it? Well that's what I'm doing. There's no need for you do harm anyone else. For the love of God, *stop*!" Eamon made the plea though he knew as he did that it would fall on deaf ears. This sick bastard had a taste for killing now and the only way to stop him would be to lock him up forever, or to put a bullet through his evil, twisted brain.

"I'm sorry Eamon but I was protecting you, the young man would have told your secret to the wrong people, you know, how you were in the school with Loyola." The bitterness was palpable when he talked about Loyola, Eamon silently noted. There was another layer to this killer's tale.

The voice continued "How you were the first of his prey in that school, though not his first I'm sure of that."

"How the fuck could you know that?" Eamon felt suddenly violated his secret on show for this demon to use as he wanted.

"The truth is a potent weapon the armoury of the righteous. *To know thine enemy is to know thyself* and I know you Eamon, better than you know yourself in some ways. I picked you for this because you need salvation and justice and punishment in equal measure" the voice was in full flow, cruel, confident and a little arrogant. Eamon hated him more by the second.

He dropped suddenly into a conspiratorial murmur. "Old Father Buckley at Augustine's was somewhat too helpful. I followed the young detective. I knew you'd set him poking around and I couldn't have that. He might well have taken this public before the work is completed and that cannot happen. I heard them talking. They worked out who you were and from there it would only have been a small leap for a clever young detective to fill in the blanks, as it were. You should never have involved him Eamon, that was a mistake and mistakes are costly in our little game."

"So it's my fault" Eamon hissed through gritted teeth. "Justify it any way you want but when I catch you, you'll pay for it in full, and when you go to hell you'll spend eternity burning for what you've done."

"Temper, temper" the tone became condescending again, then tiredness crept in that Eamon hadn't expected. "I know what I am and I pay this price willingly. The only thing that's important is getting Irish society back to a moral way of living, weeding out corruption and make us whole again, even if that means being the Devil incarnate it's an irony I can accept."

He continued his lecture. "You must not destroy the tapes, vile though they are. If you find them before I do you could use them as a weapon to force change, or if you don't have the stomach for that you could sacrifice yourself by making the whole lot public for the good of everyone, for the good of the church and for those who came after you who had no voice" The voice sounded suddenly reasonable, almost pleading.

Then a sudden change, a sneering, rage fuelled rant. "But you won't because you're weak" he used the word *weak* with such contempt Eamon actually felt guilty. "That is why I will not stop, because you aren't strong enough to do what has to be done to bring real justice. I'm going to kill every one of the men on those tapes, or their sons even unto the seventh generation, sins of the fathers, Eamon, sins of the fathers. Get to the finish line, Eamon. Stop me if you can or want to, but I will have vengeance and I will cleanse the Church." The line went dead.

Jesus Christ, he is completely unhinged. Eamon thought, taking a breath and closing his eyes to calm himself. *The violent swings from reasonable to fury to sermonising are coming from a chaotic, broken mind.* He looked at his watch. Two minutes. The whole call had taken two minutes. He knew now that he had to get that notebook, hell or high water. Glancing up he saw Marie, standing in the kitchen doorway, a pale and horrified expression on her face.

"Eamon, in the name of all that's holy, what is going on? In thirty years I've never seen you so.. so.. desperate sounding."

"Hopefully I'll be able to tell you when it's all over" Eamon sighed. "When I've delivered a madman to justice but more than that I'm not going to say. Right now, I have to go, Marie, but I pray that it'll be done soon, or else I will be."

"I'll say a prayer for both outcomes then. This is no life for anyone" she said, shaking her head.

"I agree" Eamon replied, bitterly. He rushed outside to Marie's Volvo, fumbled with the seat first and the keys in the ignition after. He turned the key, stamping on the accelerator and throwing back a shower of gravel behind him as the wheels spun and he sped out the drive and toward the Northside. He knew he'd have to break every rule of the road and every light on the way but right now, getting that notebook was all that mattered.

Arriving at the hospital, he abandoned the car and ran up the steps two at a time and made straight for the ICU. He stopped at the nurses' station where he was met by a stern looking middle aged, nurse, whose name badge proclaimed *Matron Mary Joyce*. She looked up from her paperwork over a pair of black rimmed glasses, which did nothing to soften her stare and said frostily "May I help you, *Sir*." She laboured the word, a woman not given to interruption.

"Detective Inspector Eamon Kearns" he said breathlessly and somewhat testily, pulling his warrant card from his breast pocket. He wasn't in the mood to be held up by some overbearing, menopausal despot. "I need to see the effects of the assault victim, a colleague of mine, Gavin Cantwell. It's vital that I examine his things, now!" he barked the command and the Matron was clearly taken aback.

"Sir, I will gladly assist you, but you will change your tone or detective or not, I'll have you escorted out of here for upsetting staff and patients alike!" *He might be a detective inspector*, she thought, *but this is my ward.*

"I apologise" said Eamon, not meaning a word "but I have to see his things as quickly as possible."

"The other officers are examining his things as we speak. They arrived literally two minutes ago" she replied.

Eamon's heart sank. A weight like an elephant seemed to be sitting on his chest and he could taste the fear in his mouth. "Where.. where are they now? He asked.

"Just through there, I'll take you in. Judging by your reaction it must be very important and I really would like to help, it's just I'm short staffed as usual and interruptions seem to be the order of the day. Makes it very hard to get anything organised", the Matron said either in explanation or apology for the earlier tone, Eamon wasn't sure.

She took him through the double doors to the ward and then to a small room. "In here." Eamon barged past to find two uniformed Gardaí putting Gavin's blood stained clothes in an evidence bag. They turned to him, surprise on their faces. "Oh sorry sir" said the taller of the two, sergeants stripes on his arm. "I thought I'd come down myself and make sure everything was handled as thoroughly as we could, though I don't hold out any real hope here, there's nothing even missing and the rest is both a mess or has been handled by just about every member of staff in the hospital." It was Dempsey, looking perplexed to see Eamon.

"I.. wanted to see to Gavin's stuff myself" Eamon said "I want to make sure I don't leave anything to chance. This is too important." He hoped he'd sold the lie and by their faces, a mixture of grim determination and camaraderie, he could tell they had.

"Here's his notebook" said Dempsey "I'd just gotten through looking at it this second, I'd hoped I'd be calling you with some news."

"Well, did you find anything?" asked Eamon, a little more desperately that he might have wanted, as the world seemed to stop in front of him, his eyes fixated on the small black rectangle in Dempsey's hand. That book might just have unmasked him or it held nothing, Eamon prayed for nothing.

"Just so, sir" said Dempsey, "Nothing." It seemed like he'd read Eamon's thoughts, which sent a shock through him as thou he's been struck by lightning.

"What?" asked Eamon. Dempsey's voice sounded hollow and far away, as though coming through thick fog.

"You just said *nothing*, sir. I took that to mean you thought there was nothing in the notebook, and you're right" The two men looked quizzically at Eamon "Are you alright, sir? Sir?" said Dempsey lunging forward as Eamon's legs gave out and he fell to the floor. "Quick, get a doctor, he's fainted" Eamon heard through the haze in his mind. *That's funny* he thought, *I've just fainted too. What a coincidence.*

A few minutes later he came round, to find himself sitting awkwardly in a chair with a doctor shining a light in his eyes and the concerned faces of the two Gardaí and the Matron floating into his field of vision.

"Do you know your name?" asked the doctor. The bloody stupid question roused Eamon's temper and he pushed the Doctor's hand away.

"Of course I bloody well do!" he snapped and rubbed his face while trying to reorient himself. After a moment he hauled himself to his feet, glaring at the young garda who tried to help.

"You'll be retired before I need help to stand on my own two feet, lad" he said. "I've just been working too hard and not getting enough sleep or food" he explained to the doctor who was trying to get the Matron to see about a bed. "There'll be no need for that fuss. A night's kip and a good dinner and I'll be right as rain." The Doctor didn't even get to open his mouth to protest before Eamon stopped him, waving both he and the Matron away. "Shh, I'm fine. Go tend to sick people." He turned to the Gardaí "You know me better than that, Kevin. There's nothing more wrong with me that normal. I've just been burning the candle at both ends is all."

"You have the look of it, alright Eamon. Might I suggest you go home and get a proper rest before you have a heart attack" Dempsey seemed genuine, but he had seen Eamon in worse condition for different reasons over the years. Eamon would have forgiven him for concluding that he'd been on the sauce.

"I'm on the dry" Eamon admitted, the younger Garda didn't seem to know where to look but Sergeant Dempsey simply pursed his lips and nodded.

"You're the Boss, Eamon. This'll go no further than this room" he cast a sideways look and the younger man, who simply nodded vigorously.

"Anyway, said Dempsey "there's nothing here, except to say Gavin's lucky to be alive. There's so much blood it's difficult to make anything of it. It was a frenzied attack by the look of it." He shook his head, flicking through the pages of the notebook, several of which were stuck together with dried blood.

"Bit of a wild goose chase, hoping for a connection between Gavin and the missing priest. The old lad probably has Alzheimer's and has wandered off during the night. He'll turn up in due course, they usually do." He nodded to Eamon "If there's nothing else, sir, we'll get back." He nodded in the direction of the door to the younger Garda and they both left, but before they did Dempsey turned back to Eamon. "A word to the wise Eamon, as a friend. You don't have to shoulder all this yourself, you do have back up. We all want to catch whoever did this and put them away for a bloody long time, after they get a fucking good kicking first, though. It's what Gavin would want. Mind yourself." With that he nodded again and left.

The Matron came back in with a glass of water and a stare that said *if you defy me there'll be hell to pay*. Eamon took the water

126

and drank it in one long draught. She was standing over him, still daring him to try standing. "You're going to take at least ten minutes and one of the nurses is going to bring you something to eat." Her tone said she wasn't negotiating. "When there's a bit of colour back in your face I'll happily walk you out myself. You've caused me enough delays for the day." Eamon looked up at her. She was smiling, a soft, warm smile that lit her face, removing the mask of severity.

"Yes Matron, whatever you say Matron" he saluted and sank back in the chair. She didn't leave until a nurse knocked and wheeled in a trolley of food.

"Hospital food, my favourite" Eamon exclaimed.

"You'll eat it and you'll thank me for it, if not now, then later." She was enjoying this Eamon thought, but he did eat every last bite, his hunger overcoming the meals culinary shortcomings.

He stood up and held out a hand, which she took and shook firmly. This clearly was not a woman to be trifled with. "Thank you, I think" he said smiling "but I've got to go catch a killer."

"I'll wish you good luck and god speed" she said "At least you don't look as though you're going to faint again."

As he sat back into the Volvo, Eamon breathed a sigh of relief that he thought came from the furthest reaches of his soul. He sat back, eyes closed and tried to unclench his shoulders, wincing as he twisted left and right. He'd only just realised he was holding them so tensely that they were burning and knotted. He took another long breath and then he started the car.

12.

"Delgany." That one word destination filled him with dread all over again at the prospect of meeting Morrissey face to face, another of his childhood monsters. "A chance to finally confront the bastard though" he said to himself "Gird your loins, Eamon" he said cynically. He loathed biblical quotations as much as the Church that spawned them and yet they were woven into the fabric of his brain because of the Christian Brothers education. Even that word *education* was steeped in irony, the same irony that made him understand the double entendre inherent in the phrase to gird ones loins. With Christian brothers or Catholic priests lurking you really did need to gird your loins, prepare for any danger.

He looked in the rear view mirror and thought that if anyone had looked into the car, they would have been forgiven for thinking that he wore the grave expression of someone heading to a funeral. *Perhaps I am,* thought Eamon, *the funeral of a little boy who needs this so he can finally come to terms with it and put it away, hopefully for good.*

He pulled out into Dublin traffic and headed south. Like it or not, this was the only way to either find out something that would help him heal the forty year old wounds or rule Morrissey out of being any part of this whole sordid mess. Both would be valuable and Eamon might get to give the bastard a long overdue kicking.

Enda Morrissey, or O'Muirgheasa as he had been called for many years now, was getting old, he thought as he squinted at the paper. He'd left his glasses upstairs, again. Well, they'd have to wait or his eggs would be cold and that wasn't worth the journey. He liked this life, retired now as he was from teaching. He'd play round of golf later and then off for a little discreet pleasure. His pulse quickened at the thought, but he knew to remain calm. Half the joy was in the anticipation.

He was having a late breakfast and sat in his favourite spot in the conservatory, looking out at the autumn breeze swirling the leaves about the bases of the trees in the garden. "Nora" he called "Can you get that young lad, James, to come around later. He can rake the leaves and tidy up the garden." *Ah James*, he thought, a little old for his predilections at seventeen but nonetheless, a fine specimen.

His wife came in, carrying a pot of tea and his glasses. He smiled at her as she poured "You're an angel" he gushed.

"I'm an angel? So you're off playing golf, again" Nora cast her eyes heavenward "Oh go on, I'll call James and get him round before you go, so you can pay him, at least" she grimaced, jokingly, "but eat your breakfast before it gets cold, you know you hate the eggs when they're cold."

He put too much sugar in his tea, he knew, but he'd always had a sweet tooth and what was life if you couldn't indulge your.. vices" he smiled to himself again in anticipation. Putting on his glasses he looked at the newspaper. Nothing much of interest in the obituaries, his first port of call these days, he mused, it seemed there was someone mentioned most days that he knew at one point or other, either as a Brother or as a lay man. He was about to put the paper down when a small article caught his eye, or specifically a name did. He all but choked on his tea, spluttering and coughing as his eyes watered. *It wasn't possible, was it?* He read on and his eyes widened with every word. A retired priest, only returned from a long service in the Missions, died in a tragic house fire, overcome by smoke he passed leaving no relatives and was to be buried in the local church grounds, in recognition of his long service and devotion.

"Are you alright love, you look like you've seen a ghost?" asked Nora "I'll pop up and get your tablets will I?"

"No, no, don't fuss dear" he could hardly get the words out of his mouth "it's just I thought I'd seen something in the paper but I was mistaken" he said, shaking visibly.

"Those awful death notices, I don't know why you read them, especially if they're going to upset you that much!" Nora replied, scolding "anyway, that paper is over a week old, you can't see anything without your glasses and I bet you never thought to check the date. So you see, whoever it was, is buried and gone since last week." She patted his hand and stood "I'm going to get your tablets, you're pale as a ghost."

A week! How had it been more than a week and yet he hadn't known? He had scheduled to meet Buchannan later that day. They had a strict rule. No contact between meetings and no acknowledgement of each other's existence in any way whatsoever, in normal life. Buchannan's return into his life had been almost rapturous. To rekindle the shared passion, the singular joy of finding and preparing a new conquest, made all the sweeter sharing each new experience. The thought that Buchannan might have passed, robbing him of that sweet union, was almost more than he could bear. He would have to break their silence and find out if it were true or not.

Nora returned coming down the stairs in her usual heavy footed plodding step. God how he hated that sound, but then he hated almost everything about the bitch. The mask of normalcy was in danger of slipping and that couldn't happen, certainly not now, not until he found out more. He smiled as she returned.

"Take these with a sip of tea and go lie down for a few minutes until the colour comes back into your cheeks. You look positively awful. You can't golf in that state, you'll catch your death" she handed him the two tablets he took, prescribed for blood pressure and anxiety.

He swallowed them with a smiled that betrayed his thoughts as Nora looked on, oblivious to what was going through his mind or just how close he was to snapping at that moment. He put down the cup. "Thanks love, I think I will lie down. Must have been the shock but as you say it's been over a week and no one has come knocking or phoned to tell me that it was one of my old colleagues so it's probably just a coincidence." He smiled more widely than he should have, he thought, but it was sometimes hard to gauge the correct response. In his mind he had slit her throat a hundred times and more.

"Rest well, dear. I'll give James a shout and call you in an hour" she smiled back, a far more innocent and caring smile than that of her husband of almost forty years. He couldn't eat another thing, such was gnawing anxiety and so he climbed the stairs, lay on his bed and waited for the medication to kick in. It soon did its job and he fell into an uneasy sleep after ten minutes.

He woke to the sound of a loud crash, as though someone had dropped a set of plates on a tiled floor. "For the love and honour of Jesus" he growled under his breath "What has the stupid bitch done this time?" He called out in a far more gentle tone. "Are you alright darling? Did you drop something?" There was no answer from downstairs. If that bloody next door neighbour's cat had gotten in again he was going to skin it, literally, alive.

He put his feet into his slippers and went downstairs. He looked at his watch. He'd only been asleep for a half an hour. Nora wasn't in the conservatory or in the living room and looking out into the garden he couldn't spot her either. He shuffled into the kitchen where the source of the crashing noise became apparent as the china teapot lay on the floor in pieces, tea splashed out in a brown dark puddle across the tiles.

"Nora?" he called, worried now, as she would never have just left the mess. Nora liked things to be clean, neat and tidy. It was one of the few things he did like about her, as it matched his own tendency to compulsive cleanliness and spoke to his need for order.

"Hello Brother Morrissey" a voice said from behind him. He spun around in disbelief and complete shock, his face blanching in a second.

"Who..?" the next words stopped in his throat as the figure in front of him became all too familiar. "You?" he said in shocked disbelief and then again, "you?" but the second time there was a sneer, a realisation of a shared past and an arrogance, born of a lifetime of getting away with unspeakable crimes and then surprise as the heavy baton struck him across his forehead, knocking him dazed and reeling to the floor. Blood sprang from the gash the weapon had opened, pouring freely into his eyes, making everything a bred, blurry mess. He was dragged into the hallway where a terrified Nora, her eyes bulging in confusion and fear, knelt, her hands bound to the bannister of the stair with wire and her mouth stuffed with her own scarf.

She was whimpering like some sad, pathetic puppy and Morrissey couldn't bear it. He just wanted her to shut up, as the sound went through him like a hot poker. He glared at her but she simply continued to whimper, shaking uncontrollably.

Dusk was settling in the autumn evening as Eamon arrived, an hour and a half later in a leafy, middle class suburb. Traffic had been treacle slow all the way from town. *Recession my bollocks* thought Eamon, *there must be no one left in Dublin for the night, every fecker is out on the road.* Lights were just popping to life in the windows of the red brick houses as he slowly rolled the Volvo down the street, looking for the number on the scrap of paper he'd pulled from his jacket pocket and which was now sitting on the passenger seat.

"Thirty eight" he finally saw it. The sense of foreboding grew with every second as he paused outside and switched off the car on the street. He didn't want to pull into the driveway, he didn't want to be here at all and the fear that gripped him was that of the young boy, not the adult, but it was the adult, Detective Inspector Eamon Kearns, with the full weight of his fifty two years, that got resolutely from the car, shut the door firmly and marched toward the front door. As he approached, he noticed no car in the drive and the house was in gloom. Not a light to seen in the descending darkness. He cursed having to wait or make the journey again, cursing his tardiness, Marie's misplaced concern and letting him sleep, his forced sprint to the hospital and his episode while there.

"For the love and honour of Jesus" Eamon said, impatiently. He was about to turn away when he noticed something not quite right. The front door stood slightly ajar, at odds with the silence within. He walked up to the porch and knocked on the brass knocker. The door simply swung in, slowly revealing the darkened interior but Eamon could clearly see a silhouetted shape at the foot of the stairs in the half light, an outline in a kneeling pose. The smell hit him a second after, an assault on his senses as he almost gagged and his mind travelled back in time to Ranelagh. The figure was burnt beyond recognition. The second smell to jolt his senses back in time took him straight back to being an altar boy in Mass. The smell of the incense burned at funerals mixed with the overpowering, cloying stench of burnt flesh.

He slowly went inside, closing the front door as he did. The last thing he needed was someone stumbling on the scene. He was too late, it seemed. The killer had made him pay for his delays, his weakness and his panic. The remains were blackened but more than that, they were still warm. He realised with dawning horror and rage that the killer had been here just hours ago, at most.

"Fuck, fuck and fuck again!" he shouted lashing out at the front door, but only succeeding in cutting his hand as it went straight through the opaque glass panel. "Oh for Jesus sake" he roared "fucking blood everywhere now, as if I don't have enough to worry about." He reached into his pocket and pulled out his handkerchief, wrapping it around the wound, cursing himself as he did.

He looked for a phone, finding one in the living room. The number he dialled was the one Minister Casey had given him. The recipient picked up. "Yes?" asked a voice, impassively. Eamon gave the address and the grotesque circumstances, as dispassionately as he could, while feeling both the throbbing in his hand and trying to overcome the stench of burning that still assailed his nostrils, threatening to make him gag.

"Leave the house in forty five minutes. The.. problem will be dealt with minutes after. Wait until then to ensure no one else happens on this unfortunate scene. We'd hate to have to dispose of more than one. It would be inconvenient and traffic is murder this evening." The disembodied voice seemed to enjoy the humour of its joke, however poor in taste.

"Fine!" Eamon snapped, slamming down the phone and wiping it of fingerprints. He felt as guilty doing this as if he'd killed the bastard himself, *but at least* he thought *he got what he deserved, though not ALL he deserved.*

Looking at the scene Eamon was suddenly struck by two all too familiar thoughts. The body had been burned but the fire hadn't spread beyond the bannister it had been fastened to, wire used as restraints which had bitten deep into the flesh as the figure must have tried to wrench free in the throes of agony. He looked quickly around the hall and then around the living room. The search revealed a carbon dioxide fire extinguisher. The killer had watched the body burn just long enough and then quenched the fire to ensure no one would notice anything amiss immediately. *He had made sure the fire wouldn't spread to alert anyone*, Eamon though, his brow furrowed and his head bent in concentration. He took another look at the front door. The lock was slightly worn and he found that if he didn't small it shut quite forcefully, that it popped open again after a few seconds. The killer didn't realise it hadn't closed properly. He thought no one would find this for long enough for him to get away, but why didn't he just let it burn down? Something wasn't adding up. The killer seemed to be trying not to draw attention to this murder but had made the fire in Ranelagh very obvious. The next thing that struck him was how small the body looked. A germ of suspicion grew in his mind. He remembered Morrissey being quite tall and wasn't sure that his mind had played such a trick on him for so many years. He forced himself to look more closely at the remains and then it hit him like a ton of bricks. This was a

135

woman! Morrissey had married according to Casey and Eamon knew in his heart that this must be her body, another innocent forced to pay for Morrissey's crimes.

Torture the wife to get the husband to spill his guts and then set her alight to make him suffer. Which means, thought Eamon, *Morrissey might still be alive. The killer took him because Morrissey knows where those bloody tapes are, or said he did, to save his own skin. Our killer didn't know when I'd get here but he knew I would. He can't be sure Morrissey will lead him to the tapes, though to save his own skin I'd bet on him telling everything he knows and trying to bargain his way out of this. He doesn't yet realise he's just a dead man walking. So our killer still wants me to play the game, to find the tapes. In case he can't.*

He walked outside, scanning the street. It was quiet and not a thing was out of the ordinary. A pang of envy rippled through him as he watched lights turn on in those homes that had families in them. Oblivious, going about their lives without an inkling that this horror was being visited upon their leafy, suburban world.

He also wished the 'people' he'd called would hurry the fuck along. As he stood in the cool evening air a thought seemed to drift in on the wind, as they usually did when Eamon took a moment to relax. It was what set him apart from the rest of his colleagues. Sometimes he'd just have a moment of intuition, one that lurked in the back of his mind, waiting for him to slow down long enough to hear his subconscious as it made sense of the facts or clues or jigsaw piece snippets of each case.

"This fucker thinks he can get to me if I get them!" Eamon said out loud to the night. The thought surprised him and then a second thought rushed in obliterating his revelation. *How do you get to me? Through Marie!* His shock at the thought of anything happening to her opened the gulf of fear in the pit of his stomach. This time however, the feeling was quickly drowned in an overwhelming hatred and a desire to kill the man who would try to harm her. He turned to go back inside as there was no use in attracting unwanted attention and a strange man skulking around at an obviously empty house could get tongues wagging, perhaps even soliciting a call to the local sergeant.

A slight movement behind him caught Eamon's eye and made him whip around, only a fraction too late, as the figure that had crept up behind him brought down its arm, connecting the object it held with Eamon's head, just behind the ear before he could raise his arm in defence. He saw a circle of white light explode around his vision, a violently sharp pain and his knees buckled. He fell to the ground, head spinning, unable to fight the black as it enveloped him.

A sharp slap in the face brought Eamon round. He looked up from where someone had rolled him over. The night sky was looking down on him and he thought the stars were particularly bright tonight. For some reason his head was throbbing and he couldn't get his arms and legs to move properly. *That's funny* he thought, *I don't remember being in the pub.* It was only when he lifted his head that the throbbing pain brought him clarity, focusing his addled brain and bringing him back to the present. There was someone kneeling over him, though he couldn't make out the face, only a silhouette. It took him another moment to realise the features were obscured with a scarf, wrapped around the face to eye level, and yet another to realise that the figure was actually talking to him. He strained to focus, wincing as he did, through the pain in his head, which felt as though a cannon ball was rolling around inside. His neck felt almost unable to hold the weight of his head.

"You're not supposed to be here" the voice sounded slightly muffled through the thick scarf, but Eamon recognised it as the voice on the phone that he'd rung earlier "and by the looks of the golf ball behind your ear, somebody else felt the same way. You've obviously got a very hard head." The voice was amused but also had a tinge of concern. "We're going to clean this up but you need not to be here. One of my boys is going to drive you back into the city because you really aren't fit to drive anywhere and I can't have you doing anything silly between now and the time we finish making this look more like an accident. How convincing it'll be will depend on how hard the coroner looks. Do you understand me?" The figure held Eamon's chin to see if he was being clearly understood.

Eamon nodded "I'll deal with it." He was fighting waves of nausea and felt in no position to argue as he tried unsuccessfully to totter to his feet, almost keeling over forward as he did, only for the figure to save him.

"Easy now" the muffled voice soothed, "you're in no state to do anything at all except lie down. I found these keys so I take it the Volvo out there on the road is yours." Eamon tried to nod and another flash of pain made him almost pass out again. He slumped backwards as the figure nodded to another blurry shape that emerged from the night. Eamon's eyes just would not focus properly and his head swam as the two men picked him up and half walked, half carried him to the Volvo.

"W.. wait" Eamon fought for clarity, the thoughts in his head were jumbled and he felt like his mouth was disconnected and distant. "Peter's Church, Cabra. Get me there" he mumbled before they placed him in the Volvo, lying across the back seat and the other man wordlessly got into the driver's seat setting off into the night in the direction of Dublin.

138

The rocking motion of the car lulled him and Eamon, mercifully, passed out again.

His eyes opened, slowly and he stared up at a white ceiling. The pounding in his head started anew as he raised his head to take in his surroundings. The pain forced him to lower his head back to the pillow of a bed he couldn't ever remember seeing before, in a room with which he was unfamiliar.

The door opened. Brendan's face, popped round it and Eamon could see he was worried. "You're awake, well thank God for that!" the big man exclaimed, pulling up a small, steel-legged chair and sitting next to the bed.

""You look ridiculous on that little thing" Eamon smiled weakly and managed to prop himself up on one elbow, though the effort made him dizzy, "and where the hell am I?."

"Not hell Eamon, you're in my spare room, in the parochial house of Peter's Church" he looked even more worried "You've been here all night. How did this happen, who did this to you?" There was genuine concern emanating from the big priest.

"I didn't get a look but the last thing I remember was being in Delgany looking for Morrissey and, falling." The pieces were starting to rearrange themselves in Eamon's addled brain. "Jesus Christ, how did I wind up back here?" He was confused and the images from the night before were still jumbled and out of focus.

"I arrived home last night to find you, in Marie's Volvo, outside the house. The engine was still running and you were passed out in the back seat" said Brendan, "I thought you were dead or dead drunk at first, you were grey as any corpse, but then you moved and scared the shite out of me! I got you inside and was going to call an ambulance when you almost had a fit, muttering something about keeping it quiet, no matter what." Brendan rolled his eyes "Even half dead, the job comes first."

"In that state I'm surprised I managed anything, it was purely instinct because I have no recollection at all, but it was still the right thing to do in hindsight, given the current circumstances." Eamon gave a smile and snorted, "Don't ever do it again, get me to a hospital next time and fill me with drugs so my bloody head doesn't feel like the Artane Boys Band are marching through and playing out of time."

"Did you find him, Morrissey I mean?" Brendan asked "You obviously found someone or someone found you at any rate."

"I did and I didn't" replied Eamon "His wife... had been tied to the bannister of the stairs and burned alive. Morrissey was missing and I think our maniac has him and wants the location of those tapes. If Morrissey knows where they are he'll give them up" Eamon paused before continuing "What I saw there only confirms how far this killer will go and how much he wants those bloody things."

"To the ends of the earth or so it would seem" said Brendan, gravely. "You don't think Morrissey knows where they are, do you?" Brendan was thinking, Eamon knew, as stroked his beard absently, deep in concentration.

"I'm not sure but if he does he's as good as dead as soon as the killer finds them. A man like Morrissey will try to bargain, but the killer will want his pound of flesh, literally" said Eamon, trying not to sound happy about it, but even through the throbbing in his head he still felt a pang of satisfaction that Morrissey would finally be punished for the many crimes he had committed.

"Good" said Brendan. "He will only get what's coming to him."

"That's hardly very Christian of you, what about turning the other cheek?" Eamon was surprised at the force with which Brendan spat out the words.

"I've only four cheeks and I've turned them all. He can burn in hell for eternity and I'll stoke the flames!" Brendan replied angrily. "Parasites like that are a blemish on the Church and everything a Christian should uphold."

"I know, big man, but you've got to calm down" Though his head pounded even harder, Eamon reached out. He squeezed his friend's hand, though it nearly made two of his own. "I'll rest an hour here and then I need to go back to Loyola's, back to the scene." He noted mentally that it was getting easier to say the name without feeling that mix of panic, fear, loathing and hatred. "I may have missed something because I didn't know what I was looking for." He slowly lowered his head on to the pillow again "Thanks for this. I don't know what I'd do without you."

"You'd still be in the back of the car, freezing and generally beaten up, so I suppose I'm useful in some small way" Brendan smiled, his face lightening and the anger fading.

"Give me an hour and a couple of aspirin and I'll be grand" Eamon said "I've got to get moving, soon, or the killer will get there before me and all hell will break loose."

Brendan stood up and nodded "How about a few hours. I'll ring the station for you and say you've got food poisoning. That'll buy you the day, at least"

"Again, what would I do without you" Eamon closed his eyes, sighed and fell back to sleep in seconds.

13.

Eamon woke after a few hours, the pain in his head having lessened considerably, confined now to whenever he touched the lump behind his ear or rolled onto it, which was what had woken him in the first place. He noticed a glass of water and two pills on the bedside table. He took a moment to recall everything that had happened so far in this case while he swallowed the pills and gulped down the water. His body was aching all over and he knew it wasn't going to get any better lying in bed. He threw back the blanket, put his feet on the floor and looked about for his clothes, which were in a neatly folded pile on a chair close to him. He got dressed, somewhat more slowly than normally, his head still feeling heavy and painful if he bent over or stood too quickly.

Looking at himself in the mirror he thought *Jesus! You could feature in Night of the Living Dead.* "After this I'm taking a holiday" he said to his reflection. "I'm glad we agree" he said nodding to the mirror. He went to the window, drew back the curtain and looked out. The sun was still low in the sky. *Not too late in the day* he thought *time to get back to Loyola's house and see if there's anything there.*

He didn't really expect to find the tapes but he might find a clue, anything to point him in the right direction. Going downstairs he called for Brendan but there was no answer, save the loud ticking of the grandfather clock in the hall. He thought about leaving a note but decided against it, "too many people knowing too much about where I am is not a good thing in the current climate" he advised himself, opening the front door. The sunlight stabbed his eyes, causing him to wince. His head was still not in great shape, the pain that shot through it felt like the worst kind of hangover.

He'd have to be careful driving across the city, but drive he would, because he had to start at the start and get to the finish line, and quickly too. He'd been held up long enough and now it was imperative he find those tapes and destroy them and find the killer and lock him away for eternity. The only way he could see to break the cycle of killing was to destroy the recordings, no matter who was on them, in order to stop the killer's rampage. "No tapes, no names, no names, no targets" he said as he sat into the car. The keys were still in the ignition. *Brendan would have had his hands full trying to get me inside he must've forgotten to take them out,* he thought, bemused. *He's put up with a lot in this and been such a great support I'll have to think of some way to repay the debt. How many times though has he given me hell for not locking my car? This is one time I'll get my own back!*

Eamon started the engine, looked over his shoulder to reverse out of the drive and instantly regretted it as a white hot flash of pain lanced through him. "Mirrors Eamon, mirrors" he chided, wincing again "That sent a sweat out through me" he told no one in particular. He knew he was still feeling fuzzy and felt just a little drunk. "Not to worry" he said looking in the rear view mirror, "You've often driven home in much worse state than this, be grand!"

He decided to go to the station first, both to check in and to enquire if there was any news on Gavin. He hoped and offered a silent prayer that the lad would be alright. If Gavin pulled through he'd be able to retire with a full pension if he felt like it, *the silver lining so* he thought, *but it won't change the fact that you sent him there and it's your fault he's lying in a hospital bed, fighting for life.* He vowed silently that when he caught up with this twisted bastard he was going to make him pay for that crime above all others, both for Gavin's sake and, he admitted, *for your own.*

He arrived at the station, feeling more human, the pills were obviously doing their job. The first person he met on entering the office was Sergeant Dempsey, who looked somewhat surprised to see him. Eamon remembered he was supposed to be out with food poisoning and simply said "Nothing a good shite didn't cure." Dempsey just shook his head, smiling.

"He's not awake yet, sir" Dempsey answered before Eamon could frame the question "but the doctors said his heart beat is stronger and he looks a lot less deathly" said Dempsey. "He's going to be ok, I can just feel it." There was a relief to his voice that Eamon shared.

"I pray you're right Kevin, I really do" said Eamon "He owes me a tenner, he better be alright" he joked. "Listen, Kev, do we still have keys for that house in Ranelagh, where that poor priest died in the house fire?" he asked, conversationally. "I think I left my torch there, and if it's been locked up since there's a good chance it'd still be there. I don't want to shelling out for another one."

"I think so, let me check" said Dempsey.

At that moment Ray Carroll walked down the stairs, took a look at Eamon and with a curt nod, motioned for Eamon to follow him. He turned on his heel and Eamon cast his eyes to heaven "What fucking now!" he said under his breath. Arriving at Ray's door he remembered their last conversation and deciding that

144

discretion was indeed the better part of valour, he knocked and waited

"Come in" the voice sounded amused. As Eamon entered Ray motioned to close the door behind him. "Wonders will never cease, you actually can teach an old dog new tricks."

Eamon grimaced, the sarcasm not lost on him. "Apparently so, *sir*" he continued the performance, though he was getting more anxious to be back out there, tracking down the killer.

"I'm not going to ask how things are going at present Eamon, for many reasons" said Ray, sitting back in his seat and swivelling until he almost had his back fully to Eamon and was looking out the window. "Firstly" he continued, "because I've been expressly told to give you free rein and not to interfere, secondly, because I genuinely don't want to know because this is now your shit show" he smiled, "and thirdly because by the look of you, it's going badly, very, very badly. Tell me I'm wrong and that you're on top of this, please."

"I'm doing what I have to do to get this finished, quietly, quickly as I can and that's all I can say. If this all blows up, it's on me, not you, sir" Eamon was tired of being the whipping boy and as he spoke a germ of an idea was forming in his mind. He filed it away for later. It would need thinking about.

"Very good, Eamon. I'll take that as a yes in a conversation we never had" again Ray smiled, relieved that the ramifications of any blunders or any public light shone on this mess would be shone directly on Eamon Kearns and not he. "And young Cantwell? Was he also involved?" The question set Eamon's mind on edge.

"No sir, it seems it was simply a case of being in the wrong place at the wrong time or perhaps an old grudge with someone he put away previously. Our investigations, as I'm sure you are aware, are on-going."

Ray almost laughed as he looked at Eamon "A very politically aware statement, worthy of the press office. I see you're learning the finer points of police politics. I'm surprised. I didn't think you had it in you."

"I'm full of surprises, Ray" Eamon replied "but if that's all I have to get back out there, before there's another murder I have to cover up." He watched the colour drain from the Superintendent's face and turned before he could make any comment, taking the door with him with a slam.

"Prick, cover your own arse and hang me out to dry if everything goes tits up" muttered Eamon. The idea was growing quickly in his mind but he had to resist it. He didn't have time to dwell until he had those tapes in his hand. "Then we'll see who winds up sweating and who's hung out to dry." The killer was right in one twisted way, those tapes were a weapon, or perhaps a deterrent. He just had to get them and work out the details later.

Dempsey was at Eamon's desk when he returned. "You got lucky, they're still here. The house is to be returned to the diocese today but we haven't a uniform to spare to return the effects, such as they are." He placed a small box on Eamon's desk, opened a large brown evidence envelope and took a pair of house keys from the contents.

"The diocese?" queried Eamon.

"The house is owned by the Church, for retired priests who were sent out foreign to the Missions" said Dempsey. "When they returned they'd be housed there until they found someplace else to put them. Seems they never got around to doing that with the last poor fellow. If they had, he might still be alive"

Eamon nodded as though it was just a simple fact but in his mind his thoughts were racing. *Did the Archbishop know that Buchannan was Loyola, and if so, did he keep him there to make sure he wasn't put anywhere else that he might stir up trouble as he had in the past. Does this mean he's got more to hide in this than I thought?*

Again Eamon resolved to file the thought away until he had those tapes in his hand. One jigsaw piece at a time, until the picture started to become clear.

"Here, I'm travelling that way anyway. I'll drop that lot to the local priest in Ranelagh. He can get them back to wherever" Eamon said, helpfully.

"Cheers, Sir. That would actually be a great help. I've got all the uniforms I can spare working on canvassing and interviewing in Gavin's case. If there's anything to be found we won't rest until it is." Dempsey's voice was earnest.

"I know Kev, I just wish I wasn't snowed under with my other cases so I could be out there too so it's the least I can do, for Gavin" said Eamon apologetically.

Dempsey nodded and clapped Eamon's shoulder in solidarity. "I'll get the rest, there's only a small box of bits and pieces, glasses, rosary and a few pictures. We'll leave no stone unturned until we get whoever did this. He's one of our own." He left to get the box and Eamon breathed a sigh. Being economical with the truth talking to the brass was one thing but to your own men, that went against the grain. Dempsey returned and handed Eamon a cardboard box, full of items from Loyola's house, anything that would have a print, show a picture, or give any indication at all of who he was. It was all Eamon could do not to throw the lot in the rubbish bin. Instead he hefted the box, slipped the keys into his jacket and headed back for Ranelagh.

Eamon turned the key in the lock and entered the house for the second time. He'd arrived and parked his car at the end of the row of neat, semi-detached houses. Scanning the avenue he had waited a few minutes before he walked to the house. As he entered he was once again greeted by the smell, all too familiar now, of burning, still pungent but stale now and less intense. He went into the kitchen, the same scene greeted him, save for the grisly image of the charred body and he found himself grateful, he'd seen enough gruesome killings since this started and that one was imprinted in his mind in detail.

He stood in the kitchen, surveying the possible places someone might hide a number of video cassettes. He saw nothing that made him think they would be there but he still made a point to searching behind appliances, in drawers and cupboards, under the scorched table, everywhere and anywhere, but to no avail. He performed the same searches in the living room, bathroom and hall cupboard before tackling the bedrooms. There were two, one was Loyola's and the other a spare room. He checked that first but it was simply furnished to the point of looking spartan and there were simply no places to hide anything, certainly not something as bulky as a number of tapes.

He'd left the priest's own room until last. There was a loathing and revulsion so strong that he found it difficult to admit. He was afraid to go into that room. It wasn't like before, before he knew that the poor victim was not what he seemed, not a victim at all, but rather the personification of evil.

148

"For fuck sake, get over yourself and get in there!" Eamon scolded himself. He put his hand on the door handle and taking a deep breath, turned it and pushed the door open wide. Everything was just as he remembered. He looked around the room, willing something to reveal itself. There was nothing he could see in any way out of the ordinary. He decided to look in the less obvious places. Firstly he checked the mattress for any cuts or tears that might be big enough to slip the tapes into. Nothing. He checked the wardrobe. Nothing. He took down and checked the suitcase he found on top of the wardrobe. Again, nothing.

He rifled through the pockets of the jackets and trousers in the wardrobe. Nothing. He was becoming frustrated. Then, just as he was about to close the doors, he noticed a small slip of paper on the floor of the wardrobe. He picked it up and saw it was a bus ticket, to Delgany!

"So Loyola and Morrissey *did* find one another! Jesus Christ the two of them after all these years" Eamon spoke aloud to the empty room, trying to talk himself through a possible scenario in which both the evil bastards were complicit in dealing with those tapes. "It makes more sense that they're in Delgany, hidden where no one knew they even knew each other, ever!" he exclaimed, slapping his forehead with the palm of his hand. He knew he had to go back to Delgany and search the house.

Eamon drove as quickly as he dared through traffic, out of town. The miles dragged by interminably, his impatience causing him to feel such pressure that he thought his head would explode. It wasn't helping that traffic was heavy and the rain had started again, adding to his frustration. By the time he reached the country roads he was where Marie would refer to as 'high doh', his heart thumping and jaw clenched as he threw the car into bend after bend.

Finally, he reached the same street, just as the rain stopped. Its tranquil setting lost on him as he pulled up just before the house. He jumped out of the car hurriedly, causing his head to pound and his pulse to thump in his ears. He winced, placing a hand on the roof for a moment while he calmed himself. Looking up he was greeted by an image that dropped his heart into his shoes. A yellow line of police tape cordoned off the front gates. Beyond that, he house was in ruins. The obvious signs of a fire that had engulfed the whole building, blackening windows and charred front door, told him that there was nothing he was going to find here. He slumped back against the car and closed his eyes, feeling totally defeated.

"Are you alright there?" a voice called from the path just to his left. An elderly man, wearing a flat cap, overcoat and scarf against the autumn breeze stood on the path, holding a small dog on a leash as it strained to sniff this interloper.

Eamon was snapped back to reality. "Do you know what happened?" he asked in an innocently shocked tone, "I'm a friend of the family" he added, seeing the man's mistrustful expression.

"For a moment I thought you were a reporter, like that other fellow. Awful business. It seems that poor Nora was overcome by smoke from a fire that started yesterday evening, late on. Such a terrible way to go" the old man said, shaking his head. "I'm so sorry that you had to come here to find out, it must be awful. They're such a nice, pleasant couple, she and Enda." he said consolingly, "He wasn't there himself but he's away quite a lot. I'm sorry for your loss, if Nora was a friend."

He was about to continue on with his small companion when Eamon asked "A reporter? Surely not? You'd think they'd have better things to report than a tragedy like this!" He was laying on the indignant expression as heavily as he could, hoping the elderly old fellow would warm to the conversation. He did.

"Little runt of a man, with a northern accent" the old man said, adding "Probably a protestant, not that I've much against Protestants but you just can't trust them." Eamon nodded in agreement with the mildly bigoted statement. One he could wholeheartedly endorse if the reporter was who he thought.

"Did he give a name, I think someone ought to complain. Not even giving people time to grieve before showing up like vultures" Eamon fed the line and the old man took it, seeing what he took for a like-minded soul.

"Oh you know, Mac.. something or other, I don't recall. I wasn't that interested in hearing his wheedling voice go on" the old man replied with distain.

"I wonder what he wanted." Eamon asked absently, again baiting the old man. In his mind he was silently screaming, that fucking ferret McGinn had been here. That meant he knew something more than Eamon wanted him to know. How in the name of all that was holy...? The same idea as before was bobbing to the surface. Could he use McGinn to his advantage though, that was a point to ponder.

"He stopped me this morning almost exactly where you are as I was taking George here" he nodded to the little terrier "and asked almost as many questions as you have" his voice carried suspicion, "how did you say you knew the O'Muirgheasa's?."

The lie that tripped off Eamon's tongue was no more than the truth with good lighting. "Enda was a teacher of mine many years ago and I lost contact until recently, I was just calling hoping to catch him."

151

The old man's expression brightened, his suspicions of Eamon allayed. "Ah, that's such a pity. Such tragic circumstances and him not home, though I'm not sure if that was a blessing or a curse, in the circumstances. I only hope he has good friends around him like yourself when he does hear this awful news."

Eamon pursed his lips and nodded gravely. The old man approached him and removed a glove to extend his hand "I am truly sorry for your loss" he said. Eamon took his hand and just nodded. He hadn't the stomach for continuing the charade and a large part of him wanted to scream at this old man that Morrissey was nothing more than a perverted monster and anything that brought him pain was ok in his book.

The old man nodded, seeing turmoil in Eamon's eyes perhaps, and with a final squeeze of his hand, continued down the path.

"If only you knew, he's not going to have to worry about this at all. If the killer has him he's as good as dead already and good riddance" Eamon muttered watching the man heading away down the path, being almost dragged by the terrier. When he was out of sight Eamon walked to the house.

The front door had been broken in by the fire brigade and inside there were nothing but soot stains and puddles of oily looking water. The fire had consumed the stairs almost entirely, leaving no trace of the murder scene. Eamon's memory of the man in the scarf came back to him, "A thorough clean up job. Make it look like a simple accident, as long as the coroner doesn't look too closely." He'd have to contact the State Pathologist, Cavanagh, as soon as possible, to prevent this getting any limelight. "More loose ends to tie up than the bloody Gordian knot" he said through clenched teeth.

Looking up the ruined staircase he decided that there wasn't going to be any point trying to get up there. The whole lot had incinerated, several of the beams had burned through and were in halves hanging from the second floor. The ground floor wasn't much better, between smoke and water there was little left of the house he'd seen yesterday. He shook his head and carefully walked through each room, in case by some miracle he's just stumble across the tapes, *though knowing my luck recently, I'd find Lord Lucan faster in here* he thought to himself, bitterly.

He had resigned himself to the whole exercise being a waste of time. If the tapes were here then they'd be a molten plastic mess. He picked his way out through the debris and through the door of the conservatory. The glass had been shattered, either by the heat or the firemen, and Eamon was able to step through the remaining blackened shards to go out into the garden where the late autumn sky was still leaden with rain.

It was then he noticed the garage. It was set back far enough that he'd never noticed it coming from the road. He walked over and tried the handle on the overhead door but it was locked, then the side door, which swung open a few inches before stopping as something was barring the way. Eamon was in no mood to fight his way in but he needed to rule out any possibility that those tapes were in there. He put his shoulder to the door and gave a push, moving it an inch. Again but with more impact he shouldered the door, sending a stab of pain through his head and neck. It gave another inch or two, and a third time, the door opened enough for him to squeeze through if he pushed against the door frame, though he was paying for the effort with the pain in his head and now in his shoulder too.

Eamon looked down at the obstruction that had blocked the door. In the strip of light falling in through the open door he needed a moment to adjust his eyes. The obstruction resolved itself into the shape of a man or what was left of a man. Someone had beaten him more furiously than anything Eamon had ever seen before.

"Jesus Christ!" He exclaimed, taking a step back in shock at the sudden revelation. He'd thought it might be a bag of old clothes or even a roll of carpet but another body was the last thing he expected to find. What was even more disturbing was how badly it looked. The face was beaten to an unrecognisable pulp, and both legs were bloated and seemed twisted at odd angles.

Eamon squatted down to see the extent of the injuries more closely. There was a flap of skin hanging over the eyes where it had come away from the scalp of the forehead and both nose and teeth were destroyed completely. The jaw was either broken or dislocated and Eamon thought the collar bone was probably broken too, given the sharp angle of the discoloured skin of the body. He guessed this had to be what was left of Enda Morrissey.

The body was barefoot and several toes were crushed too, on each foot. "Ooh, no little piggy going to market there" Eamon mused, trying to make sense of the ferocity of what had happened while at the same time wishing he'd gotten the opportunity to watch at least. How many times had he wished for exactly this scenario but with him wielding the implement of destruction? He felt a twinge of jealousy, of having been cheated somehow, before coming back to himself and thinking that at least some sort of justice had been meted out.

He'd have to cover this up as well and it was beginning to sicken him. These evil perverts would be remembered well by those that knew them and that was beginning to irritate his conscience. They should be publicly named and shamed for all time. How though, could he do that without risking everything? If only he had those bloody tapes. He could destroy whatever he might need to if he was identifiable and maybe then hand the rest over so justice could actually be served, even if that did mean the end of his career. *At this point,* he thought, *what career. The hypocrisy of doing all of this makes a mockery of everything I hold sacred.*

His anger rose and he stood, kicking out the outstretched, mangled foot.

Eamon heard a soft, whimpered moan from the body and saw the slightest movement of bloodied fingers, silhouetted against the light in the doorway. He jumped backward as if he'd been electrocuted and swore at the top of his voice "Sweet Jesus fucking Christ!!" His heart was hammering in his chest.

The man's left eye opened no more than a slit, Eamon almost missed it but the head turned slowly, almost imperceptibly, and he knew the broken figure was looking at him. Overcoming his fear, shock and revulsion he drew close to the body. Again he heard the whimper, faintly as it pleaded with shallow breaths "help me, please." Eamon leaned closer.

"You won't know me but I do know you, Brother Morrissey, and believe me when I tell you that you had more hope of the person who did this helping you than you ever had of me doing anything" Eamon's pent up hatred spilled out and he gripped the man's arm, squeezing tightly and eliciting another moan. "You know nothing about pain but I see you are learning, though I fear the lesson was too quick. If you want help I suggest you pray to your God! The only thing that will help you now is if you can tell me where the tapes are. Did you give them up? Did you?" Eamon's voice was feral.

The destroyed face of Morrissey tried to swallow, again moaning in pain at that simple action. There was no way he could speak properly but he did seem to be trying. Again Eamon drew closer, pressing his ear close to Morrissey's bloody lips, straining to make sense of the whispered, half words, while every fibre of his being strained against his proximity to him. He closed his eyes to concentrate on the sounds, drowning out his revulsion.

"Save me.. promise me.. tell you where tapes are.. " the words came slowly, through what must have been agonising breaths yet Eamon didn't care how hard it might have been. This bastard knew where the tapes were and was still trying to bargain for his sorry, pathetic life.

"You tell me where they are and I'll do everything in my power to help you, you have my word" Eamon said gravely, hoping that the words were understood and a bargain struck. The faintest nod accompanied by another moan was his reply, then another whispered half slurred word, along with a tiny cough that released blood down his chin "Ca.. Cat. Morrissey's eye closed and he went limp. Eamon reached for a pulse but only found the faintest trace. Morrissey was close to dying and most likely wouldn't last long enough to help anyway.

Eamon stood up. Cat, Cat? What the fuck did that mean? He hadn't seen a cat or any evidence of one in the house before it burned, so how was he supposed to find one now. He looked around the garage but nothing jumped out at him. He was about to try rouse Morrissey one more time when the cat carried caught his eye, on a high shelf. Beside it sat a plastic bowl but both were covered in cobwebs. If there had been a cat it was long since dead and buried, he thought bitterly, gritting his teeth and giving a silent scream. Then the thought hit him. Buried! They'd most likely buried the cat in the garden as so many people did. He made for the door. The figure of Morrissey moaned again, attempting to reach out a hand only to fail in the attempt, fingers opening to claw the empty air. Eamon looked down and said "If you told me the truth I'll be back." He stepped over Morrissey and out into the afternoon light, blinking slightly. He scanned the garden, walking from bush to bush and tree to tree, looking for any sign of where one might bury a cat. In the end it had been a simple task, there was even a small headstone for *Fluffy*. The earth had been freshly dug and the sod replaced carefully. Taking a quick look around to make sure he couldn't be observed easily, Eamon hunkered down and pulled at the sod with his bare hands. It came up without much resistance. *Eureka!* he thought, as it came away, revealing a rectangular package covered in oil cloth, wrapped tightly and bound with string.

He lifted it out of the earth and shook off the dirt as best he could, where it had become stuck by the rain. He couldn't open the string as the knots were wet and impossible to untie. "Jesus Christ" he muttered, frustrated. He carried the package back to the garage, stepping once more over the figure of Morrissey and looking for anything that might be used to cut the cords.

Eamon looked down and saw a shears. He grabbed it and only then he noticed the blood on it. In a flash of realisation he knew why. "You came out here telling our friend the tapes were in here and then you tried to stab him with these so he beat you to death, or so he thought. He's not very stable is he? Got something of a temper?" Eamon was taunting Morrissey but he didn't care. He was also remembering all the times Morrissey had taunted him, whispering in his ear as he raped him. "Well you might have done him a mischief but you paid dearly for it." He was so relieved that Eamon felt somewhat giddy. He cut the strings and pulled back the oil cloth to find six VHS tapes. Tapes marked with dates. The dates, he noted silently, starting with the year he had been in Augustine's. That one was going to be destroyed, now and the next one until the dates matched when he'd left Augustine's and his chance at life began.

157

Morrissey's fingers were moving, grasping the air again and his moaning was growing fainter. This was it for him, Eamon knew but some perverse need wanted to have the last word. He moved to stand over Morrissey and looked him in the, barely open eye.

"A bargain's a bargain." He reached into his pocket. "I said I'd do what I could. Here's two aspirin. Call me in the morning." He threw the pills Brendan had given him at Morrissey and stepped out into the daylight, savouring the moment. He pulled the door closed and tapes in hand headed for his car, feeling as though he'd finally gotten some measure of peace, justice even, if just for a minute.

14.

Eamon drove back towards Dublin, leaving Morrissey to his fate, and he knew it. He had written the man's death warrant. A tiny part of him tried to feel some measure of guilt for not helping the man but it was quickly overwhelmed by the sense of natural justice and liberation he felt.

He was going to go back to the station but before he did he needed to make a stop. He pulled into a petrol station in Stillorgan. He had put the tapes into Loyola's evidence box and now threw his overcoat over the lot. *Better keep these out of view,* he thought, *no telling who's watching.*

He saw a phone box outside and stepped inside to the usual smells of stale cigarette smoke and urine. "Why does every drunk in Ireland think he can just take a piss in a phone box?" he complained to himself, shaking his head, before remembering the odd occasion he had been caught short himself while wandering home from the pub and relieved himself in the first opportune place he could find. He pulled out a small notebook from his breast pocket and thumbed through until he found the name and number he was searching for. He picked up the receiver but hesitated for a moment.

"Fuck it, enough is enough" he said firmly and punched the numbers on the keypad.

"Express, McGinn speaking" the voice was unmistakable, Eamon thought, managing to make possibly the most melodious accent in Ireland sound irritating.

"Hello Trevor. We need to talk." Eamon didn't have to introduce himself as the surprised silence on the other end of the line told him that McGinn knew exactly who it was.

"Eamon Kearns!" said McGinn incredulously "To what do I owe the distinct honour?"

"Don't be a prick. We both know you're nosing around in my investigation" said Eamon, irritated by McGinn's sarcastic tone.

"I've been doing my job, uncovering the truth, truth you seem to be going to great lengths to keep under the radar, Eamon. Would you like to make any comment, for the record, for the story I'm working on?" Again his tone incensed Eamon but he bit back the desire to snarl at the little prick.

McGinn continued "I'm sure you'll like it, it's a cracker! It seems several elderly priests, old boys on their last legs, have died in tragic yet, what some might consider sinister, circumstances over the past few weeks." He paused for Eamon to comment but hearing nothing decided to plough ahead, hoping to bait Eamon, no doubt. "Aye, one had a nasty fall, another dies in a house fire and another just up and disappears from his home, and not long after your young colleague gets almost killed on the same street! That's an awful lot of coincidences, don't you think, Eamon?" McGinn was clearly enjoying this and Eamon was suppressing the desire to slam down the phone, but he needed to know what McGinn knew before deciding what to do next. "Oh, before I forget, add the tragic death of that poor lady in Delgany, you know, Nora, the wee girl who died in a house fire. You know, married to the former Christian Brother and one time friend of the

160

old boy who, coincidentally, also died in a house fire. That's a lot of coincidence, Eamon, don't you think? It'll make for a good piece."

Eamon marshalled his emotions before he spoke, otherwise he'd have exploded in an avalanche of expletives and threats. McGinn had been doing his homework, but he still had nothing more than conjecture. Not that it would prevent him from writing a sensationalist piece that might open Eamon's own life to scrutiny. He needed to manage this in such a way that the story was directed away from him and toward the killer.

You still there Eamon?" McGinn asked smugly. "Cat got your tongue?"

"I'm still here, listening to a lot of hot air, supposition and coincidence. You're fishing, Trevor, but you don't know what you're fishing for" Eamon replied. "We need to meet and when we do I will give you a story you can print if you've the balls, with evidence to back it up, but there's once condition and one warning." He waited for a reply.

"Go on, Eamon, I'm listening" McGinn's tone had changed to one of earnest concentration. He could smell the story and if Detective Eamon Kearns was telling it, a man who he knew clearly hated him and his brand of journalism, then it was going to be worth any risks or strings he might attach.

"You'll be going up against the Church, State and police force. It will not be pleasant" Eamon warned "and you will keep my name out of this completely" he was bargaining with his own life now and he had never felt quite so vulnerable in his professional career before. "Agree to this and I'll meet you and give you everything. There's one more thing, you can't publish anything until I give you the word. If you try to, or try to double cross you

161

I promise you I'll make sure that you're stitched up, locked up and the key thrown away" Eamon couldn't resist the threat. He needed McGinn to know that this was his way or he would bury the little ferret.

"I'm from Belfast Eamon, I grew up fighting Church and State in an effort to tell the truth of what was happening there" McGinn said indignantly "and I don't doubt for a second that you could bury me but remember it was you who came to me today. I give you my word, you'll not be named or mentioned or referenced in any way. I protect my sources." His tone was a mixture of pride and anger.

"Then get ready for the story of a lifetime. Where do I meet you?" Eamon said. The cat was going to be among the pigeons after this but now that the two of his tormentors were dead, he felt like it was time to lift the lid, finally. Finally he might feel clean, the one thing the killer had said that had silently resonated all this time. He needed to get it out and let people know what had happened, though he still felt he had to protect his family from the shame of his homosexuality. *It's still a sin in the eyes of God and illegal in the eyes of the law so I'm damned on both counts if it ever gets known.*

"Tonight at nine o'clock" confirmed McGinn "I'm going to assume you already know the address."

"Of course" said Eamon "Nine it is" and he hung up the receiver.

At the other end of the line, Trevor McGinn sat back into his seat, letting out a long breath and sat wide eyed for a moment trying to digest what had just happened. For Detective Eamon Kearns to have come to him meant this was huge and for him to offer this big a story meant he had something to hide himself. Whatever it was, Trevor McGinn was going to uncover it. He might not be able to name Kearns in this article but there was nothing to stop him digging into Kearns life and finding another one. It was there and Trevor knew it, his instincts were rarely wrong and he could taste the blood in the water. Smiling to himself he decided he was heading home early and going to enjoy a glass of wine before he and Eamon got down to it. He reached into the desk drawer and took out a small Dictaphone. All this was going to be recorded on tape. That prick Eamon just didn't need to know that it was.

Eamon stood in the phone box a moment longer, still holding the receiver in its cradle. He knew he couldn't really trust McGinn but he also knew that the little bastard didn't have enough, yet, to put together a story, but that it would only be a matter of time before he might.

To calm himself he decided there was one person he needed to call, even just for the reassurance that he was following the right path. He lifted the receiver, fed a coin into the slot and dialled.

"Hello, St. Peter's, Father Quinn speaking" the rich, deep tone of Brendan's voice always set Eamon at ease. Its depth reminded him of something he couldn't quite put his finger on. His own father maybe, though he doubted that, after all he'd left when Eamon was just a small kid.

"Brendan, its Eamon. I found them. I found the tapes" he couldn't hide the relief or elation he felt sharing the news with Brendan, "and I'm going to do what we talked about. I'm going to make sure they see the light of day. You were right!" He said allowing the excitement to release.

"Eamon, by Christ that is good news, but are you sure you're ready? You know you could be opening yourself to condemnation and shame. You're prepared for that?" Brendan sounded worried but also excited. "To be honest I didn't see you

163

coming to this decision but I'm glad you have" he said softly "you will be the better for it."

Eamon didn't know how to tell his friend so he just said "The tapes are dated. I'm going to destroy the ones from the years I was in the school. Everything else is fair game. I'm going to give them to McGinn and he's going to publish the story, without reference to me at all. It's the best I can do to protect my family and my career" he said apologetically "I know it's not ideal Brendan but the two of them are dead, Loyola and Morrissey, and no one else but you and I know anything else." He was willing Brendan to understand.

"I see you've made your decision, Eamon. I'm not going to try changing your mind. Only you can decide to do what's right and how much you're prepared to live with. I only hope when it's all over that you can look yourself in the eye without shame or regret" Brendan said gravely. "We're only free in this life if we can fully accept the consequences of our actions and put ourselves in God's hands. That's our real power."

"It will come out Brendan, this way the guilty will pay for their crimes, while my family are shielded from it" Eamon said, again hoping to convince Brendan this was the best option.

"But not all of them will pay, will they? What about whoever else might be recorded on the evidence you destroy to save yourself. They get away with their crimes and get to go to Mass every Sunday and contaminate everything they touch." Brendan sounded angry and Eamon could understand why. The Church was everything to him and the thought that those monsters might sit in Mass, infecting it, was more than he could bear without feeling a towering anger.

"It's the best I can do Brendan. I know it's not perfect but neither am I. I'm hoping you'll see it is enough, in time." Eamon knew he was fighting an uphill battle to convince Brendan but he wanted to secure his friend's blessing or if not at least his understanding.

"I know, Eamon. Believe me I know" Brendan sighed. "You do the best you can, we all do and at the end of the day you just hope you have done the right thing. Do what you have to do. See it through to the end and take the consequences on the chin. That's all the advice or blessing I can offer."

Thanks big man" Eamon said, relieved. "I'll do my best and it will work out for the best." The line went dead. Eamon knew Brendan wasn't happy but he also knew him to be a pragmatist who would come round in the end that this was for the best.

He made two further calls. The first to the faceless voice that had arranged poor Nora's accident, informing them of Morrissey's location and directing that he be disposed of in similar fashion, to which the voice simply chuckled "Why detective you are a man full of surprises. When I was told I might have to do some cleaning up I never envisaged there would be as much as you seem bent on creating Keep up the good work!" To which Eamon hissed loudly into the phone "I didn't bloody well commit either of these acts, I'm just like you, covering someone else's arse, so if you'd just make this go away I'll do my best not to have to call you again!"

His temper was rising and so was the pounding in his head, throbbing from behind his ear and cutting through him like a knife. He felt nausea rising and had to concentrate to prevent himself throwing up in the phone box. He hung up the receiver and placed his hands on the walls to steady himself before making another call, this time to the pathologist's office.

"This is Detective Inspector Kearns. I need to speak to Professor Cavanagh, immediately" he said in his most authoritative voice. He had no time and no patience for any more delays.

"Yes sir, one moment" said a flustered sounding receptionist. HE was put on hold to the sound of *Green Sleeves* and was reminded how little he liked hold music. After what seemed an eternity and having fed two more coins into the phone the receptionist came back on the line "I'll put you through now, Detective Inspector."

"Hello Eamon" Cavanagh sounded irritated. "How may I be of assistance today, since I couldn't possibly have anything better to do than being interrupted at your whim?"

"I'd much rather not to be interrupting you, believe me, Richard, but that Ranelagh case has spilled over into another…" Eamon was interrupted by Cavanagh's increasingly irritated voice once again.

"Oh I know Eamon, you're the second person to call in relation to that particular incident today. Very early this morning I received a call from the Commissioner no less, directing me that for all concerned this latest death would be better being classified as yet another tragedy. The poor woman died of smoke inhalation. I believe that's going to be the official COD and I'm in no position to argue. As I told you before I like my life and its…" he paused "perks, which I'm in no hurry to give up. So if that's what the very highly powered in Church and State want me to say I will say just that, just like you. Now, if that's all I have an actual autopsy to perform on someone of whose death I can actually tell a non-fictional account." He didn't raise his voice or change inflection but Eamon was left in no doubt that the pathologist was finished with this conversation. Eamon hung up feeling relieved. It seemed that all the heavens were aligning. The murders and

166

bodies covered up, the case almost put to bed and soon the tapes would leak to the newspaper and Eamon could simply walk away saying he knew nothing about it, never found the tapes and it would be too late for anyone to do anything about it. That was the thing about covering up the murders, as long as those at the top were possibly implicated, they insulated themselves but that self-same insulation would ensure nothing stuck to Eamon either.

He realised he hadn't eaten since the day before and was in fact weak with hunger. He decided to go get something before going to see McGinn. That was one conversation he wanted to have feeling a lot less shattered than he did at that moment.

Driving back into town, Eamon felt more tired than he thought possible but he knew he'd have to keep going for a while longer. He pulled into the station at six o'clock, hoping that the shift change would mean he was missed in the transition but Dempsey met him as he reached the front door.

"The Super said for you to give him a shout as soon as you got in, seemed pretty urgent" he said giving Eamon a pained look. "Oh, one bit of good news, they took Gavin off the respirator and he's breathing by himself. The doctor's say he's likely going to pull through. He's one tough young lad!" he said with a smile as he left for the evening.

Eamon headed straight for Ray Carroll's office, knocked and entered. "Dempsey said you were looking for me, sir?"

"Take a seat Eamon" said Ray, reaching for the phone. He dialled and waited. Eamon could hear a voice on the other end of the line and Ray said "Yes sir, he's just arrived." He stood up and handed over the phone, coming around the desk and as Eamon spoke to say "hello?" he heard the door to the office close and Ray was gone. It seemed he wanted no part of this conversation either.

"Good evening, Eamon. You've been both busy and hard to pin down" the voice was that of Commissioner Flannigan, who sounded too much like a benevolent uncle for Eamon's liking. He sensed that the Commissioner was putting him at ease before he went for the jugular and in this instance he knew he wouldn't have to wait long so he took the initiative.

"Good evening Commissioner, I think we can dispense with the fencing and get straight to the point. I've been following leads and they've lead me to two more bodies. I take it the *cleaning person*, if I may use the euphemism, has informed you of the latest developments and that's why we're chatting now?"

"The cleaning person, how very droll. He has told me about both instances. I only hope you didn't involve yourself in the second of these. I believe you *knew* Brother Morrissey in your youth. In fact it seems you knew Father Buchannan also, or should I say Loyola. You left out those pieces of information when last we spoke. I really hope Eamon, that you don't have an undue personal interest in this case that might, shall we say, cloud your judgement." It was a question framed as a statement, giving Eamon the opportunity to answer or ignore it but he was so completely struck from out of the blue he couldn't think for a moment. His gut sank and his heart threatened to jump straight out of his chest. He was sure the Commissioner must be able to hear it over the phone.

"I'm doing exactly what I said I would do. I'm chasing down the video tapes and the killer. I'm not responsible for what befell Morrissey, though I freely admit I'll lose no sleep over him. He was a teacher in the school I attended, and a bully, but that was forty years ago. I hardly remember him at all or Loyola for that matter." The lie came easily and he hoped his voice hadn't betrayed his terror.

The Commissioner had obviously been doing his own investigating and Eamon now feared the worst that he had started to put two and two together and realised Eamon's secret. All feelings of relief he'd felt for the past hour or two instantly evaporated in the moment of having his name spoken in the same sentence as both the rapists who had caused him so much pain.

"I'm sure. It was a long time ago and coincidences do happen. If you'd told me about the association I might be less concerned but as you say you are doing the job you were tasked with and I daresay it slipped your mind. How are you getting along with the job at hand Eamon, do I need to be concerned that you aren't up to this?" The Commissioner sounded again like he was talking to a favourite nephew, conversational, warm and wise. "I can get another detective to take over if you can't resolve it soon. God knows what they'd dig up in the course of an investigation, though, so I'd hate to have to resort to that. It wouldn't look good for your career prospects either, I'm afraid. If a case proves too weighty then the responsibilities of command might be a stretch too far as well."

There it was. He knew something and the veiled threat was that if Eamon didn't perform, and soon, he'd dig deep enough to out him, one way or another, putting paid to any prospects of career or advancement.

"Results, Detective Inspector, results are all that count. Everything else fades in the face of a positive outcome. Some things almost disappear into the ether like they were never really there at all. Do we understand each other? Good."

Eamon didn't have the opportunity to reply before the Commissioner hung up, leaving him listening to silence and feeling the world spin. His idea, it seemed, to publish and be damned was going to be trickier than he thought. He'd have to do more than just hand over the tapes. An idea came to mind. As long as the tapes were destroyed he'd done his job for the Commissioner, Casey and the Archbishop and as long as the tapes were published he'd out the twisted filth that had to face justice, even if that justice was in the shape of a lynch mob and disgrace, but the real task was to use the tapes as bait to draw out the killer. That sick bastard wasn't going to stop killing just because the perpetrators were in prison. He'd already said he'd make their children pay, if necessary. No, Eamon would have to wait for the killer to make contact, tell him he had the tapes and somehow trap him for Casey to throw in the deepest, darkest dungeon the State had to offer, for the rest of his miserable life, and Eamon was alright with that, because it would mean that all the loose ends were tied up before he gave McGinn the green light to publish.

The strain was almost too much. He had such knots in his neck and shoulders, coupled with the pain in his head, that they'd become like constant companions. He stood, left the office and made his way downstairs. Ray met him on the stairs "I often look that way after I finish talking to him, and that's just in a normal day. God help you Eamon" he shook his head and simply continued on his way.

Eamon watched him go and silently cursed his boss's upcoming retirement. He was going to get out of all this with a golden handshake, a fat pension and no bloody cares in the world. Eamon envied Ray Carroll's ability to ignore the things he needed to ignore in order to play the game. He left the station and sat into his car, lifting his overcoat and checking again to ensure the tapes were still sitting there. He set off into the darkening sky, full of rain, hoping it wasn't a portent of something to come.

15.

The rain was bucketing down. Trevor McGinn watched its windblown sheets from the big Georgian living room window of his third floor flat, overlooking Kenilworth Square. He loved the view, both a cityscape and with a nod to the countryside. It drew him back into the past on nights like this, and how the city must have looked back then, with no cars lining the street, just the occasional carriage. A simpler time, for sure, and one he sometimes wished he'd lived in.

He had a large glass of red wine in his hand and was sipping as he waited for Kearns to arrive. This was going to be big, he knew that much, and more than that it was also going to be satisfying. He'd spent years getting nothing from Kearns but abuse as the high and mighty Detective hated journalists with a passion. Trevor always thought it meant that someone had something to hide, a skeleton in the closet, when they looked down on his profession. They were afraid of what he might find out about them, which suited him to the ground, as more often than not they did have something to hide. He'd never found what Kearns might have stashed away, but mostly that was because he wasn't foolish enough to ruffle too many feathers in the Gardaí. He knew well how much he depended on their good graces to write the more probing stories he did. His *raison d'être,* as it were. Probing the soft underbelly of Irish society, bringing its denizens into the light wasn't just his stock in trade, Trevor revelled in it.

Leaving the window he went across to the couch and armchair he'd moved into just the right position for the interview. Interview or perhaps confession? He was slightly giddy at the prospect of finally getting dirt on Kearns, bringing him down a peg or two.

Trevor reached under the cushion on the armchair where he was going to sit and pressed play on the Dictaphone he'd hidden there. He wasn't going to let the opportunity pass to record every word, even if Eamon wanted this off the record. He was going to have evidence to back up any story he'd write afterwards, undeniable evidence. It always paid to be safe rather than sorry. He'd gotten a new tape and new batteries just to be sure.

"This is a test" he said in a conversational tone, keeping his voice level and quiet. If the tape recorded that he'd have no worries about it picking up the full conversation later. "Detective Inspector Eamon fucking Kearns, asshole, his is your life." He removed the recorder, rewound and replayed the piece. It was perfect. All he had to do now was wait.

Trevor's watched showed eight thirty. He could afford to finish the glass of wine but decided against another. He wanted to be relaxed but still sharp, on his toes, to get the most from this opportunity. He heard footsteps descending the stairs of the floor below and went back to the window, looking down just in time to see the couple from downstairs run down the stone steps outside and to a taxi that had pulled up. The man was shaking an umbrella and trying to close it in the rain before getting into the car. He could hear her shrieking and laughing in the downpour, complaining she was getting soaked and her hair would be ruined, as she jumped into the back seat, joined by her partner and watched as the car sped off into the night.

The knock at his own door startled him. Trevor looked at his watch. Kearns was fucking early. Typical bloody Garda. No thought of time keeping or how he might be inconveniencing anyone else, just everything on his terms. He went back to the couch, pressed play on the recorder and took a breath. *Showtime!* he thought.

He walked out into the hall to the door, excitement mounting but taking a long slow breath to calm himself. *This is like the arrival of a first date* he thought smiling. He opened the door and looked at the figure standing there. His smile froze and was replaced on his face by annoyance but before he could frame a question a hand shot out punching him square in the throat, knocking him off his feet, full length back along the narrow hall, eyes watering, choking and gasping for breath. He only just managed to look up at the figure to see he was wearing a scarf wrapped tightly around his face, before the hammer appeared as he stepped over Trevor's outstretched body.

The hammer swung high above the figures head, seeming to move in slow motion and Trevor realised he was going to die as it began a downward arc. He raised a hand to ward off the inevitable blow, trying in vain to plead as he watched the scene in horror, through tear filled eyes, but no sound would come from his throat. He turned his head, squeezing his eyes shut reflexively as the single blow caught him on his temple. The instant of pain was accompanied by a burst of white light in his head. Then everything faded, his body felt so far away, so heavy. He fell back, a breath escaped and soft blackness enveloped him.

"You've told your last lie" the voice was muffled by the scarf "but you've a story to tell yet, tonight." The figure stood over the body for a moment, then knelt, checking for a pulse before standing, turning and closing the door.

Ten past nine. He'd be late but he didn't care. He doubted if McGinn would either. Eamon hated driving in the rain. He usually got Gavin to do the driving in conditions like this, not wanting to admit that his eyesight in the rain was poor. *Getting old* he admitted to himself in his mind, though not quite ready yet to voice the sentiment out loud.

Trying to find parking close by had been a nightmare, as usual. Eventually he settled for a neighbouring street and having to walk in the rain. He had remembered to 'borrow' an umbrella from Ray's office before he left. The old man would be apoplectic but that just made Eamon smile in a bloody minded moment of spite. "Fuck it, better off him getting wet than me."

He never noticed the figure watching him as he parked. Had he been more observant he might have seen a shadow standing sheltered under a tree across the road. The rain, the tiredness and the need to get to McGinn meant he missed it. As he walked hurriedly away the figure stepped out of the shadow into the glare of the street light, crossed to Eamon's car and tried the passenger door. It opened and he leaned in, searching. The figure then left carrying a small package wrapped against the elements in a scrap of oil cloth, disappearing into the rain soaked night.

Eamon arrived at the front door of the Georgian house, converted as so many in the area had been, into three flats, a floor apiece. He looked for a bell and was about to buzz it when he noticed the door was ajar. Well it was teeming down so he wasn't going to stand on ceremony in the rain and pushed the door and went inside, closing the umbrella and shaking it off as he backed into the hall.

McGinn lived on the third floor, of course. Eamon was as tired as he ever though he could be in his life and the prospect of more stairs seemed to drain his last reserves. He climbed, heavy footed, to the top floor. McGinn's door faced him and he took a breath, glancing down the three flights ruefully. *I used to be able to take steps like those two or three at a time without even breathing heavily* the grimaced, *now I can barely make it to the top without wondering if I'm having a heart attack.* He took another breath and composed himself. He knocked on the door and to his surprise it swung inward, revealing a darkened hallway beyond.

"For fuck sake, he's not even here. Trust the little ferret to be late" he exclaimed throwing his head back and closing his eyes to stifle his temper. He reached out and flicked on the light switch to his left. He walked to the first open door on his left. The room beyond was also in darkness. HE felt for the switch. The wall lights in the room flickered on and Eamon could see McGinn, sitting in an armchair, his head lolling to one side. For a second Eamon thought he was asleep but in an instant realised the posture was an unnatural one. He crossed quickly to stand in front of the apparition, confirming what his eyes could hardly believe.

"Christ on a bike" Eamon groaned, sitting heavily down onto the couch. He held his hands over his eyes and threw his head back, groaning loudly, as if not wanting to see the image anymore. *What the fuck is going on?* He thought, silently straining his mind to focus.

He couldn't wrap his mind around any of it. He was so tired he couldn't think straight. Who? How? Had someone known he was coming here? It all seemed too coincidental and given what was happening in this case he had to first think this was part of it. Someone knew he was going to talk to McGinn but for the life of him he couldn't understand who it was. He'd only told Brendan and it was beyond ridiculous that he would have said anything to anyone, wasn't it? Had McGinn shot his mouth off and then

175

someone tipped the killer off? Had he let something slip to the Commissioner? He was so tired he could barely remember what they'd said. If he had, he didn't really think the Commissioner would have McGinn killed, would he? Or was this cover up to be so thorough that anyone looking at it at all was fair game? If that were the case where did that leave him? The only thing he was certain of was that those tapes might be the only thing between him living or dying like anyone else in this case, though now he knew he'd be using them as bargaining chips instead of releasing them to the public. As long as he had them or it was thought he might find them, neither the killer nor his superiors would move against him.

Eamon sat back, resting his head against the couch, feeling his leaden body wanting to give up. After a few moments of wishing for the whole mess to be over he sat up, looking at the reporters face, smeared with blood down one side from a wound to his skull. Before he went any further he reached into his coat, deciding it would be best to wear gloves beyond this point. Fingerprints everywhere were not going to be easy to explain, especially given his history of intense dislike for McGinn.

"Tough I'd never have wished this end on you, you poor bastard" he said to the corpse. He could see bone where the skin had been torn open and blood glistened in his hair and had streamed onto his shirt. His eyes were half closed, glazed over closed but his mouth hung open. *The blood was wet!* This had happened only minutes before he arrived. He jumped up in shock, looking about the flat, as though the killer might be lurking in a corner. He'd made the mistake once and he wasn't letting the bastard creep up behind him again.

Eamon cautiously moved around the living room through into the small kitchen and picked up the first weapon he could find, a long kitchen knife. Holding it in front of him he began searching the flat, room by room. Two bedrooms, hall and bathroom. All silent. He flicked on a light in each one expecting to meet the killer at any moment, his heart pounding with anticipation, adrenaline coursing, leaving the familiar metallic taste in his mouth, again. After a few minutes of searching behind doors, pulling open wardrobes and looking under beds and behind the shower curtain, every fibre on edge at the prospect of someone jumping out at him, he determined the flat was empty. He kept a firm grip on the knife until he caught himself in the mirror at the end of the hall. "You look ridiculous" he told himself out loud, shaking his head. He went back into the kitchen and put the knife into a drawer. When he stepped back into the living room he looked again at the body and at the trail of blood along the carpet from the front door all the way to its current resting place. Why take the time to place him here? Why risk the time? Why not just kill him when he opened the door and then walk away?

Eamon's subconscious mind was screaming. He knew this scene was set for him. He was always going to walk through the open door. He was always going to find that body. What was he supposed to see now? He walked back to the doorway and looked at the blood smears on the carpet where the body had been dragged before being seated in the armchair. His eyes followed the trail and he walked slowly forward. It was only when he reached the body he noticed what he'd missed before. The right hand had been placed in the lap and curled into a fist while the left hung to the side. Eamon knew he was going to have to open that hand, however much it repulsed him to do it. The fingers were still pliant, rigour wouldn't set in for hours yet, and they opened easily, though Eamon's stomach churned as he did. *Jesus, but for all the dead bodies I've seen, actually touching them still gives me the heebie jeebies* he thought, fighting the urge to retch.

177

He noticed blood on the index finger but on none of the others. As the fingers opened he saw what he was looking for. A piece of paper folded several times into a square, crisp, white and unblemished. It was obvious that it had been placed in the hand after McGinn had been put sitting in the armchair. Eamon stood and began to unfold it, unsure of the contents but sure that he wasn't going to like them. The killer was playing a macabre game and forcing him to play along. He slowly opened the paper, his sense of dread increasing and then looked goggle eyed at the note written there.

Colour drained from his face and he sank to his knees, staring blankly. A low moan escaped his lips and he couldn't think. His head was spinning and his brain had shut down. It suddenly dawned that the killer had used McGinn's own finger to write the note. His stomach, finally overwhelmed by the shock, heaved and he threw up. He fell onto all fours clutching the note. When he stopped retching violently, he looked again at the note,

On the paper, written in Trevor McGinn's own blood, were three simple words that seared like a white hot brand into his soul, *COME HOME EAMON.*

16.

Eamon didn't know how long he'd knelt there, staring at the paper, before the thought of Marie came to him, wrenching him back to his senses. *Come Home! Oh dear God, Marie!* The thought roused him to action and he sprang up, all feeling of exhaustion evaporating in the instant. He scrambled to his feet, almost tripping over McGinn's feet as he did, such was his hurry. He raced from the flat, pulling the door firmly behind him and half running half falling down the three flights and out into the heavy rain yanking the front closed with a slam. He ran as fast as he could to his car, saying a silent prayer as he did, *Pease God, not Marie, please, I beg of you.*

His lungs burning and legs tying up with lactic acid he reached the car, jumped in, fumbled for keys in terror and, starting the engine sped away into the city traffic, caution thrown to the wind as he jinked in and out, narrowly avoiding a number of collisions and pedestrians who jumped out of his way, shouting expletives after him as he left them in his wake.

Traffic was too heavy on a wet night and he didn't get home for almost half an hour. He cursed every obstacle, every red light and every lost second behind buses or trucks loudly and with increasing desperation and rage in equal measure.

"Get out of my fucking way!" he wound down his window and leaned out to scream at a cyclist who, having decided to take his bike out for a jaunt through Terenure late on a rainy night, was hell bent on taking up as much road as any car. "Go fuck yourself, pal. I've as much right to the road as you do!" said the cyclist, a middle aged man carrying one if not two spare tyres around his midriff. He reached out a hand and raised his middle finger before continuing.

Eamon's patience ran out at that moment and he simply overtook and then pulled in quickly ahead of the cyclist, clipping his front wheel as he did, sending him sprawling to the tarmac. "Fuck you" Eamon snarled, dropping a gear and tearing away, wheels spinning. In the rear view the cyclist was standing in the road, fist shaking ineffectually in the empty air.

He took the last corner far too aggressively, even for a driver as experienced as he, mounting the kerb and narrowly avoided clipping the neighbour's pier before slamming on the brakes and coming to a shuddering halt. He aimed the car at the driveway and sped toward his house, throwing up stones as the wheels spun, trying to find traction. He stopped, abandoning the still running engine and sprinted for the front door. Seeing that it was open and no lights were on inside, he knew he was too late.

Eamon burst through the open door. The scene that welcomed him chilled him to the bone. There were broken vases, a side table overturned, a picture on the floor, glass broken and strewn about. "Marie, Marie for the love of God answer me!" he bellowed, his panic rising with each syllable. He knew she wouldn't, couldn't answer. The house felt empty, the emptiness of an unoccupied space where his words carried the faint echo of intrusion. He ran from room to room, checking downstairs then up. Nothing else was out of place. Save for the carnage in the hall it might well be an ordinary night. He half ran, half jumped down the stairs and looked again. He closed his eyes and took a long, slow breath. Exhaling he looked at the scene, not as the husband, but as the detective.

The door, though open, hadn't been forced. The heavy duty lock he'd had installed when they bought the house was designed to keep a coppers mind at ease. Whoever had intruded had not broken in the door, which meant that either Marie had known them or had been taken completely by surprise and given that her hearing was as acute as he knew it was, that meant no one came or went up the gravel drive to the house without her knowing, often telling from the way the stones crunched exactly who it was. Eamon knew that well enough, because he could never quietly tip toe into the house after a few pints without waking her.

He was still visually examining the scene when the phone, neatly sitting on the floor, receiver in place, rang out. His heart skipped and he jumped before diving for it.

"Hello, who's this" he demanded.

"Hello Eamon" For a second the voice didn't register, as every other time he'd heard it, it had been heavily muffled. "I see you're home, but that's not home really, now is it?"

"Brendan?" Eamon gasped incredulously "What in God's name....?"

"In God's name, exactly Eamon. You've forced this in the end. I would have preferred not to involve anyone else but if you can't bring yourself to do what needs doing, then I'll have to do it for you." Brendan's voice was eerily calm, matter of fact even. "You were supposed to find the tapes and eventually find me and I was going both get justice and also help you pay for your sins and me for mine. A three for one deal you couldn't refuse, but you did."

"What choice did I have? If I made all those tapes public, I would have been humiliated, my career destroyed and my family disgraced, not forgetting the killer.. you.. *you're* the killer.. you wouldn't have stopped and more innocent people would die and that would be on my conscience! " Eamon screamed into the phone "If you've hurt Marie, I swear before your God I will kill you."

Brendan laughed. A sound that Eamon found so chilling he felt weak listening. "Hurt Marie, how could I ever hurt her as much as you? If you think about it Eamon, it's you who deserves to die. You're weak and selfish, self-absorbed and spineless. You didn't even give a second thought about those of us who came after you, did you Eamon?"

Eamon could feel the malice coming out of the phone. "Just tell me she's ok, please" he begged.

"Marie is fine, I just needed you to have something you were not prepared to lose, and Eamon, God forgive you but I know you do actually love her, in your own demented way" Brendan replied.

"What do you mean *came after me*?" Eamon was struggling to be calm but he needed time to collect his thoughts.

"Come to me, Eamon, come home to where it all began. Get down on your knees at the altar and beg for forgiveness. Then I will tell you everything.. now that I have the tapes." Brendan let those words sink in before continuing. "You left them in your car Eamon, but as luck would have it you didn't lock it before going to see McGinn. The tapes are safely tucked away. Away from you, Archbishop Flood, Commissioner Flannigan and Minister Casey. Only when the job is completed will I make them public, so everyone will know why the evil of men was cleansed." He sounded confident and earnest and Eamon knew he was telling the truth, cursing himself for being too tired, too distracted and too eager to get the story off his chest that he hadn't thought to lock the bloody car!

"Oh and Eamon, be sure you come alone, or Marie pays the price." The receiver clicked and the phone went dead. Eamon stood, rooted to the spot for what seemed an eternity, before he placed the receiver back in the cradle. He paused, picked it up again and hearing the dial tone punched in a number with the deliberate care of a man who knows the number by heart but hasn't used it in a very long time.

"Is he there?" he asked when the phone was answered. The all too familiar voice at the end grunted in reply. "Tell him I'm on my way over and I need a real favour."

Eamon drove calmly. No need to draw any more attention tonight, he thought. The last thing he needed was to be pulled by an overzealous member on traffic duty, though every extra second was a struggle. He took the back streets until he was sure he wasn't being followed by anyone and after a half hour of crisscrossing himself, arrived at McGettigans. He noticed the harsh neon sign as its letter 'e' blinked on and off erratically, as though in warning. He knew he was about to cross a line but what choice did he have. He dragged himself out of the car and quickly crossed to the narrow double doors. Putting his hand on the handle he closed his eyes, let out a pent up breath and entered.

In the soft light inside the bar he could see Cyril and Butler in the same spot he'd left them last time, at the table to the back in the dimly lit corner. He approached and Cyril stepped forward, placing his hand square on Eamon's chest. "You've got some nerve, copper. I should just knock your fuckin' teeth in and let some of the lads finish the job."

"I'm not here as a copper, and you're boss knows that" Eamon hissed, looking around Cyril's shoulder at Butler, who was sitting palms down at the table, leaning forward to hear.

"Eamon, you seem distressed. Cyril always looks out for me when he sees people who look distressed, in case they might try to vent their distress in my direction" Butler was smiling, a soft and dangerous smile.

"I'm his right hand man" said Cyril.

"Is that so?" said Eamon, not taking his eyes off Butler.

""Absolutely" said Cyril, pride lighting his growl.

"You're right handed, Butler, aren't you?" Eamon enquired, still boring his eyes into Butlers and ignoring Cyril.

"I am indeed" Butler replied.

"That'd be the one he wipes his arse with then?" Eamon looked at Cyril, knowing he was on the thinnest ice and any second now it was either going to break or he was going to step to safety.

"I suppose it is, I know I do." The big man replied, perplexed.

Locking eyes with Butler again Eamon said "So a right hand man, then, can be an important person or can be someone who cleans up your shit for a living." Cyril hesitated and it was a moment before he appeared to understand what Eamon had said. His big fist grabbed Eamon by the lapel of his jacket as the other came up to deliver a blow Eamon knew would knock him senseless. Still he kept eyes on Butler.

"Cyril!" Butler's low snap stopped him mid swing. "Eamon's just playing a game. A very odd game." He glowered and shook his head briefly to Cyril whose barely controlled rage checked and then appeared to disappear as his fist fell and he pushed Eamon toward the chair in front of Butler. "Get yourself a pint Cyril while I chat with my good friend." Butler's cordial mask was back in place as he smiled warmly. *Like a shark smiling at a fish* thought Eamon. "Eamon, I am so happy you are about. It makes life.. entertaining" he mused. "Now, how can a person such as me be of service to one in your exalted position?"

"Fuck you, Butler. You know I wouldn't be here if I had any choice but I'm desperate and I know you are the only one I can all but guarantee can get me what I need" Eamon spat the words.

Butler nodded slowly, still smiling. "You really are living on the edge aren't you Eamon?" Leaning closer to Eamon across the table he said quietly "Give me one good reason why I should even consider it, after what happened to my brother."

Eamon blanched at the mention. He'd known Butler held the grudge and maybe this was the moment he finally got Eamon back for putting his brother behind bars, though that had been just the start of it. Inside the little shit had fallen foul of the wrong people. He'd wound up having an 'overdose' of heroin, except that he hadn't overdosed but been executed by injecting him with a dose that would have killed a horse.

"I didn't put him in the frame for those robberies. That was all on him. He beat the last person half to death. That's why he got seven years, for assaulting a pensioner so badly she almost died. That and the string of.. what was it.. nine robberies?"

Butler tapped the table with a finger "He was family" he said quietly but with such an intense glare that it threatened to erupt at any second.

"Well this is family too, I know who killed the priests and beat my colleague into a coma.. and .. and he's got my wife." Eamon explained, half standing and leaning in toward Butler. "I need your help, please" he pleaded, wide eyed. His fists, pressed knuckles to the table, were shaking and clenched so tightly it seemed they might explode if he released them.

"I see" said Butler softly "That does change things a little. I may be more disposed to listening after all. I hate people who bring.. civilians.. into the game. It's not right. Sit down Eamon, before you fall down. I really don't need the scene."

Eamon slumped back, defeated. Here he was at the mercy of the one person who had absolutely no need to help him in any way, begging for just that.

Butler motioned Cyril over and whispered in his ear. He disappeared through a back door without a backward glance. To the casual glance they appeared to simply sit, waiting. Waiting, Eamon hoped for Cyril to return, talking in hushed tones. After a few minutes he reappeared, nodded almost imperceptibly to Butler at which the smile returned "Thanks for dropping by Eamon. It really has been an experience. Cyril, please show Detective Inspector Kearns to the door."

Cyril moved quickly and grabbed Eamon by the collar, sinking a ham sized fist hard into his midriff. Eamon doubled over with a gasp, clutching his gut and before he could do anything about it or even catch his breath, Cyril had half marched half carried him to the front doors, kicked them open and launched him into the street, where he landed in a crumpled, gasping heap. "And this time don't come back, copper" the big man snarled through clenched teeth, stabbing a finger in Eamon's direction. Turning on his heel he left Eamon to recover on the footpath.

186

After he caught his breath, Eamon stood gingerly, arms still wrapped around his stomach, and stumbled back to the car, throwing himself inside. Only then did he look down. In his lap sat a small, string bound and cloth covered package. He untied it and slowly examined the contents.

"A Walther PPK semi-automatic" he snorted "that'll do nicely Butler." Thanking God for the gun, he checked its magazine for the eight rounds and prayed he wouldn't need any of them while resolving to put all eight in his oldest friend if he had harmed Marie. Placing the weapon on the passenger seat and covering it with his overcoat which he rummaged from the back seat, he started the car and pulled out into the night, heading back to where it all began, almost forty years after he'd left.

17.

As Eamon drove, the sense of dread became more oppressive, every red light an increasingly frustrating and infuriating delay and yet every delay was keeping him from the memories that were floating up through the murk of his teenage memories. As he finally turned onto the leafy avenue the heavens opened again, rain pouring heavily onto the windscreen. He could just make out the silhouette of the church at the end of the street against the glow of city lights. He pulled up a hundred yards from the gates and sat quietly for a moment, feeling the pulse hammering in his chest, up into his throat, pounding into his head. He felt as though he might faint but he gritted his teeth until it felt like they might break and breathed out a long, slow growling breath.

He opened the door, stepping out and grabbing his overcoat and let the rain and night air hit him. The street itself was quiet, thankfully he thought, given the circumstances he didn't relish any eyes on him. He quickly put on the overcoat, sliding the Walther into its deep pocket.

"Whatever happens next it ends tonight and the scales are balanced" he admonished himself. "Whatever it takes."

He patted the gun in his pocket, its weight a comfort as he forced himself to walk toward the church. He stopped, half hesitating before putting his hand on the cold, wet steel of the gate. He pushed them open and stepped into the last place he'd expected he would ever go again. The rain was starting to come down more heavily and he needed to wipe his eyes with his sleeve. As he did he could see a thin shaft of light from the church door, open a fraction, falling out onto the wet paving. An invitation he'd rather have declined in any other circumstances. The thought of Marie in the hands of someone who could do the things Brendan had done gave him a grim resolve and eyes fixed on the light he closed the gate behind him.

"No way back" he thought. As he stepped forward in the rain he felt the fear fading, the dread being replaced with an odd calm, a cold resolution to get Marie to safety, no matter the cost.

"*Accept the consequences of your actions and you can accomplish anything*" the last thing Butler had said to him before Cyril returned and he'd been so unceremoniously dumped onto the street. Right now he knew he would have to do just that. *Fas est ab hoste doceri* he thought moving forward, *it is right to be taught even by an enemy,* The old Latin phrase returning to him after all these years seemed both ironic and yet fitting as it was right here he'd learned it. "Who'd have thought I'd be taking life lessons from Butler of all people" he muttered to himself as he put his hand on the heavy oak door and pushed it open. He stepped into the light.

"Eamon, come in, you're running a little late" Brendan's voice carried from the altar, echoing through the vaulted, empty gloom. "I don't have to ask if you're alone. I can trust you that much can't I, for Marie's sake?" Eamon thought he sounded a little too animated, almost panicked, a tone Eamon recognised from long years' experience in the force and encountering people at their most desperate. Brendan was on the edge and there was more than a hint of menace when he referred to Marie.

189

Eamon had moved past the glare of the light at the foyer door and having it now at his back, his eyes were becoming accustomed to the gloom ahead. Framed by the open double doors of the main church could see the altar and his blood ran cold when he saw Brendan towering over a figure in front of him, a figure he noticed wasn't moving which sent a pang of dread through him.

"Closer Eamon, closer" ushered Brendan in a soothing tone completely at odds with the situation, as he turned and lit several heavy candles on the altar. "Do you like my mood lighting, really adds to the ambiance" he waved expansively as Eamon slowly approached, still looking for any sign that Marie was still alive. As he drew within twenty feet Brendan put up a hand, "Far enough, Eamon" Brendan was almost casual in his speech "Oh I see you're worried about poor Marie, well don't be she's just.. napping, she'll be fine, as long as you make all the right choices in the next few seconds." He smiled in a way Eamon thought was more frightening than almost anything he'd ever seen.

"Brendan, for the love of God, Why?" Eamon asked, an all too real desperation in every word.

"Exactly, Eamon, for the love of GOD" Brendan bellowed, his face contorted into a grim mask in the candle light, giving him a demonic look. "You think this is how I wanted matters to turn out?" he roared again, his bulky frame shaking in anger as he jerked around to face the altar, looked up at the cross hanging above it, his own arms outstretched in supplication, mirroring the crucified Christ.

"Tell me then, make me understand!" Eamon shouted in response.

"Understand? If you don't understand by now what can I say that'll make you?" Brendan spoke over one shoulder as his arms dropped, suddenly deflated or maybe realising he was not receiving the necessary absolution from the oblivious carved face of Christ.

"At least tell me why Father Mitchell? Eamon matched his tone, quieter and calmer. ""What was his sin?"

"The same sin as yours Eamon, but born of a different motive. You want this to go away for your sake and to avoid humiliation for you. He at least only wanted to do what he thought would save the Church" Brendan's shoulders slumped further as he continued "I never meant for him to die, that is a sin for which I must pay, and dearly." He stepped round Marie's still unconscious form and came to the front of the altar. "You want to know every detail don't you Eamon, like a good copper" he sighed "Well then, this is my confession and I'm glad it's just you here to receive it. It seems fitting."

Brendan placed his hands together in a prayer pose and bowing his head to his chest, paused for what seemed eternity to Eamon, before he spoke in a low, even soft, voice. "Bless me Lord, for I have sinned. It has been some time since my last confession and I have many things to confess and to atone for." He looked down at the floor while continuing "When Father Mitchell came back to Ireland six months ago we arranged to meet. He had been a mentor in this hell and its corridors and later, when I took up the calling, he'd kept in contact over the years, less frequently as he grew older and travelled more in his missionary work but still the odd card from the farthest flung reaches. I often wondered if he was trying to get as far away as possible from this place and its poison." He sighed closing his eyes as though to see more clearly.

"He was very agitated when we met in town. It was by the statue of *Oscar Wilde* on Stephen's Green, and he was clearly upset. I'd remembered him as being a sporty kind of man, a good looking fellow who women would notice despite the collar, if you understand" Brendan looked up at Eamon smiling softly.

"But the man I met was old, frail and looked... frightened and angry. He insisted we take a walk in the park while he composed himself and so we set off. It was a few minutes before he had calmed down and we just.. walked.. in silence. Then he stopped, put his hand on my arm, looked me in the eye and with such earnestness just said *'I'm sorry, Brendan. I was not strong enough and I want your forgiveness before I die'.*

Brendan snorted "He completely took me by surprise. I could feel the hand on my arm, gripping tightly and shaking like a leaf." *'You've nothing to be sorry for Father'* I said but he kept holding my arm, his eyes pleading for the words he needed." Brendan sighed, "This is going to be a long story Eamon, take a pew" he motioned Eamon to sit, which Eamon did, slipping his hands into his pockets, his right finding the grip and trigger of the pistol.

Brendan put his hands together once again and continued "He was shaking so much I thought he was going to have a stroke, so I sat him down on a bench and asked him what had happened." He looked up at Eamon again "Loyola, Eamon, Father Mitchell had seen Loyola and was desperate to tell our current Archbishop, Francis Flood the politicking fool, the whole story, our whole history and then he said something I couldn't believe."

Brendan snorted "He actually said *'For the good of the Church he'll have to be quietly moved away again. The thoughts of anyone making this public and hurting the Church even more than things that are coming out now are more than I could bear. I've given my life to her and to God. For God's sake we must tell the Archbishop and get him moved'* " Brendan's tone was incredulous, his mask of calm slipping momentarily before he gathered himself again and went on.

"We argued, I wanted to make the whole thing public and damn the consequences but he, my mentor, my friend and the only person who could have helped bring proper justice to that animal and his cohorts, wanted to deny me vengeance" he was speaking in a strangled hiss, teeth gritted and his jaw muscles bulging.

"Vengeance is mine sayeth the Lord" Eamon interrupted "Isn't that scripture? What made you think you had the right?"

"The Lord spoke to me then, made me see that this was both the ultimate test of my faith and my chance to save the Church. It was my mission to make sure she was cleansed of these demons." Brendan's eyes looked toward heaven and his voice had the fervour of unthinking devotion in every syllable.

"I offered to take him home and said I'd think about what he'd asked. We went back to my car and I drove him out to his lodgings in Walkinstown." Brendan paused again, swallowing hard. "I had to stop him talking to the Archbishop, I had to convince him so I asked if we could continue our conversation inside. He agreed and we wet in" He sighed heavily. "I helped him upstairs to his room and we began to talk. I tried, Eamon, I tried everything I could think of to get him to see sense but he just become angry and more entrenched, a fearful old man at the mercy of the powers that be in the church, afraid to go far enough to save her from them."

Brendan's disgust was palpable "I told him as much and he told me to leave. My blood was boiling and I told him I'd find Loyola myself. I made my way to the stairs and he followed me shouting and pulling me back. I swung my arm and I hit him. It was an accident but he fell back, knocking over a side table and spilling the contents. When I tried to help him up he grabbed a candlestick, of all things, from the floor and hit me with it. I saw red and I wrestled it from him and before I realised what I'd done I hit him with it." He continued, "He fell back, his eyes staring at me but unseeing and at that moment I knew I'd killed him so I pushed him down the stairs and left before anyone else arrived, not that an old priest gets many visitors" Brendan said critically, as though that were the important element to the story. "I had to find Loyola, had to start the work of cleaning God's house!" His voice cried out in a lament, wishing to be believed, Eamon thought, like so many he'd encountered before over thirty years. They never meant to do anything. Things just happened.

"So you threw him down the stairs?" Eamon demanded. "A frail old man. You killed him in a fit of rage and dumped him like a bag of rubbish"

"I DID!" Brendan dropped to his knees, "God forgive me this sin, but he had to be stopped. This was a sign that God was bringing Loyola back so he could face God's wrath. I am his instrument!" He jumped up again, all trace of guilt erased in a second, which told Eamon that he really was unhinged. His grip on the pistol tightened and he thought he'd end this as soon as he knew all the details of Brendan's crimes. "I found Loyola, eventually, as I didn't know he'd gone back to using Buchannan. It did take me a couple of weeks, visiting Father Mitchell's haunts until he popped up one afternoon in the park in Ranelagh."

"Funny turn of phrase that, his haunts, do you think he's haunting them now, or does he haunt you instead?" Eamon asked bitterly, unable to stop himself.

Brendan's tone had become animated again and he seemed to ignore or not hear Eamon's taunt. "I knew it was him

194

immediately and I knew he wasn't going to spend another day living and breathing the same air as the rest of us, so I followed him home and when it grew dark I slipped into the house. The demon hadn't even locked his front door" he looked at Eamon "He was a demon, you know, masquerading as a man. How else could he have done the things he did?"

"Humans are the real demons in my experience and the evils we inflict on each other that I've witnessed over the years lead me to believe that with great certainty. We don't need God or the Devil to create hell or heaven. We do that to ourselves" Eamon surprised himself momentarily, giving form to feelings he'd harboured for many years.

"So you'd add blasphemy to your list of sins?" Brendan retorted.

"I bloody well would, yes," Eamon raised his own voice "but not murder, or two murders, or is it five now? The priests, Morrissey, even if they *were* to blame, the others had nothing to do with any of this. How do you even begin to explain what you did to that poor woman, Nora or even to McGinn? They deserved life not torture and death by your hand." Eamon wanted Brendan to admit to everything, to somehow see how the man was thinking. "Not to mention Gavin Cantwell. If he survives this he will be blessed indeed!"

Brendan seemed to flinch at the accusation before he looked at Eamon, a look that mixed guilt and righteousness, "I never meant to harm Father Mitchell, he was my friend and I will face judgement for that, but Loyola..." his face contorted into anger once more.

"I found him" Brendan sounded almost proud. "I told him who I was and for the first time in his life he knew fear. I saw it in his eyes as I nailed his hands to the table."

That voice again, thought Eamon, *he almost sounds as though he enjoyed it.*

"Oh I did, Eamon, I did" Brendan replied as though reading his thoughts or maybe just his reaction. Eamon wasn't sure but the thought ran across his mind *"as long as you don't read that I have a gun in my hand."*

"And the crucifix? Hardly a thing for a man of God to do, defile a cross?" Eamon asked, trying to nail down every detail.

"He sodomised children in the sanctity of the church and had the audacity to hang an image of our Lord over his bed. It disgusted me and when I found him he'd just come from the shower. It was the perfect moment to begin his voyage of purification. To know what it felt like for someone to harm you at the very core of your being and beliefs."

"And what? You bent him over the table, drove a metal cross almost eight inches into his arse, nailed him to the table and set him alight." It was a statement, not a question and Eamon delivered it in the dead pan tone of an interview room.

"Did he not deserve it? He pleaded for his life while I doused him. I wanted him to know what was going to happen." That voice again, relishing the memory, "He told me everything then about the films he had made, how there were important people on them, how I, we, could make a lot of money if I'd just let him live. How he'd sent a copy to Casey, Flood and Flannigan. They'd pay to keep this scandal quiet. It was what the Church and State owed him for the life he'd been robbed of. He'd waited until he retired to bring them out of hiding because the Church was losing power now he could bargain whereas before they'd have silenced him." Brendan shook his head "The animal disgusted me and had to be put down."

"Did you bring the petrol, hammer and nails?" Eamon asked flatly "or did you find them there." Again, the interview, crossing off each detail.

"Of course I brought them" Brendan sounded almost indignant "I knew exactly what God wanted me to do and I prepared accordingly."

"A premeditated murder, then?" Eamon simply asked.

"It was and I won't regret it for a millisecond. It's not as if you can't understand why I did it or argue that it wasn't deserved" the tone was now defensive.

"That's why we have laws, trials, juries and prisons" Eamon answered sounding hollow to himself, he thought, as he would have wished much worse on that animal over the years.

"With those tapes hidden away he'd have gotten away scot free and you know it" Brendan sneered "I did what your justice never could and I did it for my Church."

Eamon wanted to remind Brendan that his crimes stretched far beyond what he could possibly justify, no matter what his defence and no matter how much Loyola deserved it, no matter how much Eamon agreed that he did deserve it he couldn't allow Brendan to gloss over the innocent victims of his own rage, his own depravity. "Nora, Gavin, Trevor McGinn" he listed the names venomously, "how do you justify their deaths, your actions, the sheer malice in what you did to them?"

"Nora, yes her.. passing... was difficult and not what I wanted" Brendan said, shaking his head in disbelief, "but I had to make Morrissey talk" he explained with a pained look. "He wouldn't tell me the location of those damned tapes even after I threatened to burn her as I had Loyola. He wouldn't give them up and told me I could burn her for all he cared as the only person he ever cared about was already dead. I had no choice but to show him I was deadly serious. As she screamed he caved in and told me he'd hidden them in his garage. He was lying, but I think you know that, he couldn't but lie to save himself. He tried to attack me with a shears." Brendan sounded bemused at the thought.

"He managed to stab me in the arm, but not seriously enough to save his miserable existence. I lost control then, regretfully, and beat him for every child he'd harmed in his life. With every hammer fall I could see faces of boys I knew, boys who'd suffered, and before I could stop I had broken his body and killed him. I don't regret killing him, Eamon, only that I couldn't get him to tell me what I needed to know. I think he took a perverse pleasure in the end, not telling me." He said quietly, his voice strained and his gaze haunted by memories that screamed on the edge of his vision.

"Gavin, your young colleague. He was an unfortunate necessity. He would have gone to your superiors after he discovered you were a past pupil in the school while Loyola was there. If they knew about your involvement they might have you taken off the case." Brendan sounded as though he were explaining to a child. "He couldn't be allowed to stop this coming out or interfered with your involvement." he rubbed his eyes and resumed his pose in front of the altar, hands clasped again to his chest.

"McGinn is on you, Eamon. You should never have gone to him. That parasite, as well you know, would have sensationalised the whole thing. Even if he named the men who were filmed doing what they did, they'd be imprisoned at best or they'd have bought their way to freedom. Neither option would have brought them to real justice. They will all die, Eamon. The tapes will convict them in a higher court than yours and they will burn for their crimes, every last one of them. If not them, then their children, to pay for the sins their fathers wrought."

Eamon fought to control his anger at being implicated in McGinn's murder. The image of his body was one of the ones in this case that would haunt him forever. Brendan was fully wrapped in his righteous fervour and as indignant as Eamon felt about his accusations concerning McGinn, he knew he'd have to change tack, to bring him back to earth. He decided to bring Loyola and the tapes back again.

"But you didn't find the tapes. I did. For all your torture Loyola never gave up the information. Why do you think that was?" Eamon was genuinely curious. "Someone like Loyola would have done anything, said anything to save himself."

"No I didn't find them" Brendan snapped. "I lost control of my temper and I set him alight. Before I knew it he was engulfed and all he could do was writhe and scream. He paused, pointing a finger at Eamon and smiled conspiratorially, "That's where you came in."

"Oh yes?" Eamon wanted to draw him on every fact.

"When I went there I knew that you'd be the senior detective working a murder case. It was right on your doorstep and I knew that you'd find out who he was. In fact I counted on it" Brendan said "You've been part of this from the start and I wanted you with me at the end. You needed this as much as I did" he explained, sounding perfectly reasonable, which scared Eamon even more.

"Finding out about the tapes was both a godsend and a problem. I needed them to show me the way but I couldn't find them by myself" he paused again. "But you, you could go places and do things that I couldn't to find those tapes. Hence the need for phone calls and direction to talk to Casey, all of it to get to the truth" he sounded positively brim-full of pride.

"Jesus Brendan, you could have just told me about Loyola and we could have found a way to bring him down, protecting everyone, you and me included" Eamon said, leaning forward in the pew.

"Eamon, you don't get it yet. You have to pay as much as he did. Do you think God was going to let you get away with being weak, lacking faith, blaspheming, being a pervert or for letting them do what they did without fighting back? You weren't the only child they defiled. Many other children came after you and because you didn't stop those animals they had free rein. I was one of those kids but I did try to fight back. They beat me half to death. I ran, they brought me back and then Eamon" Brendan hesitated, words catching in his throat, a sight Eamon recognised only too well. "Then they shared me like a toy to be passed around in their sick circle" the words were a low snarl.

The next words hit Eamon like a truck and he slumped back against the pew, open mouthed. "Eamon, you are an abomination against God for allowing them to continue doing what they did and to get away with it for so many years without having the strength or the faith in God to come forward, even as a detective you could have done more to bring them to book."

"Fuck you, Brendan. I am human, frail as I may be, but I am a child of God. The last I heard he didn't make mistakes. I *have* made mistakes but I haven't murdered the innocent in pursuit of any truth!" Eamon was shouting. Not good he knew but he couldn't contain it any longer.

"You must do penance" Brendan exhorted.

"And give up my auld sins?" Eamon actually laughed at how ludicrous it all sounded.

"If you won't accept that your suffering is the only way to salvation then I'll add to it until God sees that you have paid a price worthy of atonement" once more the fervour had returned, with even more intensity. Brendan turned quickly and leapt over Marie's still unmoving body. From the altar he grabbed an axe Eamon hadn't noticed in the gloom which made a metallic scraping sound as it dragged across the marble table top. He turned and stood over Marie and hefted it in his big hands like a child's plaything. Eamon drew the pistol from his pocket and pointed it. "Stop or I'll shoot" he thought it sounded an oddly stupid cliché, surreal even, in the moment.

Brendan didn't seem surprised "Your choice, Eamon. You can save Marie by putting a bullet through my beating heart, but if you choose to save her you know you'll never find those god forsaken tapes before they're used and they *will* be used to cleanse the Church. Then they *will* be made public so nobody will ever be in doubt as to why those animals were punished and your shame *will* be exposed to all. You will suffer humiliation and in doing so you *will* do the penance you deserve." He paused, staring at Eamon for any hint of reply but he stood rooted to the spot. "Or you can watch her die to save yourself and protect your secret and I will give you the tapes you want after I have used them. You keep your secret but carry the weight of Marie's death as your millstone. Either way you lose and will carry that loss forever as your penance. May it be as heavy as the cross and as agonising as His crown of thorns." He took a breath and swung the axe with a roar.

The gun spat an explosive reply before Eamon had time to hesitate or think. Brendan was thrown back, dropping the axe mere inches from Marie's head where it struck the stone steps with a clang that reverberated around the church.. He heard someone screaming "Stop" but only realised it was himself when the echo of the discharged weapon fell silent. After a moment where the shock froze him to the spot, a statue as inert as any of those looking down from alcoves around the church, Eamon realised what he'd done and then ran to the altar to see Brendan lying across the two steps, blood pouring through the fingers clutching his chest. Eamon Pressed down instinctively to stem the flow but it was too late and he knew it, the wound was quickly draining the life from the big man.

"I knew I could count on you Eamon, to make the right choice" Brendan gasped coughed a gout of blood "You do really love her in your own demented way" he smiled, grimacing "and now I pay for my sins, as we all must, just like it says in Romans." He tried to laugh but grimaced and spat up more blood instead.

"Just tell me where the tapes are hidden, for all our sakes. I swear before God that I'll bring the whole lot into the open. Nothing is worth this!" Eamon was pleading, desperately but Brendan just gurgled a laugh between hacked breaths and half choked coughs of dark red.

"The truth will set us free, Eamon" he tightened his hand around Eamon's, "Don't worry old friend. Did you think I was alone? Call us Legion for we are many." He coughed again, a thick gout of blood bubbling up from his throat.

"Blest are the dormant, In Death, they repose" Brendan was drowning slowly, choking as he spoke and gripped Eamon's hand fiercely. "From bondage and torment, from passions and woes", again he gasped for breath, struggling for every word "From the yoke of the world and the snares of the traitor, the grave, the grave is the true liberator." He attempted a final gurgled laugh, sputtering bubbles of blood and air before his head slumped back, the light left his eyes and his hand fell limp.

Eamon knelt in silence save for the rain falling on the roof above.

He realised Marie was still lying on the steps to the altar. As he turned to her he thought something didn't look quite right. How she was lying seemed too stiff, lifeless. The bolt of fear shot through him in a heartbeat and threatened to overwhelm him. He scrambled over to her and then realised the cruel trick Brendan had played on him. What he thought was Marie was actually a mannequin, dressed in her clothes and wearing a wig, angled in the candle light to be just convincing enough at a distance. *Brendan had counted on me firing the gun and knew he would die here tonight which means he knew I'd have a gun with me. Damn you Butler, what did you do, you bastard?*

A mannequin, a dead priest, a murder weapon, no reason to fire the gun. It could be construed that he had lured the priest here and killed him, along with a quintet of murders that he was definitely implicated in if the right questions were asked, especially if those questions were being directed by Casey, Flannigan and Flood.

Eamon stood, looking at his blood covered hands and snorted in disgust. Not tonight. He searched Brendan's clothes as delicately as he could, finding a set of keys, one of which was a large old fashioned thing which he thought had the look of a front door key. He walked back to the pew he'd been sitting in and reaching down, pressed the stop button on the Dictaphone he'd taken out of his pocket as soon as he sat down in the pew. "A full confession. Bless you father for you have sinned."

He heard a muffled scrabbling sound coming from the door to the sacristy. He jumped up and ran toward the sound. Opening the door he found Marie, bound hand and foot and gagged with her own scarf. "Oh the irony" he thought giddily, half realising that he was indeed in shock.

He lent down and gently removed her restraints. She grabbed him in a ferocious hug, huge uncontrolled and uninhibited sobs convulsing her body. "When.. w.. when I .. heard.. the shot .. I thought .. "

"Shhh pet, I know. It's alright. I'm here and it's all over." He held her close and rocked her gently as she cried, the muffled wails pressed to his chest. He told her over and over "It's alright, pet, it's going to be alright" and yet, as much as he wanted it to be true he knew that it was far from over and even further from alright.

18.

Eamon helped Marie to her feet and walked her slowly out of the church, locking the front door behind them. He'd have to call the same number again to hide yet another body. This one though, was a killing that literally had blood on his hands. He threw his coat over them both as they went out into the torrent of rain and managed to get her to the car, albeit slowly as she seemed to be in a daze, shuffling along only because of his arm around her. He sat her into the back seat and didn't comment when she lay down and pulled her knees to her, curling up in a foetal position. She was glassy eyed and in a lot of shock and he knew he'd have to get her to hospital, though how he would explain any of this was a mystery at this moment.

He sat in and sat for a moment, just listening to the rain and trying to focus. His body seemed numb, the knots in his shoulders giving way to heaviness, a leaden weight that said, *it's over*, and yet the fear that those bloody recordings were out there and that he could be on them, sickened him and were eating away at the edges of his rational mind. Scenarios came unbidden, where they might surface and how they might be used. What would he say to explain any of it? His thoughts were circling and getting faster and more panicked, threatening to overwhelm his already shattered mind and body when a low whimper from Marie brought him back to the moment.

He stared around, not knowing where he was for the briefest time, before everything came into focus. "Hold on pet, I'm here and I'm taking you to the hospital" he said, striving to sound calm, to soothe her and reassure her again that it was all going to be fine. He started the car and drove towards Beaumont hospital. The roads were quieter, night time traffic sparse in the rain.

As he drove his thoughts wandered from scene to scene, murder to murder and to how many things he'd missed or covered up after the fact and drew one inescapable conclusion. He was guilty of perverting the course of justice on numerous occasions, complicit in several other crimes. The roads were quieter, night time traffic sparse in the rain.

As he drove his thoughts wandered like a shoal of frightened fish, darting from scene to scene, murder to murder and to how many things he'd missed or covered up after the fact and he drew one inescapable conclusion. He was guilty of perverting the course of justice on numerous occasions, complicit in several other crimes including leaving Morrissey to die and if he wanted to get out of this without shit sticking to him he'd have to both find those tapes and do some fairly hard-nosed bargaining with the three headed hound of Casey, Flannigan and Flood. Having the confession of a dead man on tape might exonerate him from the murders directly but it wouldn't save his arse from a bacon slicer if asked about how and why he covered up everything else. His thoughts then turned to Brendan, his oldest friend and how unhinged he'd become. How he never saw the signs Eamon would never know, perhaps a mixture of his own involvement, guilt and a blind spot where Brendan was concerned, his confidante and the only person to whom he felt he could tell his story, lead to him missing the signs. As he ran through the events of the night something nagged at him but he couldn't quite put finger on it, some forgotten thing that lurked beneath the surface but wouldn't come up to the light. It was infuriating to know he'd missed a detail and his subconscious was trying to dredge it up, without success.

He stopped at a junction just long enough to take his hands off the wheel, rub his eyes and stretch his torso. As he did the wipers began to squeal as the rain had stopped and the rubber was scraping across dry glass. He switched them off and looked at the road sign. A left turn and they'd be in Beaumont in ten minutes. Below the sign there was another smaller one, erected mostly for tourists, directing them to Glasnevin cemetery. It took a second as he rounded onto the road for the hospital before the thought finally clicked with him.

"The bloody poem" he said grimly, "James Clarence *bloody* Mangan, buried in Glasnevin cemetery" he half snarled, half smiled as he recalled the last thing Brendan had uttered before dying in his arms. "The grave, the grave is the true liberator" he recited and as he did he knew Brendan was not only having the last word, but also giving him an opportunity to redeem himself, if he just listened carefully. He found himself considering for a moment going directly to the cemetery, barely fifteen minutes from where he was before a soft moan from the back seat changed his focus back to the hospital. Whatever else, Marie came first tonight. When he was sure she was safe he'd go straight there. The miles between his decision and the hospital were a blur of lights, turns and impatience as Eamon strove to keep his mind clear. He arrived at the hospital and abandoned the car at the front steps, running up and directly into security. He flashed his warrant card and announced he had a passenger who was in need of attention. The security guard gave a curt nod before following him back outside. Marie had managed to sit up but looked completely bewildered and was trying to fix her hair when opened the door.

"Eamon, where are we? Are we home?" she asked in a confused voice , full of fear and uncertainty, "Who is this?" she asked as Eamon and the guard helped her from the car "You might have told me we had company, I'm in no state to receive visitors" she scolded but her voice still sounded far away, disconnected. The guard looked at Eamon sympathetically as he explained "This is my wife, she's been in an accident and she's in shock. Can you call a nurse or doctor, someone, anyone?" The guard ran ahead and as Eamon guided Marie gently up the steps he was greeted by the familiar face of Matron Mary Joyce.

"Come along" she ordered in a business like voice but he could see her expression was one of concern as she scanned them both. She took Marie's arm and led them into the lobby, past the security guard who was hovering in case either of them fell over, because to him it seemed they might. Marie might have been confused but Eamon looked grey with exhaustion, haggard and drawn and more in need of medical attention.

"So nice to see you again, Detective. Will you be staying with us for long?" the matron asked in a sarcasm laden tone "I see you've managed to look even worse this time round." She turned her attention to Marie "and who's this lovely lady. It seems she might need a lie down and perhaps a cup of tea" she said soothingly. Marie just nodded and allowed herself to be escorted inside where two younger nurses, both wearing the same expression of care and worry, took her and sat her into a wheelchair and away.

Eamon tried to pass the matron to go with Marie but she put a hand firmly on his chest, stopping him in his tracks. "Oh no, you're coming with me. Angela and Ruth there are two of my very best" she said with some pride "they'll take care of her as though she was their own mother." He took him firmly by his elbow and half pulled him down the corridor to another room.

"Wait in here, I'll be back in a few minutes when we've had a proper look at.. Marie, was it?" Eamon just nodded. He was spent and couldn't argue. The last adrenalin that had kept him going was used up and the enormous weight of tiredness came crashing down on him. He sank back into the comfortable armchair she directed him to before she turned to go. As she reached the door she turned back to check one last time but Eamon was already passed out. "Poor man, whatever demons you've been chasing have really done for you" she said softly. She left but returned a few minutes later carrying a blanket which she draped over him. "A few hours sleep will do you no harm, whatever else" she said, turning off the light.

In his sleep Eamon's mind was anything but quiet or resting. He dreamed of Brendan, Morrissey, chasing, gunshots, fire, the terrible look on McGinn's dead face haunting him, as did Gavin's accusing stare. When he finally saw the sign in his dream, Glasnevin cemetery, he woke with a start. He looked around the room and it took a moment for everything to come back to him but it did with the force of a tidal wave. He sat bolt upright, every muscle aching and stiff protesting as he forced himself out of the armchair.

The door opened and the light blinked into life, stabbing his bleary eyes. "Oh good, you're awake" said the young nurse who's head popped around the door "Matron said to check in on you every half hour or so but to let you sleep until you woke by yourself."

Eamon's head throbbed and his mouth felt like a cat had used it for litter tray. "I'll get you a cup of tea and some toast" she said in a bubbly voice "It's all I can offer at this hour. Sit right there and I'll be back in a sec.." Her head disappeared, thankfully, as Eamon wasn't coherent or awake enough to cope with her bubbly

209

personality. A second later she reappeared "I almost forgot" she said "Your wife is fine but she's had to be sedated, I'm afraid. She suffered a nasty blow to the head and was quite confused." Seeing Eamon's stricken expression she added "It's all going to be alright, she just needs to rest for a few days." The relief on his face must have been very evident as the young nurse gave a beaming smile and disappeared again. She brought him tea and toast as she had said and took his pulse as he drank. "Hospital tea, arguably the worst in creation" he said, draining the cup and taking a slice of toast.

"I agree, if I had my way it'd be Lyons loose tea" the nurse replied enthusiastically.

"Can I see my wife?" Eamon asked, a mouthful of toast making him mumble.

"Of course, but wait for a bit. She's sleeping and won't even know you're there right now" said the nurse.

"But I will" Eamon said, stubbornly and stood up, his head swimming as he did. He put a hand on the arm of the chair to steady himself as the nurse crossed quickly to him.

"Wait just a minute and I'll rustle up a wheelchair and take you down. You look as though you could faint at any minute. When was the last time you had something to eat?"

"I had tea and toast not two minutes ago" he said pointedly "and now I'm walking out that door and going to see my wife."

The young nurse hadn't been trained for belligerent policemen who wouldn't take no for an answer and just said "As you wish, sir. I'll take you down there now if you're fit to walk." She turned on her heel and held the door for him to follow. After several second waiting for the spinning world to stop, Eamon went with her and soon arrived at Marie's room.

She was in a private room and looked very pale, lying unmoving, connected to a drip. The nurses had indeed taken good care of her as her hair was neatly tied up and her face was relaxed and clean, tear reddened eyes closed and unmoving.

Eamon stood by the bed for a moment, the nurse beside him and then he turned to her. "Thank you" was all he could muster to say.

"You are so welcome" the young nurse said, "She really will be fine, try not to worry."

They stood a moment longer in silence, Eamon studying his wife's face and holding her hand. In his mind he needed the anchor of her touch to keep him going and he knew it. No matter what the future brought he'd try his damn best to make sure she knew what she meant to him.

"Is there a phone I can use? Not a pay phone, it's a rather private call I need to make. I'm sure you understand" he said to the nurse in a voice that was as paternal and caring as he could make it.

The young nurse positively beamed in response. "Of course, I'll bring you down to the matron's office. She's gone for a break before the breakfast rounds."

"Breakfast rounds?" queried Eamon, suddenly sounding alarmed, "How long was I asleep?" He looked at his watch and was stunned that he'd lost a whole five hours and it was almost six in the morning. "Jesus wept" he said throwing his eyes to heaven, "It's very urgent that I get that phone straight away and I'm not joking when I say it's a matter of life and death."

The nurse said "follow me, I'll get you sorted in a jiffy."

With a moment's hesitation and then stooping to kiss Marie on the cheek he whispered "I'll be back soon, love" he followed the nurse as quickly as he could walk to the matron's office where she pointed to the phone and seeing his hesitancy in making the call, left him in peace.

His call was answered by the same flat voice. "I have one last mess that needs cleaning up" he explained. "You'll need to get to St. Augustine's Church in Raheny" he gave directions and a description of what they'd find. "Be quick, it's not as if it won't be noticed. I've locked the front door so you'll have to find another way in and for God's sake don't burn the place down." The voice simply replied "thirty minutes, Detective, best I can do. I must say you're leaving quite a litany of carnage in your wake."

"Not in *my* wake, I'm just following the killer's trail and he's not a person who cares a lot about the carnage. That's the madness in him. He shot poor Father Quinn as he was trying to help me find the thing I am searching for and snare the killer." Eamon didn't know why he felt the need to tell the voice on the phone anything but the inference that he might be in some way responsible was more than he wanted anyone to think. As for lying about Brendan, they'd been friends for his whole life, and if nothing else he wanted to balance the scales and save his friend's reputation. He felt they were even now. If the voice believed him or not he wouldn't know as the line simply went dead.

Eamon knew he had to at least try the cemetery, and he had to hope Brendan hadn't told whoever else was involved if indeed the tapes were there. It was a long shot but it was the only shot he had. He quietly left the matron's office and out of the hospital. The same security guard was still on duty and he gave Eamon a wave as he approached the main doors, holding up his car keys. "I left her parked in the bay over to the left. It wasn't goin' to be disturbed on my watch" he nodded to Eamon "Your wife ok?"

"She will be, thanks for asking and for taking care of the car. I have to get back home and pick up a few things for her" the lie telling Eamon that he actually would have to do just that, after he'd done what he needed to do. The guard handed him the keys and patted him on the shoulder before continuing on his way.

He walked casually to the car, leaving the hospital grounds calmly and heading into the early morning. The sun was just breaking the horizon as he turned on to the main road and he fought the impulse to speed to Glasnevin, arriving at just after six thirty. He parked up and surveyed the gates. They'd be locked for hours yet but he knew well that he was getting in there now, though at fifty two he didn't fancy the climb over them. Five minutes later he had negotiated clambering over the wall a little further down with the aid of a lamp post. He'd climbed it with a lot more grunting and sweating than he'd ever have wanted to admit but he was at the top and looked for a place to drop down without breaking an ankle. He saw what looked like a soft enough mossy spot and a second later landed heavily, falling back to come to rest sitting in the dew covered grass. He picked himself up slowly and wiped the seat of his pants.

"I really am getting too old for this" he muttered, looking around to get his bearings. Over the years he and Brendan had walked these very paths, chatting and visiting graves of significant figures from Irish history. It was their one shared interest that he would always remember and knowing he would never do it again caused him more pain and regret than he thought Brendan deserved. "You bollix, I hope you're happy" he grunted as he set off in the direction he thought he'd find Mangan's Headstone.

213

It took him another half hour of wandering to and fro before he recognised some of the terrain where Mangan was buried. They'd walked here before, he and Brendan, he was sure of it and stood scanning the labyrinthine forest of limestone, granite and marble before noticing a movement in the distance. He crouched down, hoping he hadn't been seen and crept towards the closest headstone, slowly peering over it. In the early morning light he first thought he must have been mistaken before he saw it again, a man, dressed in dark clothing, going from grave to grave and at that hour of the morning Eamon was sure of the reason for its hurried search.

"Not here for the scenery, is he?" he said between gritted teeth and slowly began to traverse the distance between them, keeping out of sight behind the taller memorials. Brendan had been telling the truth, there were more people involved in this affair than a lone killer. How far did it extend? At that moment he decided he had to just do the job in front of him and not worry about the tangled web he was caught up in. Eventually Eamon could see the figure clearly, though he was wearing a heavy scarf and on overcoat, so he couldn't get a proper look at his face. Then Eamon spotted it. Twin headstones, side by side, coming together at the base. The left one was James Clarence Mangan's, a poet he and Brendan both shared an interest in, while the stone to the right was.. Plunkett, yes that was it, though why he remembered that was anyone's guess.

The figure had stopped in front of the two headstones and then walked straight up to them and removed an object that had been wedged between them. Eamon watched from only twenty feet away as the man looked around and then unwrapped the too familiar oil cloth revealing the contents. Eamon knew without needing to see that it was the same prize they both sought. He knew too that the man standing there was a good bit bigger and probably younger than he was and wasn't likely to be as close to complete exhaustion either. He needed some way to even the odds.

Looking down Eamon noticed a glass ornament, a globe about six inches in diameter sitting on the grave. He picked it up and hefted it, testing its weight. Inside a miniature statue of the Virgin Mary stood giving what Eamon hoped with a benign blessing. As the man walked away from the gravestones he passed the far side of the tall monument Eamon was hiding behind and as he did Eamon stepped out. The man barely had time to turn before the ornament hit him square between the eyes. The solid glass gave what Eamon felt was a very satisfactory crack against the man's nose bone. The figure fell back immediately, stunned and with blood gushing from his nose. He was groaning and tried briefly to raise his head before falling back again, breathing heavily through his mouth and sending ragged plumes of misty breath into the cool morning air, blood pumping from his nose, across his face and onto the wet grass.

Eamon wasted no time checking on his victory, following up with a soccer kick to the groin which doubled the man into a foetal position, rolling away from Eamon groaning loudly and gasping for breath. Eamon kicked him again in the kidneys, drawing another yelp, though it was muted by the lack of air in his lungs. He stooped and picked up the tapes which had spilled out onto the ground, wrapping them again. The man tried to roll back towards him, grabbing at his foot. Eamon looked down at him and at his profusely bleeding face and into eyes which were still glazed from the impact of the ornament. "I have already been through hell to get these, you're not having them" he said simply. The man's outstretched hand locked onto his ankle and Eamon felt a jolt of rage. "Tell whoever has you doing this that you failed." He drew back his free foot and kicked the man in his mouth, knocking his head back and breaking several teeth. He slumped back, blood spatter streaking the ground from his ruined mouth and nose. As his grip loosened Eamon pulled free, walking away from the unconscious form as though he'd never even noticed him.

Eamon made his way back to the wall and managed to find an ivy covered area that afforded enough hand and foot holds to climb over while guarding the package. At the top he stopped, sitting astride the wall and looked onto the street which had sprung to life in early morning traffic. He looked briefly back at the spot where the man still lay and thought to himself that he got exactly what he deserved. He let himself down the other side of the wall, landing on the pavement with a knee jarring thump. There was a woman standing at the nearby bus stop watching him leaving the cemetery. Eamon looked at her and smiled a smile of relief "They we're dying to get me in there but I was dying to get out" he chuckled as she looked on wide eyed as if seeing an apparition. Eamon crossed the road and jumped into his car, speeding away.

He put the tapes back into the box containing Loyola's effects. A box he intended to get rid of that morning come hell or high water. They spilled out of the cloth again but this time he simply let them sit where they fell until he reached a set of lights with a line of traffic in front of him that meant he was going to be stuck for a few minutes at least. He fumbled in the box, lining up the tapes and trying to secure them, while keeping one hand on the wheel. He picked up the bible to wedge them in place but it slipped from his grasp as he kept one eye on the traffic. He leaned over into the foot well and picked it up again. Then he saw something that both frightened him and excited him in equal measure. There was a key taped to the inside of the back cover, obscured by the leather bookmark until now. Eamon pulled it away, taking some of the paper with the tape, indicating it had been there a good length of time. The key was old and tarnished. A short hollow cylinder with a metal plate on one side which held the teeth for an old fashioned lock he hadn't seen in years. He tried to remember seeing anything at Loyola's home that might have used that kind of lock but nothing came to mind. *Better to be safe than sorry... again* he thought, swinging the car into the lane that would take him Southside in the most direct way. The city traffic was still light and he made good progress, slipping into the cul de sac a little after eight. He hoped the residents might still be asleep and he could come and go unnoticed but no sooner had he pulled up near the house than he saw a curtain twitch next door. "Oh here we go" he muttered. He picked up the box of Loyola's things, placing the tapes under the passenger seat and making sure the door was locked after getting out of the car.

The front door of the neighbour's house opened and a very elderly man tottered out, assisted by two walking sticks. "Hello there, you're the detective that was here the night poor John passed" he said "Did you find any family, only I was hoping to go to the funeral but I've heard nothing at all, not even from the local priest. It's like he dropped off the face of the planet" he slowly made his way down the step in front of the house. "It's not right, he shouldn't just be forgotten."

Eamon wondered if the old man was more worried about himself being forgotten than *John*, and was tempted to say as much but he bit back the comment, seeing the old man shake his head slowly. He decided a lie might do what the truth never would, provide the old fellow with a bit of peace. "John, oh dear nobody told you" Eamon said in a grave tone, "His family are all abroad and they had his remains sent to the family plot. Somewhere in the States I think, or was it Australia? I'm afraid I don't remember." He walked closer to the old man to save him taking any more unnecessary steps. "I'm just here check if there are any final effects left behind and bring them to the Church" he held up the box to demonstrate the truth of his assertion. "We found a key but nothing that it might fit so I said I'd come by and see if we missed anything. Least I could do for the poor fellow." Eamon showed the key and the old man nodded.

"You won't find anything in there that fits that key" he said in a very definite tone.

"Why is that?" Eamon's curiosity was in overdrive and his subconscious was shouting in his ear. The old man knew something, "You sound very sure. Is there a reason?"

"Because that key fits the strongbox that John left in my attic" the old man said simply. "I only came out to ask if you wanted to take it with you as I didn't know what else to do with it and it's just taking up space."

"Why not? I can deliver the lot at the same time. It's very good of you to care enough about your friend to mind his things" Eamon said, fishing. Was this another one that he needed to know about, another evil old man?

"Neighbours more than friends, really. He kept to himself, mostly but I got the impression it was valuable to him. I can trust you to deliver it, can't I?" the old man looked at him with suspicion before breaking into a wheezy laugh "Course I can, I'm only having a laugh. If you can't trust the Guards who can you trust? Come on in and you can get it down, I'm afraid I'd be no help at all in that regard" he said raising the two sticks.

Eamon didn't need to be asked twice. He opened the garden gate and followed the old man as he slowly made his way back inside, helped him up the step and into the house as gently as he could while still trying to hurry him along.

"He said his friend Enda might come by one day and to keep it safe in case he wasn't around, that Enda would know where the key was, but seeing as you're here and are a detective, you might as well have it." The old man went into a small sitting room and sat down slowly, grunting with the effort as he did.

"If you get the steps in the kitchen you'll be able to reach the trap door there in the hall" he said pointing with a cane.

Eamon set down the box and found the steps, opened them and lifted the trap door, peering into the dark. Almost directly in front of him was a metal box, about eighteen inches long and on the front of it was a long narrow slit that he guessed would fit the key in his pocket perfectly. He lifted it down carefully, surprised at how light it was.

"Are you going to open it?" the old man asked eagerly, clearly curious as to the contents, as was Eamon but shaking his head he said "No, it's not mine to open. I'll just take it with me and the Church can take it from there." It seemed lying was becoming part of his daily routine, *but sure haven't you lied to everyone, including yourself, your whole life?* He grimaced at the thought.

The old man nodded though he looked deflated "Probably for the best" he sighed "At least I can rest easy knowing it's where it should be."

"Oh don't worry. I'll make sure it gets to where it needs to go" Eamon said. The old man didn't seem to hear any other inference than the one Eamon seemed to be implying. He thanked the old man, telling him not to get up, he'd see himself out and left as quickly as he could without seeming to hurry. As soon as he sat back into his car he thrust his hand into his pocket, retrieved the key and inserted it in the lock. It turned first time and the lid popped up a half inch. He lifted it up and inside was a sight he'd

219

hardly hoped dream for. In neat rows were boxes for reels of film. He carefully lifted one out and pried it apart, feeling all the trepidation of a kid at Christmas. Inside was a reel of film. He quickly closed the metal case again and looked at the cover which was dated nineteen fifty two.

"Oh fuck, it's really them" Eamon exhaled deeply. The sense of elation and relief washed over him like a wave, clearing the anxiety and fear that he'd been holding on to like a drowning man to a life ring. In the moment of letting go his eyes welled up and tears fell freely down his face. There was a twinge of sadness and regret but it was overwhelmed by the knowledge that he could now decide his own fate, control the narrative without the ghosts of his past coming to strangle him in the night.

He picked up several more, noting their dates. Each tape was four inches in diameter and Eamon estimated there were probably thirty reels in the box. He looked for the dates on the tapes that corresponded to his time in the school but many of them had worn away over the years. At the bottom of the box he found a small notebook. Written in its pages were names, names of men who were now at the very pinnacle of Irish society. As he thumbed through the pages some of the names didn't surprise him as much as others but some confounded him completely. At least one of those men he'd voted for and another he'd looked up to as a humanitarian. Sick, corrupt bastards, all wearing masks while they preyed on children. "By Christ, you will all pay in one fashion or another" he swore to himself. Maybe Brendan and whoever else had not been too wide of the mark wanting to kill these perverts but Eamon had to follow the law. To do otherwise would have gone against everything he believed in. Somehow he had to expose these monsters, but how? He added the half dozen video tapes to the box and locked it again, putting the key into his pocket and patting it for reassurance.

Eamon decided he needed time to think so he was going to go back to the hospital after he made a brief pit stop. He headed into the station. The morning shift had only just come on duty and he nodded a wave at Dempsey as he casually strolled in, his overcoat covering the box and its precious cargo.

He waited until everyone was busy and took the box into the old document store room where cold cases, old records, long forgotten files and reports went to gather dust and moulder. He took an old case file from thirty years before, swapped out the papers in the box and put the metal box inside. No one would ever be likely to come in here to look for it. The room was virtually unused in all the time he'd been in the station.

As he left for the hospital he felt he had finally found the end of this case, the one that had cost him more than any other. Yet he knew he still had loose ends to tie up and wouldn't, *no, couldn't,* let it go until he had everything put to bed.

19.

The drive back to the hospital was the most relaxed Eamon had felt in weeks. He could feel his constantly burning muscles begin to unknot in his shoulders and the ache diminishing as he let the tension out. He might yet have to fight his superiors but the sense of powerlessness and the secret fear of being discovered had faded noticeably. His main focus now was on getting Marie safely home and in making sure Gavin was not only okay but well taken care of too. That responsibility, he felt, was his to shoulder. The poor lad would never have been in his current predicament if not for Eamon. Then there was Butler. He wasn't yet sure what part he'd had to play but clearly he knew more than he'd let on, but that was a conversation for another day, *but I won't be forgetting you*, he thought ominously.

He made his way to the ward where Marie was still sleeping. He was worried at first until a young nurse who, Eamon noted, had the reddest hair and the most freckles he'd ever seen, told him the sedative she'd been given had been quite a strong one.

"Poor dear, she must have had a nasty shock but a couple of days rest and she'll be right as rain" she said, comforting Eamon on seeing his worried expression. "She's lucky to have you."

Eamon snorted "Thirty years of marriage, is that good luck or bad luck."

"Seeing how much you care I'd say definitely good" smiled the nurse "I'll leave you for a little while but if there's anything I can get you just let me know." She left, closing the door softly behind her and Eamon pulled up a chair to sit by the bed.

"All in all Eamon, I'd say good luck, the last week or so notwithstanding." Marie opened her eyes and smiled softly.

"Jesus Marie you put the heart crossways in me!" Eamon exclaimed. "Have you been awake the whole time?"

"I woke just a few minutes before you came in but I didn't want the nurses prattling on or fussing so I just pretended to be asleep" she said, smiling again. "I need some quiet and I suspect you do too. I really can't remember too much but I know Bren.." she stopped, the name catching on her tongue "Brendan was mad, totally bonkers, wasn't he? Did you..?" she couldn't bring herself to ask and instead just looked to Eamon inquiringly for an answer.

"I did what I had to" he said simply. "We'll talk about it in a day or two. There's a lot to tell you but now's not the time or place. When you get home, then if you want I'll tell you the truth about everything."

"Good" Marie answered. "It's about time you finally introduced yourself. We do have a lot to think about, talk about and to decide but that's rightly for another time. Now, off with you and do whatever it is you have to do. I can see the impatience in you like ants in your pants." She smiled and laid her head back. "This is the first time in as long as I can remember that I don't have anything to do or anyone to worry about, but myself. I'm going to enjoy the rest."

"Yes dear" Eamon said quietly. He gave her hand a squeeze and stood to leave, looking back as he left and realising he was amazed by this woman's resilience and her capacity to cope. He opened his mouth to speak but she spoke first without lifting her head or opening her eyes. "It's rude to stare, Eamon. Now shoo!" He smiled, closed his gaping mouth and left, shaking his head.

As he passed the nurses' station the freckle faced nurse looked up from her paperwork and smiling said "You're the detective who was here before. You're colleague had surgery didn't he?".

"That's right" Eamon nodded "how is he?"

"He's awake, that's how he is. Good looking chap when he doesn't look like he's been hit by a bus, I say" she smiled again and winked at Eamon who just smiled back and read her name tag. "Sarah Winstone, is it? I'll be sure to tell him you took very good care of him. God knows he needs someone to, being a single lad and all". Eamon let the emphasis drop on the word single and returned her wink with one of his own. "Do you think I could see him for a few minutes?"

"I don't see why not. It's not visiting hours but I'm sure you might want to talk to him in a professional capacity." Again she smiled and Eamon couldn't help thinking that Gavin would be doing well to land a woman as pretty as she was when she smiled. There was devilment in it. "He's upstairs, turn left at the top of the stairs and third door on the right" she made the motions with her hand to guide but Eamon had already turned and was half way to the stairs.

He took the steps two at a time, feeling lighter of foot than he had in weeks. The weight of everything seemed to be sloughing away like an old skin that no longer served its purpose, only constricting and holding him back.

He knocked on the door and turned the handle cautiously, looking round the half open door, afraid of what he might find. What greeted him was less than he feared but still jarred him. Gavin's face was stitched in several places, his head wrapped in bandages still and his skin was a mixture of colours ranging from purplish black to green and yellow. His complexion was still pale and waxen too but his eyes were open and he attempted a smile when he saw Eamon.

"Jesus boss, you look worse than I do" Gavin said through his teeth, the bandage around his jaw restricting his speech. "Here, pull up a pew" he motioned to the chair at the wall with his eyes and the slightest nod of his head.

Eamon got the chair and placing it close to the bed sat down. His expression was grave and Gavin smiled slightly. "It's okay boss, don't go beating yourself up over it. No way could anyone have seen this coming".

"Should never have let you go out there on your own. That's on me and you'll never know just how sorry I am." Eamon looked his young colleague in the eye and every fibre of his soul begged for the absolution he would deny himself. Gavin must have seen his bosses need because he just waved one finger and said "Don't. The job comes with risks. Just tell me you have some good news about the whole thing and I'll be happy."

"I owe you Gav. I owe you an explanation of everything that's happened both before and after this" he waved his hand over Gavin's battered and bandaged body. "If you're able I'd like to tell you everything now, and if you don't want to forgive me or ever speak to me again I'll understand but you deserve to know every last detail".

Gavin, examining Eamon's pale and lined face, his eyes, red

rimmed and dark circled and full of sadness and regret, nodded his assent and Eamon began. He began with a story forty years in the making and it took him a surprisingly short time to lay it all out for the young man who simply lay back, occasionally furrowing his brow, giving a quiet grunt or comment.

When he finished Gavin simply sighed. "Eamon, that's a lot to process and too much death for me to wrap my head around, let alone be part of, or almost part of" he gestured, lifting the cast on his arm as if to demonstrate. "What you've been going through would drive anyone to drink, I'm surprised you've managed as well as you did, considering. Trust me when I say this, my world view has just shifted. I was always a man to follow the lead of my superiors. They knew best and I suppose that's how I was brought up. The guard and the parish priest held sway and their word was law. I see now that I may have been somewhat naïve on that score. I will carry this story to my grave and I hope that's a long time from now, I've come close enough for the next several decades".

"I appreciate that Gavin, I really do. I don't expect you to compromise your values on my account. If it comes out in the wash, you deny any knowledge of anything and walk away. Ireland isn't ready for a gay guard coming out and won't be I suspect, for another generation at least." Eamon said rubbing his eyes. The strain of going through everything was written on his features and for a moment Gavin thought he'd crack but instead he smiled. "Maybe your generation will see the changes that need to be made but I suspect it's still a long way off. I'm going to be the only gay guard you'll hear about for a long time if it comes to it".

"The gay thing… that certainly does explain a lot." Gavin said quietly. "Though not your total lack of dress sense or personal grooming" he smiled. "I've always known there was something you were hiding but you were never a boss I'd have had the balls to approach on a personal level."

"I'm not your boss, not today, but I hope I'm your friend" Eamon said, looking at the ground, expecting perhaps to be instructed just where he could put that offer.

"As long as it's just friends" Gavin gave a chuckle, which made him wince in pain. Eamon accepted the olive branch with both hands. "Relax you don't have to worry about me making advances. I may be gay but I'm not desperate, besides I've seen your arse and it has no part to play in the sexual theatre as far as I am concerned." He smiled sheepishly at a comment he never felt he'd ever have made before that moment.

"Too far, Eamon, too far" Gavin said suppressing a laugh and grimacing in more pain. "Now would you ever feck off and finish this the way it needs to be finished, before you cause me any more distress". He closed his eyes and breathed a deep sigh. "Eamon?" he called as Eamon stood to leave.

"Yes Gav?" he replied with some trepidation.

"I look forward to getting back to work after this. There's a hell of a lot more bad guys we need to take down. You might want to think about that when you're deciding how to play the cards you have. You're not exactly without options on how you move forward."

Eamon hesitated a moment, weighing Gavin's advice. "You should just concentrate on getting well before deciding what to do next. Oh by the way, to aid your recovery you might like to know that nurse Winstone has her eye on you, though looking at the state of you I can't think why."

"Sarah? The red head? That's good to know" Gavin smiled, his face lighting up. "She's certainly someone that'd take my mind off the aches and pains."

"Jesus, is that colour coming back into your cheeks. I hope so because you can't afford blood flow to anywhere else for a while yet" Eamon joked.

"Where there's a will there's a way" Gavin winked slowly.

"Where there's a willy there's a way more like" Eamon replied, raising an eyebrow. "I can see you'll be right as rain."

"I don't know boss, I could be here for a while yet" Gavin replied with a knowing look to which Eamon just raised his eyes and shook his head.

"I'll talk to you tomorrow after I've spoken to the three stooges. Rest and think about pretty nurses. I'll do what needs to be done". Eamon stopped at the door and looked at Gavin "All joking aside, I want to thank you for listening and not judging. You'll never know how much it means to me."

Gavin raised one hand slightly "You got him, we're even on that score. You did what you felt you had to do and you protected your wife. Just don't fall at the last hurdle and I'll call it square." He gave a short wave and Eamon was dismissed, smiling.

In the hallway outside Gavin's room Eamon stood for a moment with his back leant the wall. It felt cool in contrast with the heat of the ward and Eamon was glad of it. He felt strangely unburdened, though he knew he'd passed a lot of the burden onto Gavin. He hoped he'd done the right thing but his instincts told him Gavin was the right person to confide in and that he meant it when he said he'd carry the tale to his grave.

228

"Well now, a job well done!" the Commissioner exclaimed, clapping his hands together and smiling. "That deserves a drink, Eamon" he reached into the desk drawer and produced a bottle of Ray's Bushmills and two glasses.

"Thanks Commissioner but I'm not drinking" Eamon replied.

"On antibiotics are we" the Commissioner laughed "Still you won't mind if I have one?"

"Not at all." Eamon replied again, keeping his eyes locked on Flannigan. The man seemed more nervous than anything else, trepidation in the very air around him as he poured. The phone rang and Commissioner Flannigan jumped like he'd been electrocuted. He picked up the receiver "Very good" he said, relief pouring from him.

"One moment Eamon" he stabbed the keypad with one finger and pressed the loudspeaker so that the ringing filled the silence between them. After several rings a familiar voice replaced the annoying buzzing sound "Commissioner?"

"Yes Minister, It's me." Said Flannigan nervously. "I'm here with Detective Inspector Kearns and I'm happy to report that everything has now been resolved as per your instructions."

"I'm glad to hear it. Detective Kearns, I'd congratulate you if it weren't for the simply amazing display of incompetence." He paused to let the words hit home before continuing "I've had to jump through several hoops not to mention spend an inordinate amount of money to keep a lid on your activities. Priests, journalists, a former brother *and* his wife. For God's sake man how did you let it go so far? It's as if you didn't want to catch the killer at all. In fact the more one thinks about this case the thread that seems to stitch it all together is you, and we only have your

231

word that Father Quinn was involved in any way at all". The voice on the loudspeaker became softer but more menacing "I think you see where this is going Detective. I think you'd do well to consider your position on the force. You've broken God knows how many laws, been central to at least three murders and there's not a shred of evidence to say why. Think of your loved ones if this scandal went public. A renegade policeman and perhaps his junior colleague too, not to mention what society would think of your family. This is Ireland, Kearns. Whatever way we in authority choose to spin this is how we bury you. Early retirement for health reasons is your only saving grace. In fact Eamon, who's to say you aren't the killer. You retire quietly or I'll personally see to it that you spend the next twenty years in a mental hospital, so drug addled you won't even be able to tell who's wiping the drool off your chin?"

There it was. The moment Eamon had hoped would never come but now it was here he was ready for it. They would try to pin all this on him and threaten his family and friends if he didn't fall on his sword. The smug tone was palpable and Eamon wished the bastard was there right then so he could wipe that smug expression off Casey's face.

"What about the tapes" Eamon said, appearing desperate.

"What tapes?" again the smug bastard thought he was in complete control.

"The tapes you, the Commissioner and the Archbishop tasked me with recovering. The tapes I delivered here not half an hour ago." Eamon was playing victim. Raise them up and knock them down.

"The tapes you so kindly gave to the Commissioner and so stupidly let out of your sight are now in the station's furnace. Your one bargaining chip is melting into oblivion." Casey was positively beaming over the phone. He had all the cards, or so he thought.

Eamon gasped dramatically and snarled "You prick. After all I've done to make sure this went away, you'd burn me like this?" Christ he was going to enjoy the next few minutes.

The minister's tone became matter of fact. "Nothing personal Kearns, just how this was always going to play out. There has never been a serial killer in the history of the State and there won't be one now. As for the tapes, they were never going to see the light of day. You could always go to the press I suppose and you'll be labelled a crank telling your wild story of corruption and murder and I guarantee no one will believe a word. Too many of the elite of society would be tainted and after all its ancient history. Who cares about what happened decades ago?"

"I care" Eamon said quietly. Had Casey been listening he might have picked up the dangerous growl in Eamon's voice. Commissioner Flannigan, who had sat in uncomfortable stony silence, his eyes fixed firmly on the loudspeaker up to this point, glanced up sharply, and looked shrewdly at Eamon who smiled back at him.

"If you'll recall, Minister Casey, you asked me to retrieve the VHS tapes. I did and now you tell me that you've destroyed them, destroyed the only evidence that linked all the crimes together" Eamon waited as there was a pause on the line, indicating that the Minister's smugness was fading he hoped. "Funny thing about that, Minister, the VHS tapes are only copies. What you should have asked me for were the original reels of film that the copies were made from." The silence hung heavy in the room as Eamon watched the Commissioner's face drop and his mouth hang agape. He smiled at Flannigan and winked. "Still

233

there Minister?" he knew the Minister's face probably mirrored that of the Commissioner and he was only disappointed he couldn't see it.

"I suppose you want me to believe you have these fictional originals?" Casey said scoffing but there was doubt in every word and Eamon knew he had them.

"I really couldn't give a rattling fuck what you believe you jumped up little shit but I can tell you now that you're not going to threaten me or my family ever again without some fucking serious repercussions. You know and I know that you've covered this up for the great and good of Irish society and they're not going to be happy if you suddenly fail. Not the kind of people that I'd want to piss off if I were you, I should think". Eamon was positively revelling in the moment. "I do indeed have the originals, in a very safe location, and they will make it into the hands of the press. How's that for a wild story of corruption and murder?"

"What do you want?" Casey said quietly, admitting defeat.

"I want this to go away. I want to take the next three months off with full pay and when I come back I want my own task force to root out more of these sick, barbaric predators and I want to have autonomy while I do it."

"In return I get the originals" Casey countered.

"In my hoop, you do" Eamon snorted derisively "You get my assurance that for as long as I'm left alone the originals will be kept safe. You agree now or your world, Minister, and the Commissioner's and the Archbishop's all go to hell in a hand basket. Decide, now!"

"Well played Detective, Commissioner Flannigan said you were smarter than you looked. We have an agreement but I promise you this.. if you don't hold up your end of the bargain you will pay in ways you haven't even thought of yet." Casey's voice was sullen. He hated losing and Eamon knew he was vengeful enough to mean every word he'd said.

"Alright, you've made your threats clear. Don't fuck with me I won't fuck with you. Good day, *Minister*." Eamon reached forward and ended the call.

The Commissioner sat staring at Eamon for a long moment, unable to reconcile what had just happened with how it was supposed to go. "You've made a lot of very dangerous enemies today Eamon." He cautioned "though you don't have to count me among them".

Eamon reached into his pocket and took out his Dictaphone, held it up for Flannigan to see as he pressed the off button very deliberately.

"Oh fuck off Eamon, you recorded this?" he said dismayed.

"This and our little chat in the offices when this all kicked off. Your own words will crucify you even if the film never came to light. Call it extra insurance. I'm a belt and braces man." Eamon stood up from his chair. "I'll be taking that time off starting immediately, Commissioner" he nodded as he turned for the door. He paused just before he turned the handle. "I know you're wondering how this leaves things. You are after all the Commissioner of the force. I'm hoping you simply ignore this whole mess and forget it ever happened. I want to concentrate on bringing to a close whatever kind of horror has been allowed to grow in this country. It's a cancer and the only thing to do with cancer it cut it out. I'll keep you informed as my investigations

235

progress and understand this Commissioner" Eamon turned one last time to face the Commissioner who was still sitting behind the desk. "I'll play ball as far as I can in terms of keeping it under the radar. We're going to protect people not shake their faith in what we do our in the state itself".

Commissioner Flannigan simply nodded slowly. Eamon left smiling and felt another weight drop away from him.

"Almost all done. Now Butler you prick, let's see what part you played in this".

20.

He got to the bar in the early dawn, though early was a relative term for McGettigans where the clientele might not have left until four that morning. Butler was just putting the key in the lock of the front door to leave when Eamon cocked the pistol against his ear. To Butler's credit Eamon noted, he didn't even flinch.

"We need to have a quiet word now your pet gorilla isn't here" he said quietly, glancing left and right in case someone might be passing though he doubted it at this hour, "I'd hate to have shot him. Well actually, no I wouldn't but there's been enough unnecessary death around me lately". He pushed Butler in through the door and marched him to the bar at arm's length where Eamon stood, gun trained on him all the while as he turned on the lights again.

"Now Eamon, this is all a bit silly, isn't it?" Butler said lightly. "I'm tired and I just want to go home and catch up on my beauty sleep" but all the time his eyes never left the barrel of the gun. Eamon waved him out from behind the bar and over to the same table they'd sat at when he'd given Eamon the gun in the first place.

"Bit ironic, you pointing that at me in here. I did give it to you in good faith, as a favour." Butler said as though to remind Eamon he was owed.

"Shut up with the glib comments Butler. I'm well aware you've had plenty of these pointed at you over the years but one misstep here and I won't hesitate to use it again." He let the words sink in.

"Again? So you did do it" It was a statement not a question.

"I had no choice. It was him or Marie and that contest he was never going to win but he knew that didn't he?" Eamon asked accusingly. "Why, Butler? What on earth could have made you tell Brendan I was coming and that I had a gun?"

"What makes you think I did?" Butler said, nonchalantly.

"Because he wasn't in the least bit surprised when I pointed it at him and I am a fucking detective!" Eamon exclaimed angrily.

"Fair enough" Butler said grinning as he threw up his hands in mock surrender "you got me, Eamon. I did call Father Quinn."

"Why? Why in the name of all that's holy would you do that? It's the one part in all of this that I just can't get my head around."

"I owed him, Eamon. It's really that simple. When my brother was inside Father Quinn was the priest who tried to get him to mend his ways. He'd visit every week and helped him kick the drugs too." Butlers smile faded as his face became stony and his lips thin and pursed. He paused for a moment, looking at his hands as he fidgeted with the beer mat in front of him.

"The full truth Eamon is that Brendan was there with my brother at the end when he was 'overdosed' by someone in the prison. It was Brendan who held his hand and gave him absolution as he drew his last breath. I owed it to him to do one favour at least." He paused again and gave a snorted smile.

238

"The real kicker for you is going to be that he knew you'd come to me. He really did know you well Eamon because he said if you came to me you'd be looking for the kind of help only I could give you and that he wanted me to do whatever you asked. I think he planned for you to kill him to save your wife. When I told him you were coming he said it was his way of paying for the old priest and the woman."

"What does that mean? That you knew he'd taken Marie?" Eamon's anger spiked sharply, his grip on the pistol tightening.

"No Eamon I didn't know until you told me. Father Quinn just told me you'd be coming. The one thing I couldn't countenance is involving civilians. You know that. I might not be the most moral of bastards but there are limits, women and children are off limits, even to me." Butler sat upright in his chair and stabbed the table with a finger to emphasise his point. "But that's only half the reason I helped you out, you see Eamon, I know something you don't know." He smiled and slumped back, raising his head heavenward and rubbing his palms over his face and eyes.

Eamon placed the gun on the table. "Jesus wept, get on with it man!" he said, exasperated at the theatrics and gameplay. He was in no mood for either and Butler had the only answers missing from the puzzle. "What don't I know?"

"Hah! Don't be in such a hurry Eamon. You might regret it. Fools rush in where angels fear to tread and all that shite." Butler was smiling again but this smile was somehow more nervous, like a teenager caught looking at a porn mag by his friends. "We've had a merry dance over the years, haven't we Eamon?"

"You might call it that, I suppose" Eamon replied cagily, "Though I suspect you lead for most of it."

239

"You always seemed to avoid me. Sidestepping cases I might have been wrongly been implicated in so to speak." Butler's tone was one of measured caution, like a man placing his feet carefully in a minefield. "We both know why, don't we? It's because of that little matter back in the day". He looked meaningfully at Eamon.

It was Eamon's turn to feel uncomfortable and guilty, though no smile was going to cross his face. "Go on" he said flatly. He dreaded what was about to be said but knew this day had to come eventually and it was better coming out here than in a station for the record. He mentally rolled his eyes 'coming out' was the worst choice of words, he thought, since 'unsinkable' was used to describe the Titanic.

"At the time you were about to send my brother down for his first real stretch, remember? Well I wanted to do whatever I could to muddy the waters and when I found out you were the garda on the case I knew I could make your life.. difficult and maybe even get you suspended long enough for my brother's case to be struck out." Butler snorted again "but you boys in blue do stick together, don't you. Somehow the story of you in this very pub, caught with your trousers down, as it were" he gave a snigger as Eamon's face darkened and nostrils flared, "Well, it didn't stick, which is fortunate for you and unfortunate for my brother, in the long run." He clasped his hands together, fingers intertwined and rested his head on them, pausing thoughtfully.

"We both know I wasn't lying or making up fairy tales" again he sniggered nervously "fairy... God I'm on a roll. Anyway, and here's the reason I helped you this one time.. I know you were in the toilets here. I know you weren't alone. I also know you were blind drunk and talking about how you wished you could talk to someone, anyone about how you were living a lie."

240

"Since I don't remember any of that, either you're outright lying right now or..." Eamon looked intently at Butler's face. The man's expression was impassive but there was a feeling that hung in the air, one of a dam of expectation that was about to break. The realisation dawned on Eamon's face and Butler smiled again, a softer more human smile than Eamon would ever have credited him capable of.

"Yes Eamon, I was there. I was the other guy." Butler said, almost shyly, lowering his head. "Jesus Eamon, your face is a picture!" he said looking up at Eamon's incredulous frozen stare.

Eamon simply sat back, his head swimming and thoughts reeling, unable to think coherently as Butler continued. "You have your secret Eamon, and I have mine. Yours would have gotten you dismissed and probably imprisoned if it had come out and mine.. well, mine would get me shot in the head. So we both keep our secrets and we keep on living." He winked at Eamon who simply swallowed hard and nodded slowly. Then without another word lay down the gun and stood up from the table, his chair scraping the floor as he pushed it back.

"We're even then?" he said simply, holding out his hand.

Butler stood, looking at his hand for a moment before taking it in his own and shaking it firmly. "Even" he nodded and Eamon turned and walked from the bar for what he fervently hoped was the very last time in his life, though he could feel Butler's eyes on his back the whole time.

Out on the street the wind was blowing easterly, cold and dry and the sudden chill broke the spell. Eamon pulled up his collar and walked away from McGettigans feeling lighter and freer than he ever had in his life.

21.

Eamon woke late. He looked up at the ceiling and listened for the tell-tale sounds. He could hear muffled voices coming from downstairs and he decided that he'd better get up. It was Christmas after all and the boys had both come home on Christmas Eve to spend it with their parents. They'd also brought their girlfriends and the house was as full of life as it had ever been in their younger years. Marie had insisted he stay in the house until they got over the cataclysmic events of the months previous. He'd moved into the guest room and she was of the opinion he should have done years ago as now she didn't have to put up with his snoring or other bodily functions. If the boys had any questions about the arrangement they wisely kept them to themselves.

Eamon stretched and closed his eyes for a moment, drinking in the sounds from below as the smell of breakfast frying wafted its way up from the kitchen. *Right* he thought *let's be a family for another Christmas. New Year's Day may bring changes but that's for then!* He threw back the blankets and sat up, swinging his legs over the side of the bed and into his slippers. It had been three months too, since his last drink and his body was certainly thanking him for it. His energy levels were better and his morning outlook brighter, not being dampened by a hangover.

He put on a dressing gown and meandered downstairs, to find the source of the glorious smells. As he turned at the bottom of the stairs the phone rang. He gave a start at the unexpected interruption. The sound still made him feel nervous, though he knew it was all behind him. Too many memories that were too fresh made him jump at the stupidest of things. He picked up the receiver, calming himself. It was Christmas. No one deserved his wrath today.

"Hello Eamon. I'm glad to see you're healthy and looking well. The rest has done you good." The voice at the other end of the line was all too familiar but there was nothing muffled about it this time. Eamon could only stand still as he thought if he moved at all he would fall over. His stomach dropped and his hands were instantly clammy.

"I think we need to talk" the voice said "last time we met you left me feeling a little worse for wear. That was a cheap shot with the glass ornament but it is Christmas, a time for forgiving and forgetting so I won't hold it against you." The voice sounded conciliatory though Eamon didn't think for one minute he'd be as forgiving if someone hit him in the head with a glass cannon ball. "I'll be in touch when you get back to work, Eamon. It appears we have the same agenda though possibly not the same priorities as you serve the State and we serve God."

Eamon's thoughts were bobbing aimlessly like flotsam on a stormy sea. He grabbed the only word he could fathom and held on to it for dear life. "We?" he asked, bile rising in his throat.

"Call us Legion for we are many" the voice said and hung up.

"Oh for fuck sake, here we go again" Eamon sighed. He set down the receiver grimly. Whatever shit storm was brewing could wait until the New Year. He'd be ready then, whatever this Legion threw at him. Breakfast first, problems later. He smelled bacon.

Printed in Great Britain
by Amazon

35054330R00147